THE REALITY
OF WRIGHT
AND
Wrong

BESTSELLING AUTHOR
LEDDY HARPER

THE REALITY OF WRIGHT AND WRONG

LEDDY HARPER

with poetry by
KEV MURTAGH

Brit…
You amaze me.

A SPARK TO A FLAME

I sat in comfortable darkness,
My heart an emptied hole
Drawing other people's hopes and dreams,
Scratching them into their souls.
When first I looked up and saw your spark
I thought it was too good to be true,
But as you came closer through the dark
I realized you could see me too.

Two tiny sparks in the darkness
So tiny they could hardly be seen
So delicate that even to just glance at them
May cause them both to flee.
But for fun we brought them together
As we played the lovers game,
And as our sparks were tethered
They erupted into a flame.

As fingers touched fingers
As lips touched lips
As skin touched skin

A Spark to a Flame

As hips touched hips
You solved the puzzle my heart had encoded
And as you took me inside of you the universe exploded.

They say that a flame that burns twice as bright,
Only burns half as long
And baby we burned with a furious light,
But we both knew they weren't wrong.
To save the pain of burning out
And both being shattered apart,
We decided to walk away with neither cry nor shout
And once more embrace the dark.

When I turned and walked away from you
I thought that my light would fade,
I thought that when our flames went from one back to two
It would be like walking back to night from day.
But when I closed my eyes I still saw your light
Burning like the sun
And I saw too as I looked inside,
our flames still burned as one.

It was then that I knew as I think I had always known
That I could never walk away,
It was then that I knew that our sparks had grown
And became one living flame.
I knew what was missing from my soul
And what would ease my pain,
I knew that you had made me whole
And why Mercy was your name.

—*Wrong*

1

MERCY

The universe has a really sick sense of humor.

An hour ago, I had everything I'd ever wanted.

Now, I had nothing but a broken heart and shattered dreams.

As I stumbled out of the bar, I caught my reflection in the door and groaned. I was a sight to behold. Mascara lined my cheeks in inky rivers, and every hair on my head was out of place. With a tired huff, I shook my head and carried on, not caring that the soles of my high heels slid along the concrete because I couldn't lift my feet high enough to take proper steps. I should've been grateful I could still walk, considering I'd sat at the bar for close to an hour, drowning my sorrows in one drink after another.

About the only thing I had going for me was the fact that it was late. I wasn't sure just *how* late since I didn't have the faintest idea what time it was. If I had to guess, it was after midnight. With the lights from the bar behind me and street-lamps set far enough apart in front of me, there was a good chance I'd make it out of here without anyone noticing my disheveled appearance.

There was also a good chance I'd get kidnapped.

And, after the last hour or so, I'd go willingly.

Would that still be considered kidnapping?

I couldn't have made it more than twenty feet when an older gentleman stopped in front of me—and I use the designation *gentleman* very loosely. His silver, wiry beard covered half his face while the rest hid in the shadow cast from his Gilligan hat. A large—and likely dirty—trench coat hung on his slumped frame, even though it couldn't have been cooler than seventy-five degrees.

"Excuse me, but could I bother you for a cigarette? I'm out." His voice was gruff, making me think he'd smoked a carton a day for the last eighty-four years.

Holding my small purse against my chest, I pulled on the zipper to look inside. After staring into the nearly empty bag, unable to see anything in the dark, I remembered I didn't smoke. I'd never so much as held a cigarette. Truthfully, I had no idea why I even bothered to check in the first place. The answer to his question should've been a no-brainer.

"No. I'm sorry, but I don't have any."

Rather than grumble and move on to the next person, he asked, "Got a few bucks in there you can spare for an old man to get a pack?"

"Umm…" Once again, I stared into the open pocketbook that I now held closer to my face, as if I were trying to climb in to escape this man. I wasn't sure what all I had in there, but at this point, I'd give him the entire bag if it meant he'd leave me alone.

Luckily, I didn't have to give him anything.

A deep, booming voice came from over my shoulder, causing me to freeze with my face close to the opening in my purse. "Leave the lady alone. She doesn't have anything for you tonight, Joe."

"S-s-sorry for troubling you, miss." And with that, *Joe* scurried away, back to his shopping cart that was parked at the entrance to the alley next to the club.

"You okay?" Again, the voice drifted into my ear from behind. Except this time, it was softer, quieter, and held none of the bite from a moment ago. "He didn't take anything from you, did he?"

Just then, the slightest touch met my lower back, right above the swell of my ass near my side. My body stiffened, though not out of fear. The nerves at the base of my spine began to misfire, sending shockwaves straight to the apex of my thighs. Which turned out to be *nothing* compared to the heat that enveloped me when I turned around and was struck stupid the stare of the most beautiful creature to have ever walked the earth.

Yes…*beautiful*. Beyond hot, more than sexy.

Leaps and bounds above gorgeous.

God must've won an award the day he made this man.

"Joe's harmless," the stranger continued. "If he's out of smokes, that's his own problem. I give him cash every Sunday, and I'm not the only one who looks out for the town's wanderer. So, he's either trying to hustle you, or he hasn't watched his spending this week."

His eyes never left mine while he spoke. They were quite mesmerizing. Then a smile slowly formed on his perfect lips, a single dimple popping in his left cheek.

And I was a goner.

Part of me wished this was nothing more than a hallucination caused by the ridiculous number of shots I'd consumed, because that would mean I'd get to stare at him for as long as I wanted without weirding him out and running him off.

Unable to take my focus off his face, I couldn't pay attention to much other than his impeccably styled hair. It appeared to be cut short on the sides while kept longer on the top, which he wore swept back in a don't-give-a-fuck fashion. He was metro yet edgy. Preppy with a heavy dose of badass. A dangerous combination of right and wrong.

"Really, though…are you okay?" He glanced toward the building I'd spent nearly an hour crying in, and the light from the lamppost several feet away hit a small silver ball on the front part of his ear. However, he turned toward me again before I could get a better visual of it. "Leaving? Or just getting some fresh air?"

Beginning to doubt my hallucination theory, I took a deep breath. It was the only thing I could do to get a grip on reality before I made myself out to be a mute drunk. I glanced to the right, away from the club and toward the light like my answer was somehow down the street and I had to find it. "Oh, uh…leaving."

He brought his finger to my face and traced a line from beneath my eye down to my jaw, more than likely following the path of mascara tears. After briefly flicking his gaze toward the bar again, he held my chin between his thumb and forefinger and narrowed his eyes on me. "Did something happen in there?"

Shaking my head, I pulled out of his hold and waved him off. "Nothing like what you're thinking."

"Okay…" He took a couple steps back, slowly bobbing his head, likely mulling over how much truth my answer held. After glancing to the right and then to the left, up and down the street we stood on, he cautiously returned his attention to me.

He had shoved his hands deep into the front pockets of his dark jeans, and I took him all in. Ink lined both arms from beneath the sleeves of his white tee down past the denim that concealed his fists. More color painted the part of his chest visible above the ribbed V of the shirt, decorating his throat, and from what I could tell, extended around to the back of his neck.

I needed to look away before—lacking any inhibition in my inebriated state—I stripped him bare, if only to explore every detailed tattoo on his beautiful skin.

While he gave me his complete attention, nothing else existed as we stood on the sidewalk, facing one another. "You waiting on someone?"

I feel like I've been waiting for you my whole life.

I shook that thought off before I accidentally spilled those words. "No."

His tongue peeked out and slid along his lower lip, his head tilting in contemplation—of what, I wasn't sure. But when he ran his gaze down my body to the teal pumps suffocating my feet, then back up to my eyes, a restrained smirk toying with one side of his mouth, I wanted more than anything to hear his every thought.

That was…until he spoke. "You aren't driving, are you?"

Clearing my throat, I lowered my focus to the cracked pavement beneath his white, unblemished Adidas. "Uh…no. I… um…I don't have a car. I flew in a couple of days early to surprise my fiancé."

Turns out, I was the one surprised.

Biggest surprise of my life.

And *not* in a good way.

"Oh, is he picking you up?"

I peered over my shoulder at the bright blue lights along the front of the building that filled people with false promises of a good time awaiting them inside. They should rename the place. Instead of Rulebreakers, it should've been called Heartbreakers.

When I addressed the beautiful stranger again to answer his question, I nearly melted into a puddle at his feet. The way he kept his eyes focused on me, on my face, capturing my gaze and refusing to let it go…it was sexy and overwhelming and powerful, so addicting I never wanted him to blink.

"Well, you see…he doesn't know I'm here. And I'd like to keep it that way for now."

"Okay. Maybe I'm wrong, but I have a feeling your fiancé is in there." He stepped closer, pointing over my shoulder. "And the longer we stand out here, beating around the bush, the later it's going to get. So forgive me if this is too forward, because that's not my intention. Do you need a ride somewhere? Or someone to keep you company while you wait for Uber to show

up? I don't feel comfortable leaving you out here all alone—
especially at this time of night, in this part of town."

"I appreciate that, um…" Somehow, we'd carried on a
conversation for God knows how long about a homeless man,
my fiancé, not wanting to see said fiancé, and the fact that I
don't even live here, yet we'd never exchanged introductions. I
had no idea what his name was.

Intuitively, he held out his hand and said, "Brogan."

"*Brogan*," I whispered to myself, wanting to feel the way my
lips, tongue, and throat worked together to form his name.
Then I realized he stood close enough to hear it. And if the grin
that slithered across his cheeks meant anything, then he had, in
fact, heard it. Rather than embarrass myself more than I already
had, I slipped my hand into his. "I'm Mercy."

His smile grew wider, and the glow from the streetlight
several feet away caught the glint in his eye, drawing me in
even more than before. "I'm sorry. I think I might've heard you
wrong. Did you say your name is *Mercy*?"

Thank God for the night sky and subtle veil of darkness;
otherwise, there was no way I could've kept him from noticing
my burning cheeks. Which was odd, considering I'd gone
through this song and dance my entire life. My name wasn't
something that had ever embarrassed me before, so I wasn't
sure why his confusion suddenly caught me off guard now.

"Yeah. It's a lame story. Trust me. But yes, that's my name.
Mercy Wright."

"Well, now that we've introduced ourselves, can I help you
get home safely?"

"Doubt it. Home is in Ohio—at least, for now anyway."

"All right. Where are you staying while you're here?"

Even though Brogan wanted to stop *beating around the bush*,
it seemed we were continuing to do so. Then again, my inability
to give him all the facts without waiting to be prompted
might've had something to do with it.

"I wasn't supposed to get here until Sunday, but I switched

my flight at the last minute without telling Jordan. I wanted to surprise him by being early—he teases me all the time for being late to everything. We planned to go house hunting next week since the wedding's in a month. Which, I guess, isn't happening anymore..." My voice trailed off while I once again glanced over my shoulder as if I could see Jordan on the dance floor through the walls of the building.

"Does that mean you don't have a place to stay?"

Brogan's concerned baritone freed me from the mental images of Jordan with some girl in a short red dress. "I guess not. I hadn't planned to stay anywhere other than his town-house, so I didn't bother to book a room."

"Do you have clothes or anything? A suitcase or bag you brought with you?"

"Yeah. But it's at Jordan's place. I stopped to drop it off before coming here."

He sucked in a long, slow breath and nodded through his exhale. "It's completely up to you—and if you say no, I'd totally understand—but if you want, I can drive you to get your stuff and then take you to a hotel or something."

Under normal circumstances, I wouldn't have given his offer any thought; it would've been an emphatic no. Then again, I wouldn't have even entertained his company for this long, so really, there wouldn't have been an offer to turn down. But now, with my transportation limitations and somewhat elevated blood-alcohol level, my logic seemed as clear as tar.

"I'd like that. Thank you."

———

I stared at the diamond on my finger.

Ever since Jordan had placed it there, I never once thought I'd take it off. Not only that but leave it on the table in his foyer. Along with a note. And oddly enough, it was the note I questioned, unsure if I should leave it behind or just say screw it and toss it. It would be nice to make him figure it out for himself. Maybe make him question everything until he drove himself insane. Honestly, that would be the fair thing to do.

Fair to me—which was the only thing that mattered at this point.

Deciding that Jordan didn't deserve an explanation, I took the piece of paper, shoved it into my pocket, and grabbed the handle of my suitcase. There was no telling how long he'd go before noticing the ring that sat on his entrance table, but that wasn't my problem.

From now on, nothing about Jordan was my problem.

And when I walked out the front door, I felt lighter than at any other time in my life.

That was…until I found Brogan leaning against the passenger side of his Wrangler, his hands in his pockets, staring right at me. A shadow fell over his face, so I couldn't see much, though I had no doubt his gaze soaked me in. That was the only thing that would explain the heat that enveloped me as I moved down the steps, closer to him.

He pushed off the side of the Jeep and closed the distance between us. Electricity crackled in the air when he took the suitcase from my hand, and even though it should've worried me, maybe even frightened me, I felt oddly comforted by it. However, not as comforted as I felt at the sound of his warm, deep voice when he said, "You ready?"

In that moment, I realized I *wasn't* ready.

For anything.

But especially *this*—life without Jordan.

Brogan must've sensed my hesitation, because he stilled in front of me. He sketched my face with his fingertip, running across my brow, around the outer corner of my eye, over my cheek, and along my jawline to my chin. The entire time he touched me, I couldn't focus on anything other than the intensity with which he regarded me. Even if I couldn't see it.

"You sure about this, Mercy?"

God, the way he said my name—filled with gravel and weighted with thick fog.

Manly.

Rough.

Rugged.

Dangerous.

And fucking delicious.

I nodded and attempted to curl my lips into a smile. "Yeah. I'm sure."

"Okay then. Let's go." The way he said it sounded like he knew I'd go anywhere with him.

I'd either lost my mind or had *way* too much to drink. I was a trusting person but never to this extent. Never had I been the type of girl who'd hop into a man's car just because he was hot. Hookups weren't my thing, and casual sex wasn't something I'd ever experienced.

Not that leaving with Brogan meant I'd hop into his bed.

Either way, I got into the passenger seat of his red Wrangler and took a deep breath. I had no idea where I was headed. The only thing that mattered was that I was leaving Jordan behind. It'd be scary. I knew that the second I slipped the diamond off my left ring finger and set it down. But there was no way I'd let him win.

Jordan may have thought I was a pushover—I was not.

And in a way I couldn't explain, being around Brogan made me believe that.

2

BROGAN

I stood in front of the fridge with the doors wide open, mindlessly looking through the contents to see what I even wanted to eat. There was a lot—I'd gone grocery shopping this morning—though nothing really stuck out. Then again, that might've had something to do with the fact that my thoughts were on a certain raven-haired goddess instead of the food in front of me.

I couldn't shake her, no matter how hard I tried.

Granted, it probably would've been easier to do had I not sensed her walking into my kitchen. I couldn't see anything other than the inside of the fridge, yet even without seeing her, I knew she was there. Without smelling her, without hearing her...I just knew.

I sensed her.

Mercy would end up reviving me or pulling the plug.

And there was only one way to find out which one she'd do —wait it out.

There wasn't an ounce of me that had expected her to take me up on my offer to give her a lift. So, when she'd accepted a ride, I couldn't very well change my mind. And when we couldn't find a hotel that was both safe *and* affordable for a week's stay, I'd foolishly offered to let her come home with me. Again, not thinking she'd say yes.

In all fairness, she never said yes. Instead, she'd muttered, "You'd really let a stranger stay in your house?" It was cute. And adorable. And it did something to me. I couldn't say no. *Not that I'd wanted to.* Everything about tonight—from seeing her with Joe outside Rulebreakers to being unable to find a reasonable hotel—seemed rehearsed. Planned. Orchestrated as if the universe had controlled the strings to make all this happen for us.

Divine intervention, if you will.

And I was smart enough to know not to argue with fate.

"Hungry?" I asked without closing the door to the fridge. To keep from looking like I'd just stood there for the last five minutes, undecided on what to eat, I grabbed the carton of eggs from the shelf, as well as a package of cheese and diced ham.

And as soon as I took a step back to place everything on the counter, I found her standing in front of the kitchen island, hair wet and swept off her shoulders, amber eyes dancing around the room. Still, she hadn't said a word.

"I know it's late…" I glanced at the time on the microwave above the stove. "Damn, it's almost two in the morning. But I haven't eaten since this afternoon, so I'm starving. I'm going to make an omelet; would you like one?"

Dropping her gaze to the counter between us, she shook her head and rasped, "I'm not really hungry."

I wasn't sure what had her so closed off, and normally, I wouldn't care. But something inside me refused to let this go, refused to let her shut down without knowing why. She hadn't been overly talkative earlier, though nothing close to how reserved she seemed now. Something had happened, and I wouldn't rest until I understood what it was.

"Are you ever going to tell me what went down tonight?" I asked as I grabbed a large frying pan from the cabinet. "If I'm hiding you from your fiancé, I think I should at least know what I'm getting myself into."

She shrugged while fidgeting with her fingers and picking invisible things off the granite. So I stole the opportunity to see her, really take her in—something I hadn't been able to do earlier. I wasn't sure if it was the lack of makeup, the casual clothing instead of her sexy dress, the knowledge that she had been naked in my house, or the lighting in the kitchen, but something made her look and feel like a completely different person than the one I'd picked up outside Rulebreakers.

She seemed…more innocent.

Younger.

More broken.

And while I'd *felt* something in my soul while we stood on the sidewalk outside of her boyfriend's house, it was nothing compared to this moment. Familiarity sizzled in the air. But not like I'd met her before. No. It wasn't déjà vu. The closest thing I could compare it to would be a mirror—as if looking into her eyes had allowed me to see into my own.

The oil in the pan began to smoke, pulling me from the trance she'd unknowingly put me under.

"How old are you, anyway?" I cracked a few eggs, barely paying any attention to what I was making. I didn't slow down for fear she'd suck me right back in…and then I'd end up burning my house down. "You look too young to be getting married."

"Twenty-three." If she continued to check out everything in this kitchen *but* me, I would soon take it personally and likely develop a complex. "And I guess I'm not getting married anymore, so there's that."

"About that…" I stared at her until she *finally* lifted her gaze to meet my eyes. "I don't mean to pry or anything, but I kind of need to know what to expect. If you were my girl and I found out that you were staying at some guy's house, I'd flip my shit."

"He's not like that." She offered the tiniest, shyest smirk

when I questioned her with a quirked brow and cocked head. "I just mean he wouldn't start a fight. I'm sure he'd be mad, but he doesn't have any right to be. I wouldn't be staying at another guy's house if I hadn't caught him practically having sex on the dance floor tonight."

That had been my first assumption when I found her earlier, but the last thing I'd wanted to do was jump to any conclusions. If I'd done that, there was no way in hell I would've left without taking a stroll through the bar to make this prick understand what he'd lost.

"You said you came early to surprise him?" Cooking anything seemed to be difficult with Mercy in front of me. I doubted I'd be able to toast bread in her presence.

"Yeah. I dropped my suitcase off at his house and then located him on his phone. He told me earlier that he was going out with some friends, so I figured I'd surprise him by showing up wherever he was." She sighed and mumbled, "It was quite the surprise."

"So he has no idea you're even in town?"

She shrugged while she resumed picking at the granite, as though something was stuck to the countertop. "I guess he'll realize it when he sees the ring on the table next to the front door. If not, then he'll figure it out when I don't show up at the airport on Sunday."

"You're seriously not going to tell him? You're just going to wait until he figures it out?" Damn...Mercy Wright was a badass with a halo. And it made me wonder what else she kept hidden beneath her wings.

She slid down the island enough to stand closer. Her scent consumed me. It overpowered the egg and oil and drifted beneath my nose. Lavender. I'd recognize that scent anywhere, though it always seemed to smell different on everyone. On Mercy, it smelled like dawn and brought to mind the vision of a sunrise. The burnt oranges and crimson. Warm yellows that promised a new day filled with happiness.

"I was going to." Her soft voice dispelled the daze I'd been in. She must've noticed my confusion—I couldn't remember what I had said to even know what she was talking about—because her brows drew together for a split second. "When I was there to get my suitcase...I wrote him a letter and was going to leave it with my ring. But since he didn't think I deserved his fidelity, I decided he didn't deserve an explanation."

With a smile I couldn't erase, I sprinkled some cheese over the egg before folding it in half. "I don't blame you. But what are you going to do when he calls you a million times to find out where you are? He'll probably think you're dead some-where and call the authorities." That made me laugh. Mostly because I enjoyed the thought of the cops finding her here. I enjoyed that thought better when I imagined them finding her in my bed. "Can he track your location?"

"I turned the tracking off before I got here. It wouldn't have been much of a surprise if he realized I was in town. Then again"—she lowered her voice and her chin—"that might've saved me some heartache in the end."

"At least you know the truth. It's better to find out now than after you married the jackass." I wasn't typically one who talked shit about people I didn't know. But anyone willing to cheat—especially on someone as innocent as Mercy—deserved much worse than being called a donkey. "Gotta look at it that way, or you'll go crazy."

"You sound like you speak from experience."

I cut the omelet in half, slid a piece onto two different plates, then pushed one toward her. After I put the pan into the sink and grabbed us each a fork, I decided to give her an answer to her non-question. "I have experience being cheated on, yes. Except I wasn't lucky enough to find out before the wedding."

"Are you married?"

"Not anymore." I shoved a bite into my mouth and acted as though the egg was too hot to keep talking. It was the only thing I could think of at the time to excuse my lack of explanation, and telling her I didn't want to talk about it seemed insensitive. After all, she was in the middle of her own crisis and, more than likely, yearned for support. Or at least someone who understood what she was going through.

Except I didn't understand.

Because my situation was very different from hers.

Either Mercy didn't want to pry, or she truly was hungry—even though she'd told me she wasn't—because rather than continue the conversation, she stuck her omelet with her fork and took bite after bite until the entire thing was gone. Once we were both done with our two a.m. snack, I took both plates to the sink to rinse them off.

Neither of us had spoken since she asked if I was married. However, as soon as I closed the dishwasher and turned to face her, my reason for remaining silent had nothing to do with deflection. It had everything to do with how unbelievably stunning she was. And the best part...she didn't even have to try.

Every speck of makeup she'd worn earlier had been washed away with her shower, allowing me to see her more clearly. Her dark hair had dried some, leaving it in long, messy waves—like she'd spent the day at the beach. Even her face appeared to have been sun-kissed with the cherry hue of her cheeks. She held her hands in front of her, wringing her fingers while toying with her bottom lip between her teeth. If only she'd lift those golden eyes so I could see all of her.

I'd known her for two hours, yet I had no doubt that Mercy was different.

Damn...even her name was something else.

Normally, this would've been the moment when I'd lead the girl into my room and strip her naked, lay her on my bed, and make her understand why everyone called me *Wrong*. But not this time. Not with her. She wasn't here to climb between my sheets, and I rarely had actual guests—women who spent time here without taking their clothes off or screaming my name in ecstasy. I was probably just as confused as she was, unsure of where to go from here.

I scratched at the back of my neck and cleared my throat. It worked to get her to look at me, and the second her eyes met mine, I was once again at a loss for words. "So, uh…there's a TV in the bedroom. It's connected to Netflix but not cable. If you want cable, you're more than welcome to use the one in the living room." I pointed to the open space beyond the kitchen, as if she'd somehow missed the large sectional couch or floor-to-ceiling entertainment center when she first walked through it.

"Thanks, but I'm pretty tired. I think I'll just go to bed. I didn't want to be rude and walk away if you…" She lifted one shoulder and glanced around the room. I'd seen her do this a few times, like her words had gotten away from her and she had to find them before speaking again. "If you still wanted company or something."

I wasn't sure if this was her way of hitting on me or not, nor was I sure how I felt about it. Instead of figuring out the answer to either of those questions, I offered a smile and said, "Nah, but thank you. If you were staying up and didn't want to be alone, I'd hang out on the couch or something, but I'm beat. So I guess it's best if we both turn in."

Mercy nodded and put one foot behind the other. "Good-night, Brogan. And thanks again for tonight. I really appreciate you helping me out."

"No problem. I guess I was just in the right place at the right time." I hated to think about what would've happened to her had I not shown up. Where she might've gone. Where she would've stayed.

With a sheepish smile, she turned around and slipped into the spare room right off the kitchen. It wasn't until she closed the door that I turned out the lights and went to bed—only to lay there for God knows how long, staring at the ceiling, and pondering divine intervention versus coincidence.

———

My eyes slowly opened, the bedroom door coming into focus as I lay on my side and waited for the fog of slumber to dissipate. Warm light filtered in through my bedroom window and, based on the vibrant colors it splashed across my walls, I could only assume it was still early.

Taking in a deep breath, I rolled to my back and stretched my arms above my head to rid my body of the remaining elements of sleep. Doing so had opened the floodgates in my mind, allowing every memory from last night to rush in. To sweep through my every thought until flash after flash of Mercy's face danced behind my eyes.

I jumped out of bed, more worried about whether she'd left than the time. Urgency fueled my every move as I frantically grabbed a pair of pants to pull on—walking out naked would ensure she'd take off. I didn't worry about a shirt, unwilling to waste another second.

My heart hammered harder with each room I found empty. The last thing I checked was the front door, which remained locked. That didn't mean she hadn't left, considering there was always the garage door, which she could've closed on her way out. After all, that was the point of entry last night; it made sense that would be the way she exited as well. Either way, I felt like a little boy who'd just lost his comfort blanket.

It was an unfamiliar feeling.

My feet were weighted with lead, and my shoulders hung with defeat as I trudged into the kitchen to pour myself a cup of coffee. I managed to fill a mug, grab the milk from the fridge, and add a splash before contemplating how I even had coffee in the first place if I hadn't made it. It was then that I caught a flash of red through the kitchen window.

Standing on the patio next to the pool, leaning against the glass partition between the edge of the deck and the fifteen-foot drop to the bottom, was Mercy. She had on a red shirt that hit her mid-thigh, and had she not been arched forward, ass popped out, I wouldn't have noticed the black shorts beneath it. Dark hair veiled her back, errant strands drifting over her shoulders. She peered into the distance, head turned in profile, granting me a glimpse of her tranquil expression.

Awe hung on her lips and brightened her eyes as she admired the rising sun.

Damn she was sexy.

I could stand in front of my kitchen sink and watch her through the window all day. The way she took in the scene calmed my soul. The sight before me was like mainlining euphoria, filling me with warmth and an inner quiet I never thought possible.

What I wouldn't give to wake up to this every morning.

That thought alone was enough to snap me out of my daze and push me into action. I grabbed the hot ceramic mug and stepped toward the French doors that led to the patio. It took tremendous effort to slow my movements, hide my eagerness, and feign casualty. Weakness wasn't something I was used to, so I couldn't for the life of me understand where it came from now.

3

MERCY

I had never seen anything quite as beautiful as the view from Brogan's back patio.

That was...until the door creaked open behind me, pulling my attention from the colorful sky over the treetops to the colorful chest of a god. I'd wondered last night about the extent of his ink, and now, I had a bit of a clearer picture. Granted, I still couldn't see it all thanks to the light-grey track pants that hung low on his hips and covered his legs.

I couldn't speak or move. Not even blink. The man in front of me consumed my every thought and, possibly, controlled my every action. Right now, it was as though he'd pressed pause, freezing me in time so that only my heart beat and my lungs filled with air.

"I thought you left." There wasn't a sound on this earth sexier than Brogan's morning voice. The grit he'd spoken with last night didn't come close to the way his baritone raked over each word like large tires down a gravel road.

When he moved closer, eyes narrowed and brow lined with deep creases, I realized I hadn't responded. Then again, I wasn't sure what kind of response he was looking for, considering he hadn't asked a question, and seeing me here negated his theory that I had left.

Either way, I forced my lips to curl as much as possible under his scrutiny and said, "Nope. I'm still here." And then I clenched my jaw shut to keep me from saying anything else that would make me sound stupid.

He laughed and slowly shook his head, eyes downcast and a lazy smile drawn wide across the scruff covering his cheeks. When he came to a stop about two feet away, he leaned against the glass partition. Coffee mug in one hand, the other deep into a pocket in his pants, he turned to face me. "How long have you been up?"

"Maybe twenty minutes." I peered over the ledge to focus on the scenery before me like I had been prior to Brogan coming outside. It was the only way I could communicate without locking myself in my own bubble, too afraid of doing or saying the wrong thing. "I made coffee. I hope you don't mind."

"Of course I don't mind, Mercy." There was a good chance he could bring me to orgasm by doing nothing more than saying my name. "I really appreciate it, actually. Thank you. Saved me from having to make it."

"I hope I did it right. I tend to prefer strong coffee. The blacker, the better. It was the only thing that got me through college. My friends call it my crack." Before I rambled like one of those dolls on a string, I gulped down what I had left in my mug and took a bit longer to swallow it all.

"What'd you study in college?"

His curiosity took me by surprise. Honestly, I'd expected him to continue the conversation about coffee. Rather than obsess over his interest in my life, I cleared my throat, concentrating on the pink striations that cut through the sky, and answered his question. "I recently graduated with my teaching degree in early development."

"Nice. Have you started looking for jobs?"

"Funny story…a small private school in town hired me."

He was quiet for a moment, which called my attention away from the sky and back to his face. Last night in the kitchen, his eyes had been a deep green, reminding me of a jungle. Wild and exciting—a hint of danger lurking along the dark edges. Now, standing outside with the light shining on them, his irises were more aqua. Brighter and softer. Even while he stared at me with such intensity, I found them calming. Reassuring. Nevertheless, just as dangerous.

"In town? Like...*here*?" Hope sang in his tone—or maybe that was merely wishful interpretation. "Or did you mean where you're from?"

"Here. Ironic, right? I have a job but no house, no husband, no friends, and no family."

"Have you thought about what you're going to do? With the job, I mean."

I glanced to the side and studied the forest behind his house. "To be honest with you...no, I haven't thought about it." When I found his eyes again, there was an undeniable pull within me to speak without thinking. "This whole thing scares me. Up until last night, I had the rest of my life planned out. Jordan and I were supposed to find a house this week, get married next month, and then I'd live here, where I'd start the job of my dreams and live happily ever after. Now? I have no clue what I'm doing in five minutes, let alone for the next five years."

"You should stay." Leaning forward, he pressed his forearms against the ledge with his mug captured between his hands and squinted off into the distance. "Your flight home isn't for another week, right? So you should stay and hang out. Maybe you'll fall in love with the town for reasons other than a guy. And who knows, you just might make new friends and find your own place to stay."

"Yeah...I don't know about all that."

"Oh, and Mercy?" Without turning much, he caught me out of the corner of his eye. "When I said *here*, I meant my house. You're welcome to stay as long as you'd like."

Brogan may have returned his attention to the sunrise, but I couldn't take mine off his face. I'd tried to admire him last night while we ate, but I didn't want him to catch me staring, so I'd only been able to steal glimpses. And *nothing* came as close to painting the full picture as the sight of him while he squinted into the sun. I may have only been able to see his left side, but there was more to view on half his body than on any man twice his size.

A thin, silver hoop wrapped around the edge of his nostril, so small the light barely reflected off it. Aside from a small disc that held the place of a traditional ear piercing, he had three silver balls in his ear—one on the front flap, one above that in the cartilage, and one on the inside; however, I didn't know the technical names of any of them. And as I'd suspected last night on the sidewalk, ink littered every inch of skin, all the way around his neck, behind his ear, and into his hairline. Never in my life had I found this sort of thing a turn-on, yet regarding him now, I had no doubt I'd have to change my panties.

"You trying to figure out if you should trust me?" He swung his head to the side to face me without moving his stance against the railing. "I get it. I have tattoos and piercings—some you haven't even seen yet," he added with a wink.

I shifted on my feet in a desperate attempt to clench my thighs together without him noticing. The heat between my legs was more than I'd ever experienced. "It's not that."

"Then what is it, Mercy?"

"I know nothing about you."

He hesitated for a moment, and then asked, "Do you *want* to know about me?"

That question didn't require any time to formulate an answer. "Yes."

"Then, by all means, babe, go get dressed. We can get to know each other over breakfast." He swatted my ass playfully and stalked inside, leaving me on the deck to stare at his backside as he walked away.

And oh, dear God, what a backside it was.

———

"Ask me anything." Brogan sat confidently across the table with a wicked smirk on his face. He'd been cheerful since leaving me behind on the patio this morning, even though he hadn't said much. It was more his demeanor that seemed light and happy.

I wanted to learn all there was to know about him; albeit, I would rather have done so at his house, not at a four-person table in some small mom-and-pop restaurant. The tables were so close together, I worried someone would overhear. I imagined this was what speed dating was like.

"I can ask anything? And you'll give me the truth?" I doubted that. No one was *that* honest.

He shrugged, yet when he spoke, he never broke eye contact. "Why not? If it's something I don't want to answer, I'll tell you that. I've never understood some people's motivation to deceive. If you did something, own it. No need to lie about it. If you didn't want the backlash, you never should've done it to begin with. Am I right?"

I wasn't sure I necessarily agreed with him, but that would have to be a discussion for another time. "Okay, so…what's your last name?"

"Daniels." He stared at me for a moment, as if expecting me to say something, and when I didn't, he leaned forward with his elbows on the table. "But everyone calls me Wrong."

Well, that certainly grabbed my attention. "Why?"

"From the stories my Nonna told, my mom used to tell me I was wrong all the time. Don't ask me why, because I don't remember. It could've been any number of reasons. Anyway, when I was about three, I was at church with Nonna, and someone asked me what my name was. I told them it was Wrong. It kind of followed me through life after that."

When his eyes dropped to my mouth, I realized I was toying

with my bottom lip between my teeth and stopped. "Interesting story, except I don't understand how that's a nickname anyone would want to have."

"It is what it is. I guess it's fit through every stage of my life, so it stuck around."

I wanted to know what he meant, but I decided to move along. Otherwise, we'd spend all of breakfast discussing his nickname and the many reasons "wrong" fit him. I wasn't sure I was ready to handle that quite yet. "What do you do for a living?"

"I'm a tattoo artist. Own my own shop." Again, he regarded me, seemingly expecting some sort of reaction.

And again, I didn't give it to him. "Well, that certainly explains the ink," I said with a soft giggle, which brought a smile to his face. "How long have you done that?"

"Since I was sixteen—not on a real person until I was eighteen. My uncle was a tattoo artist. He saw something in me when I was young, so as soon as I was old enough to apprentice, he had me in his garage, learning the ropes. I started working in his shop the day I turned eighteen, and then I took over the business at twenty-five."

I fought against the urge to ooh and ahh. "How old are you now?"

"Twenty-nine. Damn, Mercy…you're asking all the hard ones," he teased.

I decided to teach him not to complain. "When did you get married?"

There was a split second that I worried he'd veto this question—hesitation clouded his gaze and he lowered his eyes. But instead, he ran his hand down his face and slouched in his seat. "I married my high school sweetheart when I was your age. Nonna was sick, and I wanted her to be at my wedding, so Jessica and I had a small, private ceremony with our closest friends and family." His shoulders jumped with the slight laughter that rumbled through his chest. "It was mostly her family, since I didn't have many relatives left aside from Nonna, my Uncle Jerry, and a cousin."

Unsure which direction to go in, I went with the first question that came to mind and made a mental note not to forget the others. "You said last night that you're not married anymore. What happened?"

"Same shit that always happens; am I right? I found out she was talking to some guy behind my back. Some chump I didn't even know. But get this...the prick knew about me. He knew who I was, and he still had the fucking balls to creep up on my wife." He dropped his chin and mumbled, "Bastard."

That sounded fresh, and it almost made me change the subject, except curiosity urged me on. If he didn't want to answer, that was all he had to say. There was no reason to turn around until the tour guide said so. "How long were you married?"

"Four years." Sorrow flickered in his eyes, which created an ache in my chest I couldn't explain. We'd only just met, so there was no reason for such intense empathy, yet there I was, in pain as if I'd lived through it all with him.

Doing the math in my head, I asked, "So you've been single for the last two years?" Unfortunately, all I got in return was a chirped "Yup" and a short nod. If the waitress hadn't sidled up next to our table with a tray of food, I would've pressed for more, but I had to take that as a sign to quit while I was ahead.

While we ate, we exchanged surface-level questions and easy banter. It was nice and relaxing, not at all awkward like I'd expected. Then again, there was something about Brogan that set me at ease. There was also something about him that spiked my blood pressure and soaked my panties, but that could've been chalked up to his physical appearance and sex-laced voice.

It wasn't until we got back into his Jeep that we resumed our conversation. Before backing out of the parking space, he turned in his seat to face me. "Where to, babe? My house? Or are we only making a pit-stop there to grab your suitcase?"

If I'd thought my name on his lips was orgasmic, it didn't come *close* to the arousal-inducing way he called me babe. Granted, there was a very high chance that he called all women that to keep from using the wrong name, but I didn't give a shit. He could've used whatever term of endearment he wanted. Which should've been my first sign to run far away.

Unfortunately, I was too lost in the land of lust to see such a sign.

"Your house…*for now.*" I smiled and then prayed it was sexy rather than pathetic. "I still have more questions for you, Brogan Daniels."

He shifted the Wrangler into reverse and revved the engine while wagging his brows at me. With an effortless laugh, he backed out and headed toward the main road. "Ask away, Mercy. Because once we get home, it's my turn."

We weren't far from the house, which was out in the middle of nowhere, surrounded by trees, so I didn't waste a single second before diving in. "You said you didn't have much family when you got married. What happened to your parents?"

"Dad overdosed on heroin when I was four, and my mom killed herself shortly after. I was raised by my Nonna—my mom's mom—which was why having her at my wedding was so important. She passed away less than three months after I got married."

"What about your uncle and cousin? Are they still alive?"

"Yeah." He had to raise his voice so I could hear him over the wind whipping in through the open windows. "My uncle's a long-distance truck driver, so he's never around, always on the road. And my cousin's currently in jail for the third or fourth time—I can't keep up. But I'm pretty sure he won't make it out again. I think this one's sticking."

"Oh my God." I covered my mouth, hoping he hadn't confused my shock for judgment. "What'd he do?"

"Fucked a minor. Dumbass thought she was eighteen. She wasn't. Turns out, she was only fifteen, and the house he

26

thought was hers was actually her parents'. And the best part is…the *bed* he fucked her on, the one he thought was in *her* room was actually—"

"Her parents' bed."

Brogan peered at me out of the corner of his eye with a smile snaking across his lips. "Bingo. They came home and caught them, called the police, and that was all she wrote. I guess the apple didn't fall far from that tree. The whole reason I got Uncle Jerry's shop was that he was caught inking pretty girls in short skirts…who were *not* of age to get a tattoo. They shut him down real quick. Truthfully, he's lucky that's all he got nailed for. Had they found out about the blowjobs he took as payment, he'd probably be sharing a cell with his son."

Pulling up to Brogan's house during the day offered a much better view than I'd had last night in the pitch black and drunk. It was built into the crest of a large hill—which made the hill seem more like a mountain. The narrow driveway was easy to miss if you didn't know to look between the bushes, and without turning off the main road, you'd never see the house at all. In fact, only the roof was visible until you wound down a long, steep drive, paved with asphalt and lined with large rocks.

He either enjoyed his privacy, or I should've taken his family history lesson as a warning.

"Any other tough questions before we head inside?" He parked in the garage and turned to me with his hand on the key, as if waiting for my answer before shutting off the ignition. "Because once we go through that door, you're in the hot seat."

"Are you a criminal?" My heart pounded too heavily for me to regret voicing that concern.

With an impish grin, he shook his head. "No. I've never been arrested, nor have I ever committed a crime. And before you ask, I don't do drugs. Never even smoked pot. Hand to God. You can't possibly watch your dad choke to death on his own vomit and want to touch that shit—or *any* drug, for that matter."

"Were you there when it happened?"

His hand fell away from the key, as though he didn't have any strength left to hold on to it. And then he collapsed into his seat with dead weight. "Yeah. I have no idea where my mom was, but she wasn't home." As he spoke, he stared straight ahead, and I wondered what his mind's eye saw. "I was young, so I didn't fully understand what was going on. But the bits and pieces of that day that I do remember stuck with me and were always enough to ensure I never got around that shit."

"That's awful," I whispered, wishing like hell I could do something to wipe those memories from his mind. It was impossible, but that didn't mean I didn't wish I could all the same.

"Not as awful as finding my mom in the bathtub a month later. Now…that I *do* remember. In vivid detail. I saw a lot of therapists when I was younger, and they all believed that my mom's death was clearer than my dad's because I wasn't aware my dad had died when it happened. I don't know what I thought because, as I said, I was too young."

Instinctually, I reached over and placed my hand on his, which pulled his attention from the windshield to his thigh. His breathing slowed when he laced his fingers with mine, yet mine sped up—as did my heart.

However, our clasped hands didn't stop him from continuing. "If I think about it, I can recall the gurgling sound in the back of his throat, the color of his lips, and the officer who showed up. They're short clips that play in my mind like a flipbook. But with my mom… There was blood from her wrists everywhere. It didn't matter that I was only four. I was fully aware of what had taken place in the bathroom that day."

"It's my turn." I barely got that out, as if the emotions I'd felt after listening to his account of finding both parents dead one month apart from each other had become tar in my throat, causing my sentiment to become stuck on the way out.

Bewildered eyes met mine in the dim garage. "What do you mean?"

I nudged my chin toward the door at the top of the steps that led into the house. "It's my turn to be in the hot seat. Come on. You're wasting time, and if I decide to stay here, I plan to take full advantage of your pool."

4

BROGAN

Mercy rested the back of her head along the edge of the pool, the water hiding the parts of her I craved to see. The subtle curve of her hips and smooth skin along her inner thighs. Granted, the best parts were still covered by a yellow bikini that left more to the imagination than I would've wanted. Regardless, the soft swell of her breasts that bobbed to the surface every now and then left me drooling and dangerously close to pitching a tent in my board shorts.

"What's the story behind your name? Where'd Mercy come from?" I crouched in front of her so that the water covered my shoulders, putting us face to face.

She rolled her eyes, yet the smile that danced on her lips negated any irritation she sought to convey. "If you had to guess...what would it be?"

I stared at her for a moment and contemplated all the reasons her parents would've given her such a name. "Your mom begged for mercy while she was in labor with you."

"You're such a good guesser," she said, humor coloring her tone.

"Is that really the reason? Or are you just fucking with me?"

"You'll never know, will you, Brogan?" Not only did Mercy

look innocent, but she acted and flirted like a good girl you'd bring home to meet your mom. And for someone like me, that was a dangerous trait to have. "Or should I call you Wrong?"

My chest constricted so rapidly, so harshly that I lost the ability to breathe for a moment. The mere thought of her referring to me as *wrong* in any fashion—regardless of it being my nickname and everyone else under the sun calling me that—felt like a sledgehammer to my sternum. "No. Call me by my name."

Any sign of amusement in her expression fell away. Apprehension curled her shoulders and embarrassment caused her to lower her lashes, preventing me from seeing her eyes. I hated that she'd blocked me out. More than any other time since meeting her, this was the moment I needed to see them the most.

"Mercy..." It was raspy and low, my throat unwilling to release her name for fear it'd slip away and I'd never get it back. But before I could say anything else, she lifted her gaze. And I stopped breathing for an entirely new reason.

Two burning embers stared back at me, desperate and hungry for just one breeze to bring them back to life. Needing to ground myself, I grabbed ahold of her legs, behind her knees, and stepped between them. With her thighs against my hips, she gasped, and her eyes popped open wider. And those two dangerous, smoldering embers became two raging fires, ready to burn out of control.

"Women call me Wrong because they climb into my bed thinking I'm Mr. Right, and then leave knowing I'm nothing but wrong for them. That's why I want you to call me by my name. Call me Brogan. Not Wrong."

"Okay," she breathed out. And after a few moments of pulling herself together, she cleared her throat, shifted so that I released her legs, and stood straighter, raising her shoulders above the surface. "If that's why women call you Wrong, why do guys do it?"

I shrugged and acted as if the loss of her touch didn't affect me as much as it did. "Growing up, it was my nickname. Nonna was the only one who refused to use it. To my friends, I was Wrong Daniels. And when I took over my uncle's shop, I named it Wrong Inc—with a C, like a play on words." I shook my head, suddenly feeling ridiculous for the first time since coming up with the name. "Anyway, over the years, Wrong stuck, and eventually, that's what everyone knew me as. And after the divorce, the name took on a new meaning for women."

"Do you know what I just thought of?" Her lips curved into an infectious grin, eyes bright and dancing in the light. "My last name is Wright. Your nickname is Wrong. Together, we're right and wrong."

Damn… She fucking amazed me. The way she could change the subject as though she could read my mind was impressive. "If we get married, we should take your last name. Can you imagine how confused everyone would be if I was Wrong Wright?"

"Oh, we're getting married now?" The flirt was strong with this one…when she wanted it to be. And for fuck's sake, I hoped she never stopped. "What's next? You want me to have your babies?"

"Of course. We can name them Always, Never, Rarely, Eventually, and Sometimes."

"Five kids?" Her eyes widened dramatically, her mouth falling open. No matter how surprised she tried to act, she couldn't cover up the smile that pulled at the corners of her lips, or the amusement that sparkled like glitter in her irises.

"At least. If you can come up with other words that go with Wright, we can add to that number. But it's always best to start small. We'd make some good-looking babies. After the first one, you'll be on me like cum stains on hotel bedspreads, begging for more until we have an entire litter."

Mercy laughed so hard I wasn't sure she'd ever catch her breath.

"You think I'm wrong?"

"Well, aren't you?"

I rolled my eyes and splashed her. "Just watch, babe. By the end of the week, you'll be professing your undying love for me. And if you're lucky, I'll take you to the airport so you can go home, get your shit, and come back."

"You wish." She splashed me back and then turned around. With her elbows on the ledge, she pressed her forehead against the glass partition and attempted to peer over the side, following the water that cascaded over the edge. "Where does this go?"

"Into the back yard."

She craned her head and regarded me with pinched brows. "Seriously?"

"Want to see?" I waited for her subtle nod before taking her hand and pulling her away from the ledge. I led her out of the pool and around the corner to a spiral staircase that took us to the bottom floor on the backside of the garage. Not once did I let go of her hand.

And not once did she let go of mine.

As soon as we made it to the bottom of the stairs, the water falling from the pool echoed down the narrow hall. She gasped, which did nothing but speed up my already racing heart. And when the waterfall came into view, her grip tightened while her other hand came up to cover her gaping mouth.

"This is... Oh my God, Brogan, this is beautiful." Had we not been standing so close to each other, I probably wouldn't have heard her soft words over the rushing water that crashed into the bed of rocks at our feet.

"It goes over the edge of the pool and lands here," I said while leaning my shoulder against the wall at the opening, pointing to the smooth, grey stones. "Beneath the rocks, there's a drain that collects it and cycles it back through. The architect thought I was crazy when I asked for it, but eventually, he figured it out and got it done. It was one of the few things I demanded the house have when I had it built."

"What were the other things?"

"I didn't want to be seen from the road, and I wanted a basement, which—as you might know—isn't something many houses have around here. Those two were easy once we found this land. Well, not necessarily *easy*, but they pretty much went hand in hand."

"What was so hard about it?"

"They had to dig into the side of the hill and build the elevation a little. It was a pain in the ass, and we had to go in circles with the engineers. In the end, doing it the way we did allowed for this bottom level, which not only gave me a garage, but it also gave me a basement."

She followed my finger to the door a few feet away, painted the same gunmetal-grey as the walls and floor. Then she brought her attention back to the waterfall we stood behind. "I take it your shop does well, then. This had to have cost a fortune."

"I do well, and yes, building this house wasn't cheap. But it was right after I left my wife, so I didn't care about the price tag, just as long as it kept me occupied." Which had turned out to be a mistake, but that wasn't something Mercy needed to hear about.

Hell, it wasn't anything I wanted to *think* about.

"So she never lived here with you?"

It was an innocent question, brought on by my own statement. However, that didn't mean I was interested in answering. So, I stepped around the corner of the wall and dragged her beneath the cascading water, hoping it would take her mind off my divorce, off the darkest moments of my life, and keep her attention right here. Right now. With me.

To ensure that, I captured her face between my hands and brought my lips to hers. My goal wasn't to fuck her out here. Only to redirect her thoughts. I hadn't expected anything to come of it—especially from me. But there I was, holding her half-naked body against mine, my bare chest to hers, our tongues dancing in tandem...and I never wanted to let her go.

I'd heard and read about this kind of magnetic pull, the kind you only feel with one other person. The kind you can't fight against no matter how hard you try. And while I used to believe I'd already felt it with someone else, someone who'd gotten away and taken my heart with her, I couldn't deny how different this was. How much stronger.

More powerful.

More debilitating.

More...*everything*.

If kissing Mercy was the equivalent of two neodymium magnets coming together, then kissing Jessica would've been the same as sticking an advertising magnet to a fridge. No comparison.

Needless to say, it scared the fuck out of me.

And calmed my every fear all at the same time.

Mercy pulled away first, though she didn't move out of my arms. Her eyes, now darker than before—more chestnut than honey—searched mine. And if she saw what I did when looking into hers, then she would've seen my soul. All my hopes and dreams. My desires.

Her gaze fell to my chest, where she had her hands, her fingers splayed across my pecs. And a second later, she was gone. She pushed away, out of my hold. Out from beneath the falling water. In that moment...I knew.

Mercy had seen in my eyes what I'd seen in hers.

"I...uh..." She turned toward the staircase. "I should probably go."

My feet wouldn't move; I'd become rooted in place. There was a chance this was a sign that whatever power she had over me would drown me at the end of it all. "Where?"

"Upstairs. I need to take a shower. And I'm tired. Maybe I'll lay down for a nap."

I nodded, because there wasn't anything else I could do. At least she wasn't leaving.

———

By some miracle, I made it to Sunday without Mercy taking off.

This was now two mornings in a row that I'd woken up with stones in the pit of my stomach, anxiety eating away at me. I'd somehow convinced myself that she'd be gone. That I'd check her room and find it completely empty. And while I knew in my heart why that was, I refused to accept it. At least, not until I was sure she wouldn't disappear.

Thankfully, I didn't have to go far to locate her. When I walked out of my room, I found her seated at the kitchen island with her phone in front of her. Her eyes met mine when I stepped closer, and when her lips curled into a hesitant grin, I felt like I could finally breathe again.

"Be careful, babe. If you keep making coffee for me, I just might get used to it and never let you leave," I teased as I grabbed the milk from the fridge.

"You don't have anything to worry about, baby." She kept her eyes on her cell, though her smile grew wider, more confident. Less hesitant. Meanwhile, I nearly tripped at the sound of her calling me *baby*. "Having your children will ensure I don't go anywhere."

After the awkwardness that had followed us around yesterday, this banter was exactly what I needed. Kissing her had been instinct, though I never stopped to think about the possibility of it pushing her away. So witnessing her flirtatious side this morning calmed my worries and set my soul at ease. "I see you're coming around to the idea. What changed your mind so quickly?"

Her whiskey eyes shone like a beacon of light when she lifted her gaze and smirked, coffee mug poised just below her glossy lips. "The thought of naming one of them Mommy's."

It took a great deal of effort to keep a stern face. And even more to slow the blood rushing south at the thought of knocking her up—because that would mean I'd know what she felt like wrapped around my cock. "You'd have a sixth kid just to name it Mommy's Wright? Does that mean we get to have a seventh and name it Daddy's?"

"How about we compromise?" The twinkle in her eye should've clued me in to what would come next. "We have two kids and name them Mommy's Always, and Daddy's Never."

"Yeah…that's not going to work for me."

She laughed, but it quickly fell flat the second her phone lit up. Without needing to read the question in my eyes, she said, "He's supposed to be picking me up from the airport today." She lifted her attention to me and pointed to her phone. "This is his third message this morning."

"Have you responded?"

"No. He thinks I'm asleep."

"Is this the first time he's reached out since you got to town?" I'd purposely stayed away from asking about him. I wasn't excited by the idea of her thinking about the asshole who'd cheated on her, so I'd kept my mouth shut, hoping she'd bring it up if she wanted to talk about it.

Mercy closed her eyes, released a long sigh, and nodded. "Technically, he texted me Friday night. It was when we were in here eating eggs, so I didn't see it until I went to bed. But I didn't respond. I was supposed to be busy with a fundraiser all day yesterday, which was why I originally couldn't fly in until today. But I managed to get out of it and switched my flights. Not hearing from him yesterday wasn't surprising; he tends to leave me alone when he knows I'm busy."

I couldn't imagine any reason to go an entire day without speaking to Mercy…if she were mine, that is. "What's he saying now?"

"Nothing important—what time he'll be at the airport, how many houses he has lined up to look at this week, and this last one is making sure I remember my hoodie." A sad smile crept along her lips. "He always keeps his place super cold, so no matter how hot it is outside, I wear jackets in the house."

My first thought was why she didn't just keep one there, but I decided against asking that. I didn't really care to carry on a lengthy conversation about her relationship with him. "Are you going to respond? Tell him you aren't coming? Anything?"

"I don't know. If he's saying all this, that means he hasn't seen the ring. And I don't know why he hasn't, considering I left it on the table next to the front door. That's where he puts his keys when he walks in. And it's not like there's anything else on the table for it to get hidden behind."

"So you're just going to let him go to the airport and wait on you for hours?"

She shrugged, and I had to admit that the idea of her fucking with this guy almost made me hard. Then she dropped her head into her hands with a groan and said, "I don't know what to do, Brogan. Tell me what I should do."

On any other day, with any other person, I would've told them that it wasn't my place to tell anyone what to do with their own lives. But not this time. "Block his number so you don't see his calls or texts. Because once he realizes your plane landed and you weren't on it, he will call you." At least, any sane man would.

Then again…a sane man wouldn't have cheated on her.

"What if he thinks something happened to me?"

"I doubt the first call he makes would be to the cops to report a missing person. So, who would he call first when he realizes you didn't come?"

"Either my parents or my best friend."

"Okay then, call them and let them know what's going on."

"I'm not ready to tell my parents about it. And if I tell Stella what he did, she'll get stabby. I don't need that right now."

"Can't you just tell them you're all right? So when what's-his-face calls looking for you, they aren't worried?" To keep myself busy, I began to pull shit out of the fridge. I had no idea what I'd make, but at least I wasn't just standing there, staring at her while trying to convince her to cut off all communication with this asshole.

No need to look as desperate as I felt.

Her smile caught me by surprise—not because she didn't often do it, but because it was flirtatious, and with the current topic, it seemed to come out of nowhere. "I see through you, Mr. Daniels."

"It's Mr. Wright to you…and what do you see?"

She tucked her chin to her chest and giggled. And it took every ounce of willpower to keep from rounding the island and tasting her laughter on my tongue. "You want me to tell everyone I'm okay, so when you hack me up into little pieces and bury my remains in the forest out back, no one will come looking for me."

I twisted around to pull a piece of paper and pen out of the junk drawer behind me. After scribbling a couple lines on the blue sticky note, I made my way to her, caged her in with my arms on either side, palms flat on the granite. Bare chest against her warm back. And lowered my lips to her ear. "I have no desire to bury you out back. If anything, I'm dying to bury my cock in you…but that's a topic for another time."

Her sharp gasp brought a smile to my face.

I pushed away, uncovering the note I'd stuck to the counter next to her phone. "That's my address. If you plan to stay here —which I hope you do—give that to them, so they at least know where you are." Then I went back to the random ingredients next to the stove, hoping like hell she hadn't taken me seriously…unless she wanted the same thing.

Mercy didn't say anything else while she tapped away on her phone. She also didn't make eye contact with me. However, the vermillion tint to her cheeks and apparent strain on her lips were enough to reassure me that it wasn't a bad thing.

"There. Done." She set down the phone and leaned on the

counter with her elbows, spine curved forward, shoulders curled in. Defeat wasn't a good look on her. "Now, to wait for the hundred questions that'll surely come from either my parents or Stella—more than likely both."

I wanted nothing more than to get her mind off the situation. As well as learn as much about her as I could before I lost my chance. "Are you close to your parents? Do you think they'll give you a hard time about staying with me?"

"Yes, and yes. Which is why I didn't tell them I was with you. I gave that information to my best friend. Because, no matter how close I am with my parents, it could be days before they realize I'm missing. By then, you'll have the entire crime scene cleaned up. But Stella...we talk every day. She'll know something's up if I go silent for more than a few hours."

Women amazed me. "So you've been talking to your best friend since you've been here, yet you haven't told her about your fiancé or where you're staying? What the hell have you guys talked about for an entire day?"

Mercy shrugged and attempted to bite back a coy grin. Then she gave up, let the humor roll through her, and said, "Most of the time, we text stupid shit back and forth. Memes or funny things that happened to us or that we saw. Normally, I would've told her what happened Friday night, but I guess I wanted to process it first. Not to mention, I've been with you."

"Well, how about this?" I cracked a few eggs into the pan as I spoke. "We eat...whatever this will be, and then we get dressed for the day. I have to get downtown to find Joe and make sure he's good for the week, and then I have to stop by the shop and catch up on the books—all of which you're more than welcome to tag along for. Meanwhile, you answer texts and calls as they come in, while *not* dealing with the prick who'll hopefully be sitting at the airport for half the day."

"Are you sure you don't mind me following you around?"

"More than sure, babe." Hell, I'd make up places to go if that meant I got to keep her around longer.

5

MERCY

Silence drifted through the doorway like a dense fog, suffocating me. And if that wasn't bad enough, nighttime cloaked the house, the darkness blinding me until I couldn't breathe, couldn't see. Couldn't think straight. I just prayed that Brogan hadn't gone to sleep in the twenty minutes since saying goodnight.

The distance between the room I stayed in and his wasn't that much. But at night, in a pitch-black house—an *unfamiliar* house, at that—it seemed to be miles away. Every creak in the wood was a muted scream. A quiet confession that I didn't belong. I was an intruder. And once I stood in front of his bedroom door, I contemplated turning around and making the long journey back to my bed.

Except I couldn't.

Because I was weak and afraid, too tempted by the unwelcome darkness to unblock Jordan's number or listen to the numerous voicemails he'd left on my cell. My heart ached, and I craved a distraction. Something tangible and real. Anything to get my mind off the lump in my throat and weight on my chest. I couldn't be sure, but I had a feeling that Brogan wouldn't turn me away—especially after he'd kissed me underneath the waterfall yesterday.

I tapped on his door, light enough that he'd hear it if he was awake but wouldn't alert him if he'd fallen asleep. And then I held my breath, unsure if I truly wanted him to answer or if I wanted to slip back into bed unnoticed.

A few seconds later, when I hadn't heard him respond, I put one foot behind the other. Only to freeze in place with a gasp when the door opened. Brogan stood in front of me, looming in the doorway like a da Vinci painting.

"Is everything okay?" he asked without an ounce of sleep in his tone.

The level of concern in his husky voice melted my panties and soothed my erratic heartbeat. But when he stepped toward me, bringing his face closer to mine, nothing eased my trepidation quite like the interest that flashed in his dark eyes. It swathed me in peace and coddled me, lulling me into a state of comfort and security as real as the air I breathed.

"I'm sorry. I wasn't sure if you were awake or not."

"I'm awake, babe. What happened? Are you all right?"

In one second, we went from standing at least a foot apart to his palms cradling my cheeks. His fingers stretched and splayed around the sides of my head and along my neck. He may have only touched my face, but I could feel him everywhere. As if he'd crawled into my chest and taken up residence.

If I'd known what was best, I would've evicted him.

Instead, I pressed my hands against his pecs and allowed the heat of his skin to subdue my doubt. "Yeah, I'm fine. I just couldn't sleep. I can't stop thinking about...you know."

"Has anything changed? Have you talked to him?"

I shook my head, hoping that would be enough of an answer for him.

"Do you want to sit on the couch and watch a movie?"

Again, I shook my head. This time, however, it wasn't enough of an answer for *me*. I didn't know what I wanted from

Brogan, other than to make this ache go away. I needed the anxiety to vacate the pit of my stomach and the voices in my head, asking a thousand what-if questions, to quiet. Watching a movie on the couch should've been able to do all those things.

But the thought of his mouth and hands consumed me.

The way his lips had frozen time beneath his waterfall.

His tongue against mine had eradicated all the evil in the world.

He'd kissed me only one time, yet my heart had become a junkie. My soul craved him as if we'd somehow known each other in a past life, and the thought of losing him again was too much to bear. He might've only kissed me once, but there wasn't a single part of me that believed he hadn't touched every ounce of my being a thousand times over again.

Throwing caution to the wind, I lifted myself onto my tiptoes and pressed my lips to his. He didn't resist—not that I expected him to, but the fear was always there. He quickly dropped his hands to my hips and turned me to the side, pushing my back against the wall right outside of his room. And the instant I felt his erection along my lower stomach, I moaned into his mouth.

The last thing I expected of him was to pull away. Yet he did. He broke the kiss and pressed his temple to mine, panting in my ear as though he'd just finished a marathon. "I'm not right for you, Mercy."

"Maybe I don't want what's right for me, Brogan." I raked my nails down his abdomen and hooked my fingers into the waistband of his track pants. "Maybe, just this once—this one time, this one night—I want wrong. Right fucked me over. Now I want to fuck Wrong."

Not another word was spoken—not like there could've been with how fast Brogan claimed my mouth. He skirted his hands around my ass and down the backs of my thighs before lifting me off my feet. And within seconds, I was flat on his bed, my legs wrapped around his waist.

His tongue danced with mine.

My nails clawed at his shoulders.

It was passion and need and unimaginable desire.

Hot and desperate. Like he couldn't get my clothes off fast enough, like I couldn't get him *close* enough. I wanted to draw it out, make it last. But I was also impatient and needed it now. Fast. Hard. All of him, all over me. Inside and out.

Even though the hint of moonlight through the blinds allowed me to see what he was doing, it wasn't enough. I needed to see *everything*—his eyes, his expression, the pleasure and yearning on his face. For the first time in my life, I craved the whole experience. So when he flicked on the light next to the bed, I sighed with relief.

Then I whimpered at the sight of his dick—more accurately, at the discovery of the barbell that penetrated the head, a silver ball on the top and bottom.

And when he situated himself above me again, I moaned.

"You're so fucking beautiful, Mercy," he whispered along my lips a split second before kissing me, swallowing my choked cries of urgency. His mouth on mine obliterated every last thought in my head. His warm hand on my bare hip sent electricity throughout my entire body. However, nothing compared to the way my chest constricted when he pulled away, just enough to look me in my eyes, and said, "I'll show you wrong if you show me right."

Rather than attempt to speak—my voice wouldn't have worked even if I tried—I nodded and dragged my legs up his sides until I dug my heels into his ass cheeks. I longed to feel him inside me, and without the ability to verbally express it, I had to *show* him.

His hard length slid through my folds, slick with my arousal, except he didn't give in to me. Instead, he held my stare with such intensity I could've come right then and there without any penetration. "Tell me this is what you want, Mercy."

Again, I nodded.

Unfortunately, that wasn't enough for him. "With your words, babe. Tell me."

"I want you." My voice, thick with lust, became caught in my throat so that my words came out croaked and broken. "I want this, Brogan. All of it. With you. Right now."

He didn't waste a single second before pushing inside me. Filling me. Stretching me. Satisfying cravings I never knew I had while meeting every need I'd never admitted to him. In the end, he worshiped my body and owned my soul. He claimed my desires. Branded my heart and left his mark on every cell that was me. I lay naked beside him, spent and sated. Panting. Exhausted yet wide-awake. And in the comfort of his arms, I felt safe. Wanted. Needed.

But most of all…I felt cherished.

"Did these hurt?" I asked while carefully toying with the small barbell that went through one of his nipples. He had them both done, but with the way I was folded against his left side and partially draped over his chest, I could only pay attention to the one on the right.

"Nah." His fingers danced in circles along my shoulder while we talked. "Out of all my piercings, those were some of the less painful."

I figured his dick had been the most painful, but I wasn't about to ask. Bringing that up would only remind me of how incredible it was to feel it on the inside, stroking the right spot as he brought me to the edge over and over again. Yeah, I couldn't allow myself to get lost in those thoughts, or else I wouldn't have been able to carry on a conversation that made any sense. "What's worse…getting pierced or getting tattooed?"

"Depends on where, I guess. There's been a time or two I've had to take a break in the middle of getting a tattoo just to reset. There have also been plenty of times I've barely felt it. I have piercings that didn't even make me flinch, some that have turned me on, and one that required a paper bag." His soundless laughter rippled through his chest. "But no, these didn't bother me."

"I've always wanted a tattoo."

"Yeah? I happen to know a guy who could do you up while you're in town."

"How do I know you're even any good?" I teased, fighting off my smirk even though he couldn't see it anyhow.

Brogan shifted toward me, rolling into me, and twisted our legs together. "Babe...I'm way better at that than I am at sex. Does that answer your question?"

Holy hell. There was a chance my tired and weak body had just become ready for round two. Brogan Daniels was a god in bed, which could only mean his abilities with ink and skin had to be unmatched. However, I wasn't ready to end the flirtatious banter just yet. "So I take it that means you're only okay? Average? Middle of the road?"

Heat consumed my neck a split second before he licked a path along my jaw. I assumed he was about to say something with the way he positioned himself, bringing his lips to my ear, but as soon as I relaxed into him, ready to hear whatever lingered on the tip of his tongue, he expertly and swiftly filled my swollen core with one finger. Just enough to remind me of how good a lover he had been.

"That's not what you were saying when I was buried inside you, Mercy." His gruff voice stifled my gasp and drew out my moan. "I do believe you were begging for more. Did I hear that wrong? Or were you faking it?"

I shook my head, praying he would never remove his hand from between my legs.

"No what, Mercy? Which question are you saying no to? Tell me. I want to hear it."

"I wasn't faking it."

"That's what I thought." He took his finger away, but before I could form the first grumble over the absence, he stuck it into his mouth, wrapped his full, delicious lips around the knuckle, and slowly dragged it back out, humming as he exaggerated the pop at the end. "Does this mean you're going to let me tattoo you while you're here?"

"You can do whatever you want to me, baby."

"Mmm...that could get dirty."

For the first time in my life, the idea of getting dirty with someone excited me.

———

Stella had called several times over the last few days. Some of the calls I'd answered, others I'd sent to voicemail. To be fair, those were typically during moments when Brogan had me... incapacitated, if you will. But eventually, I knew I would have to tell her what was going on.

Even if I wasn't ready.

"You're starting to worry me, Mercy." For Stella, that was a big deal. She smoked a lot of pot, so worrying wasn't something she did often. "You never keep things from me for this long. You always tell me everything. But now, you're at some guy's house, having the best sex of your life days after giving your ring back to Jordan, and you won't give me any details."

I wrapped the towel tighter around my body and sat on the side of the bed—my suitcase had remained in this room, though I hadn't slept in here since Saturday night. "For the second time...I literally just stepped out of the shower. I haven't even fully dried off yet. Can I call you back when I'm done?"

"No. Getting dressed has never stopped you from talking to me before. Hell, you do it on FaceTime while you stand out of view of the camera. Why is this any different?" She wouldn't give up until I gave her something.

Brogan had left to run a couple of errands, and when he came back, we were supposed to get ready to hang out with a few of his friends. I had probably less than half an hour to get dressed and dry my hair. So, at this point, it was either be late or multitask like a mother.

"Where do you want me to start, Stella?"

"The sex. Duh. Always start with the sex, Mercy."

I pulled up a pair of panties and traced the violet outline of Brogan's teeth on my inner thigh. A near perfect circle. The memory of that bitemark caused my body to flush, but that was nothing compared to the arousal I felt at the sight of the faded one on my hip. "Fucking unbelievable."

"So you've said. Details, hooker. I need details."

Closing my eyes, I vividly recalled all the ways Brogan had taken me over the last four days. He'd explored my body in all the rooms in his house. His hands and the pinch they could cause my skin as well as the soothing heat of his palms. His lips. His tongue. The silver rod through his shaft, just below the head, which served several different purposes for both of us.

The thought of him left me wet and desperate.

"Never mind, I don't want to know. I swear, you sound like a cat in heat over there."

I laughed and pulled out a pair of shorts and a tank top. If I hadn't gone naked so much this week, I would've been out of clothes. Thank God for a man with a healthy appetite for sex. "I do not. Shut up. I'm trying to get dressed and talk at the same time."

"Don't lie. I get it...he's a god in the bedroom. You can tell me all about that when you come home—which you are still doing, right? You're not going to call me on Saturday and tell me you've decided to move in with the guy, are you?"

After clasping my bra, I carefully adjusted the band to keep it from rubbing against the tattoo on my ribs. The one Brogan had put there the other day. Ever since telling him that I wanted one, he wouldn't let it go until he had me in his chair, marking me with ink. I lightly ran my finger along the fancy letters covered in ointment. *Save me and have me, fix me and I'm yours.* I still wasn't sure where the line came from, but there was something so unbelievably perfect about it that I doubted I'd ever be able to fully comprehend its meaning.

"No. And maybe next time, smoke a bowl or something before you call. You're too high-strung for me today." It was a joke, and luckily for me, she knew it.

She laughed and said, "Moving on. Have you heard from Jordan?"

I rolled my eyes, oddly annoyed at the topic instead of upset by it, which was what I'd expected to still feel this soon after his betrayal. Heartbroken at the very least. Certainly not irritated and repulsed. I guess indifference was better than sorrow.

"I can only see his voicemails, which I haven't listened to. He sent me two emails, but I haven't read those, either. If he's tried social media, I wouldn't know. I've stayed off those on purpose. Completely signed out of them. Why…have you heard from him?"

"He called a few times at the beginning of the week, but when I told him that he was wasting his breath, he finally got the hint and stopped. Apparently, your mom told him to give you a little space and you'd come around. She's under the impression you're having a case of cold feet."

I'd only called two people—three, if you counted my parents individually—to tell them I was okay, but that I needed them to ignore Jordan until I could explain everything next weekend. However, I didn't tell my parents anything more than that, knowing they would repeat it all to Jordan the second he called. Worse, they would've called him the instant I hung up with them.

It might've been fucked up, but I wasn't ready to let him off the hook that easily.

And while I hadn't given Stella many of the specifics, I did assure her that my whereabouts were in my email inbox in the event something happened to me. That had only increased the number of texts and calls from her since. Then again, I couldn't fault her for that. She knew I was with a guy in a town I was only vaguely familiar with—if she'd known just how far out in the boonies we were, she would've had a much bigger issue with the whole thing. I guess I should've been thankful she hadn't gone to my apartment and retrieved my computer to get the information herself.

It wasn't that I didn't trust Stella with Brogan's information when he'd given it to me. The reason I'd kept it to myself was because I wanted to hold on to this secret for a little while longer. It was the first bold, daring, and possibly dangerous thing I'd ever done, and I wasn't ready to let anyone else in on it. Not even my best friend.

I rolled my eyes and groaned. "I wouldn't be surprised if, after finding out that I caught him cheating on me, she still tries to convince me to go through with the wedding. She means well, but my God. It's like she can't accept that I'm an adult and capable of making my own choices." It'd taken her longer to accept that I was moving out of state after the wedding than it did for me to plan the whole thing, which *included* getting a job.

"Do you think anything long-term is going to happen with this mystery man?"

"I doubt anything will carry on after I leave here. I wouldn't be opposed to it, but I won't hold my breath, either. He seems to be a bit of a ladies' man. Plus, he's not my type at all."

"Oh, you mean he doesn't wear polished shoes? Wasn't valedictorian of his graduating class? I take it he doesn't have his PhD, either. See what happens when you lower your standards? You find someone who can rock your world seven ways to Sunday and then back again." Stella tended to exaggerate to the nth degree, which I'd learned to accept long ago. "And are you ever going to tell me his name other than *B*?"

"Like I've said a dozen times…I'll tell you everything when I get home."

"Fine. But don't think I'll let you get away without divulging every juicy detail."

I laughed while slipping my top over my head. "Don't

worry. I'd never be foolish enough to assume that. But listen, I have to go. He'll be back soon, and I still have to dry my hair. I can do a lot while talking on the phone, but doing so while using a blow dryer is impossible."

"Whatever. Have fun tonight…with whatever it is you're doing."

"Thanks. I will. Talk to you tomorrow."

After disconnecting the call, I quickly rushed through the rest of my routine, wanting to be completely ready by the time Brogan walked through the garage door. I wasn't entirely sure where we were going or who we would be hanging out with, but he'd promised there was no way I'd run into Jordan or see anyone I knew—which was an easy bet, considering I didn't know many people in the area.

I'd just finished applying mascara when he came up behind me and gripped my ass with both hands. He lowered his lips to my neck, inhaled deeply, and rasped, "Why are you in here?"

"Where else would I be? All my stuff is in this room."

His next words were so predictable, I could've recited them myself. "That's because you keep taking it out of my room."

I turned to face him and placed my hands on his shoulders. "It's for the best."

He'd argued with me the few other times I'd said that, but I meant it. I knew myself better than anyone else, and if I allowed it, I'd fall for him. Head over heels. Considering my heart hadn't been broken for a week yet, that was dangerous territory.

Instead of putting up a fight this time, he covered my lips with his, proving his point with his mouth: *Live in the moment, Mercy. Don't think about it and just have fun.* Easier said than done, although it did sound nice in theory.

"You about ready, babe?" he asked and then licked his lips, his eyes lingering on mine.

"Yeah. Just waiting on you."

"Well then, let's go."

6

BROGAN

The last Thursday of every month was trivia night at the hole in the wall near the house. With Mercy being here, I'd planned to skip tonight, but the guys gave me a hard time about it. Especially since I'd taken the week off work at the last minute. I'd never done that. In all the years I'd been there—when it was Uncle Jerry's and after I'd taken over—I hadn't missed a single day.

I'd had concerns about bringing Mercy around the group. They were loud and rude, and not many women found their company entertaining. But more than that, I didn't want anyone to mention *Wrong Inc*. I'd managed to get this far without Mercy finding out that I had a bigger reputation than I'd let on, and I'd be damned if someone clued her in this late in the game.

In the end, I invited Mercy along, and she came without hesitation.

What was probably the most shocking part of the night was how easily she fell in with my friends, as if she'd been a part of the group from the beginning. It was odd, considering they weren't fond of pussy infringing on guys' night. And by some miracle, we made it through the entire game of trivia without any mention of my not-so-secret lifestyle that I'd *somehow* kept secret from Mercy.

"I got to say, man…" Robbie held my stare with slightly dropped lids, showing how much he'd had to drink. His eyes were always the first to show. "I didn't believe you to begin with. When you said she don't know about the show, I thought she must've been pulling your leg."

I glanced around the smoky, packed bar, making sure Mercy hadn't come back from the restroom and overheard. "Shut the fuck up, Robbie. I told you all not to bring that shit up tonight." I took a swig from my drink and then pointed the top of the bottle at him. "And trust me, I thought the same thing. But she honestly doesn't know, and I'd like to keep it that way for as long as possible."

Bradly let out a small snicker and kept his gaze fastened on a shapely woman bent over a pool table, lining up a shot. Normally, I would've looked, too. Hell, we all would've been commenting on other objects to bend her over.

But not tonight.

Robbie waved me off and then leaned against the high-top table we stood around, wiggling his eyebrows. "From what I can tell, she knows everything else about you. All it'll take is one search on Google and *boom*. You got a bag but no cat… because it's out of it."

I couldn't suppress the laughter that hit me in my chest, dimmed by the clamor of voices around us competing to be heard. "Don't you think I know that? I can't keep her from finding out about it, but I also don't want to tell her if I don't have to."

I paused mid-thought when the guy behind me brushed against my back. "My bad, dude," he said with a lazy smile. Trivia night was always packed. And with dollar draft beers, always full of drunks.

With a curt nod, I turned back to Robbie and Bradly and leaned in. "I think the only reason she hasn't looked me up is because she's signed out of her social media in order to avoid her ex. And to be honest, I wouldn't think to search a random person on Google. A celebrity, maybe. But not everyone I meet."

Robbie elbowed Bradly as though he was about to tell a good joke. "But you *are* a celebrity." He emphasized the *tee* at the end, making me laugh harder.

I flipped him off and fought to compose myself. "No, I'm not. And she doesn't know that."

"You scared she'll turn out like all the others?" He meant the women who saw dollar signs when they looked at me. "'Cause I'm not so sure she will, man."

Glancing around the bar, I took in the people around us. I recognized several of them—trivia night tended to bring in the same crowd every week—but a few I'd never seen before. There were women I'd fucked around with, and then others who wanted it yet never got it. Some were keeping an eye on me, while a few more had given up trying to get my attention. However, they all had the same thing in common—they may have been looking at me, but not a single one of them *saw* me. And it made me think of Mercy. Made me think of the way she took me in when she set her eyes on me.

No one had ever done that before.

Shaking my head, I turned back to Robbie. "Nah. It's nothing like that."

I worried she'd run.

Bradly had remained quiet throughout the conversation so far, but apparently, this was worthy of his opinion. He raised his glass and said, "You got it bad, don't ya?"

Staring over Robbie's shoulder toward the restrooms, I contemplated his question—or, more accurately, his *accusation*. It wasn't the first time I'd thought about it; however, it was the first time anyone else had pointed it out. Or put me on the spot. And for whatever reason, it made me delve deeper than I'd been willing to on my own.

If I had to categorize myself as something, I would've said

laid-back. Easy. Go with the flow. It took little to be content, and a lot to get me excited. Mercy excited me. Everything about her left me exhilarated. Smiling like a fool. Carefree and reckless like a teen. And it would've been a lie if I said I didn't know why.

I was a man of few beliefs, but I believed in Mercy Wright.

I believed in her presence. Her meaning. *Her.*

"It doesn't matter how bad I have it, does it? She'll leave on Saturday, and that'll be the end of it." No matter how much I'd tried to prepare for this to come to an end, the thought of it still soured my stomach and lurched me into full-fledged denial. "Maybe she'll still talk to me after she gets home. Maybe she won't. But I'm not stupid. Sooner or later, she'll realize who I am, and then everything will change."

"It doesn't have to." That was about as close to words of wisdom as Bradly could get.

"Yeah, it does. It *always* does." I didn't have to say anything else—they knew what I meant. "No matter how much I want to, I can't keep her."

Bradly cleared his throat half a second before Mercy appeared at my side. I turned to let her nuzzle closer, like she'd been all night, and then I wrapped my arm around her waist, like *I'd* done all night.

"A table only goes quiet when someone walks up if they were all talking about that person." She glanced between Robbie and Bradly. I couldn't see her face to read her expression. "So, what was it? If you're gonna talk about me, don't I at least get to know what it was about?"

Damn…her sass turned me on.

"I was just about to bet Wrong a pitcher of beer"—Bradly winked at me, and my heart sank—"that he won't ask you to marry him."

I wasn't sure what I expected her reaction to be. Maybe for her posture to turn rigid, her back to straighten. Anything to let me know just how ridiculous she'd thought his bet was. But to my surprise, she did none of that. In fact, she giggled and shook her head, probably assuming it had been a joke.

Knowing Bradly, it was not.

"A pitcher of beer to ask? You might want to go ahead and flag the woman over then, because you're about to buy the next round." I shoved my empty glass to the center of the table and pulled Mercy closer. "What do you say, babe? Marry me?"

She tilted her head back against my shoulder and let the waves of her invigorating laughter wash over me. Consume me. Sweep me under and never let me go. "Sure thing, baby. Let's go down to the courthouse tomorrow and get hitched."

With a smile so wide I worried it'd split his face in half, Robbie slapped the table, rattling everything on it, and shook his head. "You'll never learn, Bradly. Never. You have to watch the words. Be specific."

"I'll give you this one," Bradly complained, and then he turned his attention to Mercy. "You really should consider it, peaches. You just might be the one person who could make this motherfucker stop bitching about the one who got away."

Suddenly, the humor in her shoulders died, and her body turned hard against mine. This wasn't a conversation I wanted to have—here or at any other time—so I waved down the barmaid and asked for another pitcher of beer. Then I held my breath until the subject changed.

———

I didn't think it was possible to get enough of Mercy's naked body.

As I rested between her bare legs, propped up by my elbows on either side of her smooth stomach, I had to fight the urge to crawl up a little more and slip inside her again. I also had to make sure I didn't stare at her for too long; that made her self-conscious, and she'd shy away.

"Have I told you how beautiful your tits are?" I asked with my mouth hovering over one.

She giggled but didn't push me away. Instead, she threaded her fingers through my hair and gently squeezed me between her legs. "Only about a thousand times. Maybe after hearing it a thousand more times, I might actually believe it."

I'd never understand why she couldn't see herself the way I did.

If only she could…

I traced the letters of her tattoo on her side, along her ribs. The words still tripped me up—especially the "fix me and I'm yours" part. When I'd asked about the meaning, her explanation made sense. Despite what it said, she didn't want someone to take care of her. Instead, she wanted an equal. Someone just as lost and broken as she felt. She yearned for the kind of person she could grow *with*. And that was something I not only understood, but I respected as well. Damn…this woman continued to impress me.

"Why did your parents name you Mercy?" My lips curled against her skin.

"Why did yours name you Brogan?"

"It's a family name. Now it's your turn to answer my question."

Amusement hiccupped in her chest. "Why do you think?"

"They wanted you to be kind and compassionate?"

Nothing came close to the beauty that was her natural smile. Not posed or provoked, but genuine happiness that came from within. "That would've been an excellent reason."

"I don't know why you won't tell me. I answer your questions."

"Speaking of…" Apprehension invaded her expression as she flitted her sight around the room. "What did your friend mean tonight when he mentioned *the one who got away*? Was he talking about your ex-wife?"

Ironically, her nervousness enticed me to answer. "Yeah.

After I left and began to cool down, I realized I'd lost her. And I thought I'd never find that feeling again."

"Then why leave? Why not work it out?"

I pushed up on my elbows to see her face as we spoke. Needing her to see the unspoken sentiment through my eyes. The words I couldn't bring myself to say. "I left when I found out she was talking to another guy. I didn't ask questions. Hell, I didn't even fight. I read through the conversations they had online, so really, there was nothing she could tell me that I hadn't already seen for myself. There were things she revealed to him that she never told me. I gave up and walked away without fully comprehending what I was walking away from."

Not once did Mercy avert her attention or pull her calming touch from my hair.

"She never slept with him, which was something I didn't find out until way later…because I had refused to hear her out. In fact, they had never met. I guess it was just some online thing that had gone on for over six months. She had feelings for him. She couldn't deny that. Nonna always said my stubbornness was my greatest attribute…*and* my greatest weakness."

This shouldn't have been so easy to talk about, yet with her, it was like discussing the weather. Effortless and painless and…*freeing*.

"During that situation, it was definitely my weakness. I didn't care that they were never physical. I believed she'd given him a part of her that should have been reserved for me. In a way, that was worse than fucking him. I turned my back on her —on us—without thinking twice about it."

"Then what did he mean when he said she was the one who got away?"

I blew out a breath. "Over time, I began to doubt my decision, but by then, it was too late to do anything about it. She moved on—left town, actually—and cut off all communication with me. She refused to have a simple conversation. I'd convinced myself that she was it, and I'd let her slip through my fingers. The only thing I could do was sit back and wait for her to return."

"So you think she's your soulmate?"

"No." I knew that would get a reaction, so I wasn't surprised by her knitted brows or scrunched nose. In fact, I found it cute, which was why I laughed—though she likely thought it was for another reason. "One of these days, I'll explain my theory on soulmates and life partners. But not tonight."

"*One of these days*. You say that like I'm not leaving. Did you forget that you're taking me to the airport in approximately"— she quirked her lips to the side and hummed—"thirty-six hours?"

"No, I haven't forgotten. Does this mean you've decided to turn down that job at the private school in town?" I stared into her eyes, reading the truth before she could recognize it herself.

It was amazing what the heart knew, even when the rest of your being wasn't so sure. Knots riddled my stomach while I awaited her answer, yet not once did my heart rate accelerate. It didn't dip or clench. Didn't threaten to jump out of my chest or shrivel up inside. It remained strong. Steady. Keeping with the same tempo no matter how long it took Mercy to respond.

My heart just knew.

"I haven't made up my mind." While that technically may have been true, it wasn't the *truth*. She just hadn't accepted it yet. The real answer shone in her eyes, in the honey swirls that held me hostage. It was only a matter of time before her brain caught up with her heart.

"I think you have, but you're too scared to admit it."

"Why would I be scared?"

Brushing my thumbs along her sides, I smiled confidently and said, "Because the idea of moving here freaks you out."

"Because of Jordan?" She rolled her eyes.

"No. Because of me." And that widened them, pulling them to mine until she couldn't turn away. She couldn't hide from the truth. She couldn't deny it or play it off…not while looking into my eyes. Because looking at me was no different than looking into a mirror; we were a reflection of each other. "You can't understand this magnetic pull between us. You've excused the insane, inconceivable level of chemistry we have as nothing more than lust. Something to pass the time with for the week. And anytime you've attempted to dream about what it'd be like after this week's over, the intensity frightens you. *That* is why you're too scared to admit that you want the job."

"Maybe I don't want to get my hopes up," she whispered, her voice raw and aching.

I pulled myself up her body, just enough to bring my face to hers. "Don't hold them down, Mercy. Release all your hopes and dreams into the universe, as high as they can go, and trust that they won't come crashing down. If you don't, you'll never know if they're attainable."

In an instant, fear washed over her eyes, locking her within its cage. Her mask slid into place with a coy smirk and crimson cheeks. "I find it ironic that the man who's pining after his ex— who he has labeled as the one who got away—is suggesting that I let go of my inhibitions and jump in feet first. Yeah…no thank you. I don't have a problem killing time for a week, but I'm not going to sit around with you and wait for your soul-mate—or whoever she is—to come back."

If I knew she wouldn't push me away, I would've told her the truth. I would've explained it all to her. But I couldn't. Because no matter how deeply I trusted my intuition on this, it wouldn't ease her fears. If anything, it'd exasperate them.

There was always a runner and a chaser.

She was no doubt the runner.

And I wouldn't give her a reason to flee.

"Want to go somewhere tomorrow?" My question caught her off guard, which made me laugh. "It's your last day before you fly out. Let's get out of here. Go out of town. We can stay the night, and on the way back, I can swing you by the airport."

"Where are we going?"

I shrugged, even though I knew *exactly* where I wanted to go. "We could go anywhere. I hear Savannah's really nice this time of year. Have you ever been?"

"Nope, can't say that I have."

"Good. We'll go there. We'll get up in the morning, fuck in the shower, then grab our bags, fuck one last time, and then hit the road." I gently nipped at her bottom lip, knowing how much it drove her crazy.

"Why do I get the feeling you're using this to convince me to come back?"

I covered her mouth with mine, just long enough to silence her. Then I pulled away, looked deep into her eyes, and said, "Mark my words, babe...I *will* get my way. And you *will* come back."

Mercy Wright would be mine before she boarded that plane.

End of story.

7

MERCY

Within forty-eight hours, my life had flipped upside down.

Turned inside out.

Twisted around before finally settling into a beautiful chaos that excited and scared me all at once. But as I pulled into the parking space in front of my apartment building with exhaustion clinging to my lids, all I could think about was getting my suitcase upstairs and falling into bed. Well, that wasn't necessarily true. Brogan encompassed the majority of my thoughts, most of which were the very reasons I planned to crawl beneath my covers and catch up on lost sleep.

I pushed through the front door, wheeled my suitcase against the wall, and engaged the deadbolt behind me. When I turned, ready to trudge to my room, my heart stopped, and an abrasive cry ripped from my chest. A figure standing in the living room a few feet away startled me. But I soon regained my senses and realized he wasn't an intruder.

Yet relief was the last thing I experienced.

Instead, I was pissed to find him in my apartment without my permission.

"Why are you here, Jordan?" If he expected to find a broken-hearted woman, he'd come to the wrong place. Anger continued to fuel me, leaving no room for sorrow or regret. I'd left that behind on the sidewalk outside his house, right before I left with Brogan.

"You refuse to answer my calls or texts. Your mom and Stella won't tell me what's going on. You've disappeared all week," he cried, holding up a stack of mail that dated my absence. "What happened? Why won't you talk to me?"

"I take it you haven't found the ring?"

His glistening eyes narrowed, his brows stitching together. But as soon as his gaze fell to my left hand, the confusion shifted—though it didn't disappear. Now, rather than puzzled at what ring I'd meant, it was clear he was lost as to why I'd taken it off.

"I left it on your entryway table. Last Friday night when I went back to get my stuff. You see...I flew in a couple of days early to surprise you. Imagine *my* surprise when I tracked your location to Rulebreakers and caught you grinding on another woman."

No less than three expressions flashed across his face—everything from bewilderment to shock. But the one that stuck out most was the flash of guilt. Followed by the flicker of regret. "There's got to be some sort of mix up here, Mercy. I wasn't with another woman."

"Are you trying to tell me you weren't at Rulebreakers last Friday night?"

"Yeah, I was. But I wasn't with a woman. I was out with the guys. We stopped there for maybe an hour and then we left."

"What time? And where'd you go?"

He shifted on his feet, eyes falling upon everything in the room except me. "Maybe around midnight? I don't know. Terence was down the street at Eight Ball and asked us to head over for a few games of pool. I didn't check my watch, but I think it was around midnight. I got home about two thirty. Two forty-five the latest."

I had to fist my hands and clench my jaw to keep from

getting sucked in. I wouldn't have considered myself a weak person, but when it came to the people I cared about—*loved* even—I had a tendency to believe them. Or at the very least, *want* to believe them.

Unfortunately, I couldn't go back now.

Not after Brogan.

Not after our trip to Savannah yesterday.

"I saw you, Jordan. Are you trying to tell me I don't know what I saw?"

He huffed and dropped his head forward. "It's a dark club. And the whole time I was there, it was packed. Could it be possible that maybe you just *thought* you saw me? But really…it was some other guy?"

"What are the chances of two guys who look almost identical—same height and build, same hair, same mannerisms—who also own the same shirt, being at the same place at the same time? Do you think I'm an idiot? You can only pass off so many coincidences before you have to accept that it's exactly what it looks like. And Friday night, it looked like you were fucking some other chick on the dance floor." I was borderline hysterical, which was probably the reason he kept his distance.

"What shirt, Mercy?"

I groaned, frustrated with him, my inability to put an end to this madness, and the entire situation as a whole. "The one I got you for Christmas last year. The blue one with the big fish on the back."

"You mean the shirt I left here the last time I was in town? The one that's probably still hanging up in your closet? If that's the shirt you're talking about, then how could I have *possibly* worn it Friday night while out fucking around on you?"

Somehow, I'd forgotten that he had left it here, or that it was currently in my closet. The possibility that I hadn't seen him with another woman—but rather, some *other* guy with another woman—strangled me with the cold, unrelenting hands of guilt.

I'd *slept* with another man. Had allowed him to do unspeakable things to my body.

But worse than that, I'd gone to Savannah with him. Where we…

The tears wouldn't let up. Once they'd broken free, they refused to relent. But I wouldn't break. I wouldn't collapse on the floor or curl into a ball. I'd found my way into this situation, and I would find my way out.

But not now.

Not tonight.

"I need to process this." I stepped aside, giving him enough space to get to the front door. "I can't even begin to wrap my head around it all right now."

"Wrap your head around what, Mercy?"

"Jordan…" My voice gave out in the middle of his name. I was on the verge of telling him that I'd spent the last week sabotaging everything we'd built all because I *thought* I had caught him with another woman. But I couldn't. I couldn't do that to him. Instead, I swallowed my shame and muttered, "I need to be alone."

"But I just told you it wasn't me."

"I know. But that doesn't make the last week disappear."

"Did you…" He shook his head, his pinched face a detailed sketch of utter agony. "Did you do something last week?"

All I could do was nod and pray for the best.

It took him a moment, but he eventually settled in his skin. His Adam's apple bobbed, and he blinked rapidly, though once he calmed long enough to speak, he said, "It's okay, Mercy. You didn't do it on purpose. I get it. We can get past it; I know we can."

My fingertips were numb. My knees weak. Each breath moved in and out of my lungs like a toy car over a bumpy road. But even as the room around me spun and my throat nearly closed on itself, my heart continued to sing, as if its beats were controlled by someone else.

"We can't, Jordan."

"Why not?"

"Because…I got married yesterday."

———

"Do you believe him?" Stella asked from the floor, where she proceeded to contort into ridiculous yoga poses while I remained curled into the corner of her couch.

My head throbbed, and my eyes felt like they could pop out of my skull at any second. With every aching tremor, Jordan's face pulsed through my mind, only to be replaced with Brogan's. I was stuck in an emotional tug-o-war I never wanted to be a part of. "Believe what?"

"That it wasn't him? You're the only one who knows what you saw that night."

She was right. And if I closed my eyes and pictured the dance floor, the swirling lights that had crossed his face numerous times, the way he had smiled…there was no way that man could've been anyone other than Jordan.

"His shirt is hanging in my closet. The one I saw him wearing that night."

Her eye roll was exaggerated, as was the fluttering of her lashes. "It's not the only shirt with a big fish on the back to have ever been made, Best Friend. I'm not saying he's guilty, but let's not fool ourselves. It's entirely possible he owns more than one."

"I don't know what to believe anymore." After spilling the proverbial beans to Jordan, I spent the remainder of the night in tears over a decision I wasn't prepared to make. Over regrets and guilt. And over all the confusion it brought forth.

"Well, do you want to be with him? Mystery guy aside, yes or no?"

"I love him." That wasn't her question. "Until a week ago, I couldn't imagine my life without Jordan." Again, not what she'd asked. "And now...I don't know how I feel or what I want. I'm so confused."

"Come on, let's get through this so we can move on to *B*. Because I seriously want to hear all about that, and until you come to terms with Jordan—or close enough to it—you'll skimp on all the good shit."

A traitorous grin stretched my lips. "Oh, trust me, Stella... there's enough good shit to go around twice over." No matter how guilty I felt over the entire situation, whether the guy in the club was or wasn't Jordan, it didn't eliminate the butterflies in my stomach or the hiccup in my heartbeat whenever I thought of Brogan.

Stella bent forward and grabbed her ankles, looking at me through her parted legs, upside down. "Either way, hurry up. You told Jordan about your sex-filled week with a stranger, and he said he doesn't care. Well, in more or less words. Do you believe him?"

"Yeah." I didn't doubt him. I fully trusted him when he called this morning to tell me that, if I wanted, he was willing to put it all behind us. Except, Stella didn't know the whole story. We hadn't moved beyond the Jordan part, which meant she wasn't fully aware of just *what* we'd have to get past. "He wouldn't have said it if he didn't mean it."

"So really, you're stuck between whatever you have with this sex god and the future you've planned with Jordan. Am I right?" With her face beet-red, she rolled into a sitting position that didn't look anything close to comfortable.

"Basically. Yes."

"All right. We can come back to this. But first, I need to know what you have with the other one. A list to compare, if you will. So...spill the beans, bitch. What's his name?"

"Brogan." I couldn't even say it without smiling.

Which meant it took me far too long to recognize Stella's

frozen expression, brows peaked high on her forehead. "For the love of cannabis, please tell me you know what his last name is."

"Daniels."

"No fucking way," she whispered and then stared at me with wide eyes and a gaping mouth. "*The* Brogan Daniels? *Wrong* Daniels? The guy who owns Wrong Inc?"

My stomach bottomed out. "Yeah...how do you know who he is?"

"The real question should be: How do you *not* know who he is? He's got one of the hottest shows on television. Every woman in America—and at least two dozen other countries— would give their left tit to suck his dick. Me included."

"Okay, can we not talk about you getting anywhere near his genitals? Thanks."

To my surprise, I learned that Stella's eyebrows could, in fact, lift even higher. And there was a good chance she'd scare small children with her Grinch-like grin. "Did I just detect possessiveness in your tone? I don't think I've ever heard you sound like that. Like you could beat on your chest and fight off all the horny bitches of the world who want your man."

I rolled my eyes, though I couldn't deny that she was right. "Back up to the part about him being on TV. What does that mean, exactly?"

"He has his own show where they pretty much film his tattoo shop and the people he works with. And bits and pieces of his life. It's reality TV, so I guess it's not surprising that you don't know what I'm talking about. Although, I figured you would've at least recognized him from magazines or something."

"Nope. I'm fairly certain I would've remembered his face if I had."

She clapped loudly, garnering my attention. "Listen, Best Friend...I know I said we'd come back to Jordan and the decision you have to make, but that was before I knew your sex god was Wrong. I don't give a flying shit what future you might have with him, my vote is for Wrong. All the way. Screw Jordan; fuck Brogan. Literally."

"You think I should choose the unstable path over the one I've spent years paving?" Realizing who I was talking to, I laughed to myself and shook my head. "Never mind. Of course you do."

"How'd you two leave it yesterday when he dropped you off at the airport?"

It was now or never. "I told him I would come back once I had everything packed and shipped to his house."

"What the hell, Mercy? You're such a gossip-hoarding heifer." She threw a pillow at me, and I thanked my lucky stars it had been something soft instead of something hard, because I had no doubt she would've chucked anything within arm's reach. "You told him you'd move in with him?"

I glanced to where she sat, verifying that she had nothing else to lob at me, and then took a deep breath. "Well, considering I'm his wife, I didn't think it made sense for me to live anywhere else."

I'd managed to do what no one else had—make Stella speechless.

"Say something."

"*Wife?*" she asked, lunging at me. "Shut the fuck up! You're lying."

I should not have been surprised that out of all the words in the English language, those were the ones she'd picked. "Nope. I told you that we went to Savannah on Friday. And after he made me come harder than I've ever come in my entire life, he took advantage of the high I was on and convinced me that it would be a good idea to get married."

"You're lying."

I covered my face and shook my head. "I'm pretty sure he

picked Savannah on purpose because, as it turns out, there's no waiting period between getting a marriage license and saying *I do*. We threw clothes on and raced down to the courthouse before oxygen could return to my brain."

"Shut up." When I stopped talking, she grabbed my arms and shook me, not at all caring that I had a headache. "What's wrong with you? Tell me everything, dammit. Don't stop until every second has been accounted for."

"What else do you want me to say, Stella?"

"For starters, how did he ask? What made you say yes without a seven-page list of pros and cons? *Oh...*" She quirked her lips to the side, a smile twitching at the corner. "The sex. I always thought he looked like he knew what he was doing. But back to business, woman!"

I couldn't keep up with her. It was one of the things I loved most about her—even when it frustrated me. "We were just lying there, like we always do after sex, and he said we should get married. At first, I thought it was a joke, so I played along. Then I saw the look in his eyes and realized he was serious."

Her eyes widened just before she glanced at my hand. "Did he have a ring?"

"No. It's the one thing that makes me question how planned it was. Part of me believes he took me to Savannah, picked that specific place on purpose, knowing how quickly someone can get married there. He just seemed so determined, so...eager that I can't imagine he hadn't thought about it before that moment. But he didn't have a ring, nor did we exchange any at the courthouse. Who knows...maybe he's not a ring-wearing guy?" I'd learned how easy it was to take a ring off, so I wasn't overly concerned about not having one. Having Brogan was enough.

"That's okay; we've got time to work on him getting you a big rock. A big, shiny, sparkly rock that blinds anyone who looks too closely at it. One I can wear on occasion." She flicked her wrist in dismissal, as if she'd suggested we share shoes, not a diamond ring. "Moving on. How long did it take you to say yes?"

"Seconds. If that."

"Impressive, Mercy. You're not one to make such rash decisions."

I ran my hands down my face, shocked at myself for nearly every choice I'd made over the last week. "I know. That's the craziest part of it all. I didn't think twice. I didn't analyze it from every side or pick it apart. I didn't contemplate the repercussions. It was like he had asked what two plus two is. The answer was instant." I groaned and closed my eyes. "I can't explain it, Stella. I wish I could. The only thing I can say is it felt right."

She stared, blinking dramatically, waiting for more.

"That's it. I said yes, so we left the hotel, got married, and less than twenty-four hours later, I found out that Jordan might not have even cheated on me to begin with. I dumped my fiancé —without telling him, I might add—and shacked up with…"

Everything came to a screeching halt, like an eighty-four-car pile-up.

"Holy shit. Holy. Motherfucking. Shit," I mumbled under my breath.

"What? Don't holy shit me, Best Friend; tell me! Spit it out!"

I blinked a few times, and then I blurted, *"Holy fucking shit, Stella. I got married. To someone who's on TV. Oh my God…is he famous?"

"Yup. Pretty much."

"I'm going to be sick."

"Morning sickness?" Her eyes opened wide. "Oh, fuck. Are you pregnant?"

I grabbed the pillow she'd thrown at me and beat her once with it. "No, I'm not pregnant. Did you fall on your head during yoga? Are you *trying* to jinx me?"

She smacked me across the face—not hard, but enough to make me balk.

"What the hell was that for?"

Stella, still kneeling on the floor in front of me, waved me off. "Don't worry; you're not pregnant, so it's fine. I only needed you to shut up for a second. That, and you hit me with a pillow. But back to you shutting up for a second. Listen to me… you can't leave him. Got that? Are you paying attention to what I'm telling you right now? You. Can. Not. Leave. Wrong."

"Why? Is he in the mob or something? Will people come after me?"

"Yeah." She nodded slowly. "I will. I will cut you in your sleep if you leave him. He's Brogan Daniels. *The* Brogan Daniels. Do you hear what I'm telling you?"

"Uh…yeah. But I'm still not sure I understand why I can't leave him—aside from you turning into some crazed deviant."

With a dramatic huff, she dropped back onto her haunches, where she proceeded to tick off every relative point she could come up with, and a few that weren't relative at all. "He's amazing in bed, can get you off unlike anyone else, has a glorious shlong. He's gorgeous. Has a body you could lick breakfast, lunch, and dinner off of. He's got money, which means he can support you if needed. You didn't *allegedly* catch him cheating on you. He's gorgeous. Amazing in bed."

"Yeah. Now you're just repeating things."

"They deserve to be mentioned a few times. Have you seen him?"

I rubbed my chest, attempting to soothe the ache that resided in it at every mention or thought of walking away from Brogan. And as if that ache had settled there for the sole purpose of bringing my hand to my chest, a dull sting spread through my skin just above my right breast. It only took a second to recall what it was, and for the smile to take hold of my lips.

Brogan had branded me several times with his teeth, all in various places south of my bellybutton. But when he'd noticed the tank top I'd put on before trivia on Thursday night, he'd decided his mark needed to be visible for every guy in the room.

As fucked up as it sounded...it made me swoon.

And it had turned me on so much we'd almost arrived late.

"Have you talked to Wrong about Jordan?" Stella asked, to which I could only shake my head. "But you've talked to Jordan about Wrong?"

I shrugged and sighed and covered my face. Again. "Yes and no. I told him about meeting him, about spending the week with him, and about Savannah."

"*Okay*... What else is there to say?"

Staring at my best friend, I fought back the stinging tears that beat against the backs of my eyes. "I don't know how to describe it. I've tried...many times. To myself, in my head. And any which way I attempt to word it, it doesn't make a single bit of sense."

"You mean...like you right now?"

"Yes. I love Jordan. And if he truly wasn't the one I saw, then realistically speaking, he should be the one I choose. But I can't bring myself to let Brogan go just yet. Maybe I need more time to see what this is? I don't know, Stella. Help me out here."

"Are you trying to say you love Brogan?"

"No." My head throbbed as I shook it aggressively. "Not even close. But I can't explain what it is that I'm feeling, because I can't put it into words."

"Easy...lust. But don't worry; lust has created many long-lasting relationships. Look at Angelina Jolie and Brad Pitt."

"They split up."

"So? They were together for, like, fourteen years. I didn't say lust created happily ever afters. The key word there was *long-lasting*. I'd say fourteen years is about as long as you can ask when you start the relationship out doing the naked tango."

"I don't know why I ask you for advice."

She placed her hands on the tops of my thighs and held my stare. "Want real advice? Call Wrong and talk to him. Be honest about everything. This isn't the time to hold anything back. I'm willing to bet you'll know what to do by the time you hang up the phone."

She was right.

Which I found annoyingly awesome.

8

BROGAN

I should've told her before she'd boarded that plane.

In my mind, if she knew about the show and wasn't here to assure me, I'd go crazy with uncertainty. Unfortunately, she found out anyway and *wasn't* here to make it right. She *wasn't* here to silence the unease. And because of that, I'd gone certifiably insane.

The only thing that kept me out of the asylum was her voice.

I didn't hear from her much—a few minutes a day, if I was lucky.

But I'd take that over nothing at all.

The day after she got home, I found out that her ex had been there. It'd be a lie if I said I hadn't seen red when she told me. I was livid and wanted to murder the fucker, but in that moment, she needed me to remain calm. It was one of the hardest things I ever had to do. But for Mercy, I did.

The entire time she spoke, my heart had climbed its way into my throat and rocks filled the pit of my stomach. I'd convinced myself that she was running. I knew she would. Hoped she wouldn't.

But somehow, by some miracle, I'd managed to convince Mercy that a decision shouldn't be made until she got here.

Either way—with me or with the loser who couldn't keep his woman—she'd have to relocate, so it was pointless to decide anything while trying to organize the move. She'd agreed. Then she spent the last eleven days giving me heart palpitations.

"Please, Mercy, stop watching that shit." I cringed just thinking about what all she'd seen in old episodes of the show. There was no telling how the producers had portrayed me, or the assumptions she'd made while seeing it.

"I can't. I'm too invested now. On one hand, it's a highly entertaining show. On the other, it makes me sick, and I keep hoping as each episode goes on and the closer I get to the end that you'll stop fucking that chick in the shop."

My chest tightened as a groan ripped through my throat. The thought of having to watch her interact with someone she used to sleep with was enough to obliterate me, so I could only imagine how she felt watching my interactions with Indi, the only female I had working for me. "All you need to know is that I'm no longer fucking her, Mercy. I haven't been with anyone since I met you. Haven't *wanted* anyone since you. I swear on that. Isn't that all that should matter?"

"It would be…if she wasn't in love with you. And you're blind if you don't see it."

"It's television. They cut out about ninety percent of what they film, and then piece together the rest to tell whatever story they want. Trust me…it's not real, regardless of it being called *reality TV*."

"You wouldn't know, because you've never seen it." It was the same argument she used every day, throwing it back in my face as if living it and watching were somehow different. "I'm telling you…I'm a woman, so I can recognize these things. Bobblehead is in love with you."

I shouldn't have, but I laughed. Indi nodded a lot—and I mean *a lot*—and for whatever reason, Mercy had given her a nickname. She claimed it was because she couldn't remember

Indi's name, though I preferred the theory that her territorial side refused to use it.

"It's not funny, Brogan." She huffed, which was a sure sign she was about to end the call. "I've had to see you with your wife, who—let's not kid ourselves—could very well be a Victoria's Secret lingerie model. Then I had to witness how heartbroken you were when the marriage ended. That means I had to sit through episode after episode knowing how much you loved her. And now, I'm stuck in what I can only describe as softcore porn between you and the coloring book with legs."

I had to bite my tongue, wondering how many other nicknames she'd come up with for Indi. "Then stop watching it."

"I can't!" The traces of humor in her tone were the only thing that had kept me from getting on a plane just to toss her TV out a window. "I need to know these things."

"What things?"

"*Things*. About you. About your life."

A knock on the door caught my attention, and when I glanced behind me, seeing Indi leaning against the frame with her thumb hitched over her shoulder, I knew that meant my time was up. "Listen, babe…my next client's here. I would love to stick around and give you five thousand reasons to turn that shit off, but duty calls."

"Fine. Have fun."

I smiled at the phrase she used every time I had to go. "You know it."

"Was that the wife?" Indi asked as I slipped past her to get out of the back room.

"Yeah. She's hung up on the ridiculous idea that you're in love with me." I shook my head, laughter filtering out beneath my breath. Then I met Indi's smiling eyes. "You don't…do you?"

"Fuck no." She waved me off, and we went our separate ways.

It had been sixteen days since I last saw her.

Phone calls hadn't been enough—especially because most of them were her telling me all the reasons we wouldn't work, while I had to pacify her long enough to get her in my arms again. I felt confident that once we were breathing the same air, she'd calm down.

At least, I knew *I* would.

But as she pulled into the short, circular drive near the front door, rather than release a sigh of relief, I had to fight against my need to go to her and claim those lips again. Her voice through a phone for over two weeks, when I'd only had the real thing for one, wasn't nearly enough.

As I calmly walked outside to meet her at the car, Mercy stepped out of the driver's side, looking seven shades of nervous. Whereas, I couldn't wipe the smile off my face. I settled my hands on her hips, as though they'd belonged there all along, and leaned in for a kiss.

It was short.

And awkward.

Stiff and disconnected.

She turned out of my hold and took one step toward the rear door, where her luggage sat on the seat. But I didn't let her get far. I'd be damned if I'd let her push me away after I finally got her back.

Reaffirming my hold on her hips, I shifted her so that her back was against the car, chest so close to mine I could *hear* every beat of her heart. With an air of confidence, I lifted my hand to cup her cheek while losing myself in the warmth of her gaze.

"Let's try that again." I lowered my lips to hers once more, and a split second before they touched, her subtle gasp sucked me in. Held me tight. Kept me safe and promised to never let go. And the moment her mouth opened, inviting me in, there was no going back.

No *desire* to go back.

Mercy fisted the sides of my shirt as she melted against me. Her rigid posture gave way, losing all notion of unease. She'd gone from a stone statue to modeling clay. Solid to something I could mold to me.

When the need for air broke us apart, I dropped my forehead to hers. "Hey."

A sigh drifted past her smiling lips. "Hey, baby."

And I was home.

I couldn't wait one more second to get her inside. With a kiss to her temple, I stepped aside and pulled both suitcases out of the back, leaving the remaining boxes and bags for later. "Come on; let's get these put away."

I led her through the front door, around the kitchen, and into my room. Excitement drove my every step, pumping my legs faster. I was unwilling to sacrifice a single moment of having her in my arms again. Of getting her in my bed again.

Our bed.

It was crazy and made no sense—not even to me. I knew what I believed and how I felt. All the signs and indications were there. Not one ounce of me doubted her. Us. What we had or *would* have in the future. I'd never felt so sure about anything in my life, even though every bit of it was completely illogical.

However, once I had the two suitcases in the room and turned to face Mercy, doubt crept in. It slithered through the cracks and wrapped itself around my neck. Choking me. Crushing my ribcage and piercing my lungs. Every inhale strained. Every exhale ragged. The sight before me worthy of closing the casket and draping me in darkness.

The blank stare that met mine.

The fisted hands and labored breathing.

Mercy had retreated into her shell.

"What's wrong, babe?" I asked, hoping to pass off my anxiety as concern.

She shook her head, glanced over her shoulder—as though she expected someone else to be here—and then faced me again. "I guess I thought I would take the other room. Like last time."

"Why would you? We're married."

One shoulder lifted in a defeated shrug. "I don't know, Brogan. We've done everything backward. In the moment, I thought it would be easy. Like a switch could be flipped and *boom*…I'd settle in. But being back here…it feels like it did *before* I left. *Before* the marriage and the plane ride, and the time I spent away. That's where my things were before. It was a safe space I could go to when I needed to take a moment to myself. I have no idea how this is supposed to go. How I should feel. I'm confused, okay?"

I took her hands in mine, though it was evident in the way she hesitated to release her fists that she had already disconnected. "Let's talk this through. It is new and, hell, I'm scared too, but we can get through this together."

"There's just a lot to figure out. The last thing I expected was to catch my fiancé cheating on me. But I did—or I *thought* I did." Her eyes dropped away from mine. "I'm still not sure what the truth is. And ever since then, it's been one unexpected thing after another. I feel like I'm trapped in a wind tunnel, all my decisions and choices swirling around me. Sucking me in and yanking me in a thousand different directions. One minute I'm upside down; the next…I'm inside out."

Deciding to give her enough space to gather her thoughts and voice her concerns, I took a step back. I didn't want to be a millimeter away from her, let alone three feet. But if it meant she'd feel comfortable opening up, then I had to suck it up and do it.

Tears swam within her gaze when she fastened her focus back on me. "Seriously, Brogan. Where the hell did you come from that night? Why were you there? It's like you just appeared out of nowhere, right when I needed you the most. I thought I could spend one reckless week to keep me from losing myself in the pain of betrayal. I was okay with that."

When she locked her fingers together and dropped her gaze to her wringing hands, I held my breath. There was a *but* coming, and I wasn't sure I could handle what else she had to say. Yet I didn't have enough strength—or sense—to interrupt. While I didn't want to hear the rest of this, I knew I had to. I had to have faith and believe this wasn't a death sentence.

"Getting married was never part of the plan." Her gaze met mine again, and within the heavy swirls of syrup, the pain matched what I felt in my chest. Heart-stopping agony. Though I refused to search for more.

"Do you..." *Fuck.* I didn't want to ask, but I needed the truth. "Do you regret it?"

The seconds ticked by, each one pushing the knife in my chest deeper and deeper. Had I been willing to take my eyes off her, I would've checked the floor at my feet for blood. I felt ripped apart. Torn in half. Shredded into pieces I'd never recover from. I'd experienced heartache before...yet never like this. Even the *notion* of losing Mercy was more than I could bear. More than I could handle.

A tear tracked down her cheek, and she made no move to swipe it away. Just left it there as if it was meant to distract me from her words when she said, "I can't answer that. Because I don't really know how I feel about anything right now. That's what I've been trying to say, but all you've done is tell me to turn off the TV. I'm confused, and I have no idea which way is up anymore."

I stumbled backward until I met the end of the bed and sat on the rail of the footboard, unable to hold myself upright any longer. "You're confused about me?" My stomach sloshed like a rocky sea. None of what we'd done was conventional, sure, but not once had I been confused about her.

"Yes. No." She huffed out a wave of frustration. "Hell if I know. Don't you see, Brogan? I don't know anything about you. I spent a week with you, and by the end, I was willing to marry you. All because...I *felt* something."

"Like you've known me for a hundred lifetimes?"

Her eyes lit up, sparking a flame of hope in my chest. "Something like that, yeah."

"So then why are you questioning it now?"

"The show," she whispered, adding a quick shrug at the end. "You have this whole other side to you, and I don't recognize him at all. There's Brogan...and then there's Wrong. There's the guy I spent a week with. And then the guy on TV. The guy I gave myself to, who brought me to higher highs that I never imagined were possible. And then the guy who's done the same to almost every hot chick who walks into his shop."

"That's why I told you to stop watching it."

"Why? Because you knew I'd realize I'm nothing special?"

That angered me. Pulled me to my feet. Tightened my muscles into fiery coils beneath my skin, burning me alive from the inside. "No. Not even close, Mercy. Because you're watching a twisted version of my life—a life I had *before* you—and you're holding it against me. You're comparing yourself to other women. Women I never contemplated marrying, let alone have any other type of relationship with. Women I never brought to my house, let alone move in. You're taking bits and pieces of months on end that were strung together to fit into a third of that time and overanalyzing it. *That's* why I didn't want you to watch it." I had to take a slow breath to calm down before I gave her another reason to walk away. "You're more than special."

She dropped her gaze to the floor, somewhere between where I stood and where she cowered. Without looking at me, she lowered her voice and said, "I just feel like I don't know you. That's all I was trying to say."

Seeing her so broken calmed the storm within until I could

speak without raising my voice or making her retreat further into herself. "And you think that'll somehow change by watching scraps of my life that have been cut and pasted together by someone else? Someone whose job it is to create drama for the sake of viewers and money?"

Her eyes met mine.

Her heart broke mine.

But her *soul*...her soul soothed mine.

"Why didn't you tell me?" Defeat weighed heavily in her whispered words.

I scrubbed my hands over my face, tired of answering the same question. But if that was what it took to keep her, then I'd repeat the truth time and time again. "The show ruined my marriage. It's the reason Jessica sought attention elsewhere. She couldn't handle it. On top of that, I've spent the last two years in a bubble, completely unaware of who around me was genuine and who wasn't. Women come to my shop to get a tattoo in hopes they'll leave with more. Do you have any idea how much money they are willing to pay to have me be the one to ink them versus any of the other guys in the shop?"

She shook her head, her chest heaving with each labored breath.

"And if I never see another tit or ass that isn't yours again, I'll be a happy man. It gets old, Mercy. That's not what I want. *You* are what I want. I don't need random hookups to pass the time. Or fake ass friends who only hang around to get on TV— or worse, the bragging right of knowing me. I need *you*."

"Then why do the show?"

"I do it because I signed a contract, and it pays the bills. It affords me the opportunity to do things I never thought I'd be able to do. I grew up with nothing. Nonna gave me all she could, but still...it wasn't much. I was approached with the idea of having cameras film the shop and maybe follow me around a bit, and I agreed. After the first season, they came to me with a contract that had a lot of zeroes on it. Things had literally just fallen apart with Jessica, so I signed on the dotted line. Didn't think twice. Now…I'm just riding it out."

Mercy pulled in a long, desperate breath while dropping her head back. Her frustration clear as the day was long. "It's so hard to explain what I've seen, because you haven't watched it. And you refuse to believe anything I say. You pass it off as something else or excuse it as being edited to look a certain way. I concede on Bobblehead. I mean, I still think she's in love with you, but I can't be upset or jealous about something that happened before we met. However…you can't lie about how broken you were during season two. After you and Jessica split."

There was so much to say, but I wasn't sure she was ready to hear any of it. Instead, I allowed her to direct the conversation, while I stood back and answered, biding my time until I could paint the full picture for her.

"I'm not denying that, Mercy. I've never pretended I wasn't."

"You two were like Barbie and a tatted-up Ken. A pierced Romeo and his Juliet. You guys were the epitome of a perfect couple, and everyone knew it. Trust me…I've spent some time on Google. I've read the forums. Half of them had lost all hope in love, and the other half wanted to do very explicit things to your body. Things I won't dare mention. But that's not the point. The point is…I can't compete with that. I can't *compare* to that."

"People see what they want to see. I was torn up about it—I've told you that. For a while, I thought I had made the biggest mistake of my life. But I didn't. If anything, I had to go through that to get to this point with you. And if that heartache led me here—if it led me to you—then I'd go through it ten thousand times again if I have to. If it means I get you in the end."

She nibbled on the inside of her cheek, her eyes on me, though not my face. And once a thought stuck in her mind, she parted her lips, rolled her shoulders back, and squinted at me. "Are you saying you love me?"

I wanted to laugh. In fact, I had to steel myself to keep from smiling. We'd managed to fuck like pros, explore each other's bodies and limits, desires, fantasies. Hell, we'd run off and gotten married. All without once uttering the word *love*.

"Of course I do."

"No. Not like that. Like, love me for real."

I probably shouldn't have, but I had to take a moment to contemplate my response. Not because I didn't have an answer. But because my truth would have her flying out that door and never looking back. "I feel something real for you, something more real than I ever imagined I could feel for another person. Does that answer your question? Is that enough for you right now?"

She nodded and ran her tongue along her bottom lip, leaving behind a glossy finish. "I told you I would come here and figure things out. And that's what I plan to do. But I can't do that while sleeping in your bed. There's another part of this equation that you're not considering...and that's Jordan."

"I don't see how he even deserves a second thought."

"We were *engaged*, Brogan. We were supposed to get married in less than three weeks from now. I left him, only to run off and marry someone else. All while he thought we were still together. Take yourself out of it for a moment and tell me he doesn't deserve to be thought of."

"He cheated on you, Mercy. Just because he came back a week later and gave you some song and dance about how it was someone else doesn't change that fact. His shirt being left at your house doesn't change what you saw."

"I know. Trust me, Brogan...I'm aware of this. I guess I didn't expect him to fight for me. I thought he'd realize he'd been caught and just quietly disappear. But he didn't. And not only is he fighting for me, saying he's willing to get past *this*"— she motioned between the both of us—"but he's also telling me that the whole reason I ended up in your bed to begin with was false."

I realized, right then and there, that if I wanted to win, I'd have to give her what she wanted—time and space. Two things I never wanted her to have. But this was more about her than me or her ex. Somehow, she would have to come to terms with her actions. And until she did that, she would never be mine. She'd forever live in that dead space filled with regret and doubt. That was the last thing I wanted for her.

"Okay. Fine. Do what you have to do, Mercy."

But that didn't mean I had to stand around and watch her push me away.

I walked out of the room, leaving her and her suitcases behind. However, I didn't leave the premises. Instead, I went to her car, unloaded the rest of what she'd brought with her—four more boxes were coming in the mail—and then moved her car down to the garage. The rest of the evening was spent on the couch, watching TV, while she tiptoed around.

There was something to be said about walking on eggshells.

Sweeping them up would be far faster and more effective.

9

MERCY

"I guess I don't understand why you can't stay at a motel or something. Why his house?" Jordan fought to contain his anger, and he'd done a decent job of it. Until now.

I'd kept in touch with him over the last couple of weeks, though I hadn't been entirely honest about everything. While he knew I'd planned to move to town either way, I'd conveniently left out that it was sooner rather than later…or that it had already happened. Also, while he knew I had a lot to think about, he wasn't fully aware that my main decision had come down to a guy. I'd let him assume my struggles lay with whether I believed him or not, and if we'd be able to get over my "indiscretions."

He probably would've made that choice for me had he known I'd been in town for a few days and only just called this morning to meet up for lunch. Granted, he hadn't asked me how long I'd been there, so technically, I hadn't lied.

"Well, considering I can't afford an extended stay at a motel, that wasn't an option. You two are the only ones I know well enough in the area to stay with. And regardless of the situation, he's legally my husband. Staying with you is a legal issue I don't care to deal with."

"A *legal* issue?" He opened his eyes wide and leaned on the table. It was a good thing the waiter had already come for his salad bowl; otherwise, he'd be wearing ranch all over his tie right about now. "Shouldn't you be getting the marriage annulled?"

I used to live such an uncomplicated life.

"You don't understand, Jordan." I set my elbows on the table and held my head in my hands, allowing my hair to act as a curtain and protect me from seeing his face. "Until I figure my shit out, I can't make any decisions."

"So your plan is to string me along until you decide which guy you want?"

I glared at him. "No. Of course not."

"Then tell me. What is it you're doing to figure your shit out?"

Frustrated, I couldn't bite my tongue any longer. "Why don't you tell me something, Jordan? How long did it take before you noticed the ring by your front door? How is it that you managed not to see it for days?"

"I told you, it was late when I got home that night. I wasn't paying attention when I tossed my keys to the table, and it must've knocked it onto the floor. I didn't find it until after I got back from Ohio and looked. How was I supposed to know it'd be there? Why would I have even thought to look for it?" It was obvious he didn't like the accusations I'd slung at him with my question. "And I certainly didn't expect you to run off and marry a complete stranger."

I glanced around the patio, making sure the few other people dining outside weren't eavesdropping, and then leaned closer. "It's not like I woke up one day and thought the idea of shacking up with some random guy for a week before marrying him sounded like a good time. All of this started because of something I saw at Rulebreakers. None of that would've happened had I not seen what I did that night."

"So you're saying this is all my fault?"

"I wouldn't say that." I sighed and dropped my head back for a moment, letting the heat of the sun bathe me in a soothing peace before meeting his gaze and continuing. "I'd say that situation was the catalyst."

"But it wasn't me." If he could look me in the eyes and lie, that was on him.

I just prayed that wasn't what he was doing.

It would sicken me to know I'd spent so many years with a man who could do that.

"You say it wasn't. My memory says it was. I'm trying to figure out which one's telling the truth. Because I would never forgive myself if I listened to my gut, only to find out it was wrong. To know I'd hurt you beyond repair, all because I didn't look deep enough. At the same time, I could never be with a man who'd so easily forget me when I was away."

He wiped his fingers around his mouth and leaned back in his chair. With one hand on the armrest, the other in his lap, his body lopsided in the seat, he regarded me. Such arrogance. The sad part was, I used to think it was confidence. Now, it left me unsettled.

"Admit it, Mercy. It's more than trying to figure out if I'm telling the truth or not. If that's all it is, then you wouldn't be here. You'd be in Ohio, taking the time to figure it out. And you would've already filed to have that marriage annulled. That fact that you're here, and you haven't done a damn thing to reverse your marital status, proves that, at the bottom of all this, you're deciding between me and him."

I couldn't exactly deny that. Nevertheless, I didn't care to acknowledge it, either.

Unfortunately, I didn't have much choice. He didn't offer me one.

"Ultimately, yes. That's what I'm doing. Because if it turns out that you really were there that night, and you really were with another woman, then I have no desire to leave him." My throat burned as each word vacated my mouth. It felt like a lie, though I didn't understand.

Jordan simply nodded and turned his attention toward the street.

"Listen…" I took a deep breath, hoping it would settle my overwrought nerves. Anxiety flowed through my veins, and I couldn't begin to comprehend what had triggered it. I just knew I had to wrap this up and leave. "I have zero desire to drag this out. I don't plan on stringing anyone along—you or him. This isn't a choice of which guy I want more. Everything went to hell in a handbasket the moment I walked into Rulebreakers. Now, I'm just trying to figure out how to piece it all back together without losing a part of myself."

"You spent, what…one week with him? And there's even a question in your mind that you might lose a piece of yourself if you leave him? Are you listening to what you're saying, Mercy? Do you hear how utterly ridiculous you sound?"

If I gritted my teeth any harder, I'd likely break a molar. "He's also called and texted me every day. Multiple times a day. I think it's fair to say that I heard from him more in a twenty-four-hour period than I have from you since the night I found you in my apartment."

"Funny…because I haven't heard much from you, either."

"Then why do you want to be with me? What are you fighting for?"

He tossed his napkin on the table and leaned to the side to reach his wallet in his back pocket. "Looks like we both have some things to think about, huh?"

I sat in silence while he removed two twenties from his billfold and slid them beneath the saltshaker. And it was all I could do to form a smile as he stood from his chair, nodded, and then left me there, all alone.

Just me and my thoughts.

By the time I got up to leave, I'd come to a realization—this was never about who I saw in the club that night. It wasn't even about which man I wanted to be with. At the end of the day, I didn't care who was on that dance floor; the truth wouldn't change anything. And I didn't need to choose between Jordan or Brogan; I already had.

My issue was with myself.

Whether or not I could emotionally handle living in Brogan's world.

———

I arrived at the house later than anticipated, greatly in part to getting lost. As much as I loved the privacy and abundance of nature, it was damn near impossible to find my way back if I accidentally took a wrong turn.

I hadn't thought it would be a big deal since Brogan worked odd hours at the shop. That was one thing I wasn't sure I'd ever get used to—if I ended up sticking around. The last time I was here, I'd had him all to myself for an entire week. Now, I was lucky if I got to see him four hours a day. I couldn't be sure, but over the last couple of days I'd been in town, I'd wondered if his absence had more to do with my presence than his schedule at the shop.

However, I hadn't been able to bring myself to ask.

To my surprise, I opened the garage door and found Brogan's Jeep parked inside. I could've sworn he'd mentioned working late tonight, which meant around midnight, but maybe I'd misunderstood. However, the one thing I didn't misunderstand was how my body relaxed at the knowledge of him being home.

The house was quiet when I walked in. At first, I thought about checking to see if he was in his bedroom, but then I figured I'd wait it out. I needed to pee and change out of my clothes anyhow, so it made more sense to get that done first.

With my jeans off and tossed into the basket next to the closet, I moved into the en suite bath in nothing but a shirt that barely covered my panties. And as soon as I flipped on the light, I stilled. In awe.

On the mirror was a message. Written in what looked to be a blue dry-erase marker.

Tied to the mast of a drifting ship was I,
My wheel lost, years before in a tempest of my own design.
Tossed was I from shallow bay to shallow bay by the silent
storm of solitude,
Sanctuary escaped me.
To the heavens, I cried for mercy.

When dawn broke on new life's day I saw her then,
Perfect yet damaged, whole yet...missing,
A puzzle yearning to be solved,
Her pieces scattered, lost?
The only clue, a vision on my soul.
And her name was Mercy.

I must've read it thirty-seven times, trying to figure out what it meant. I traced the slanted lines of the letters with my eyes, the places along the loops where the marker grew thinner. The curve of the commas. The harshness of each period, as if he'd stabbed the mirror with the blue, felt tip. I broke it down and read each verse by itself. Then two at a time. Then the whole thing from start to finish.

My eyes were dry, though my soul wept.

Not caring that I hadn't used the restroom or washed my face. Or even put on pants. I ran out in search of Brogan, finding him in the kitchen with his back to me. My ears rang, so I couldn't tell if I was just really quiet, or if he hadn't turned to face me on purpose.

I opened my mouth to speak, and nothing came out.

No sound.

No word.

Not even a cry.

Keeping my eyes on Brogan, I took a moment to organize the unraveled parts of myself so that I might make sense when I found my voice. My emotions had been slain, hacked up into tiny pieces that riddled the floor around me like tarnished bits of glitter. My thoughts had been split in half until my mind became filled with incomplete notions.

Then he turned around, met my stare, and said, "Hey."

With that one word, that one look, the mess was gone and my head was clear.

"The mirror…" I pointed behind me, as if he wouldn't know which mirror I'd meant. "What is that? The writing. The words. You did that?" All I got was a nod, right before he moved his attention to the island. I stepped forward to try again. "What does it mean?"

"You said you don't know me." He flicked his eyes toward the bedroom I was staying in. "Well, that's more than I've ever given to anyone other than Nonna."

"I still don't understand. Please, Brogan. I'm not trying to devalue your effort or sound ungrateful…I'm just really confused." I must've been too wrapped up in the sentiment he'd left behind in my bathroom, because I just now realized he was in the middle of making dinner.

He grabbed a spatula and stirred the hamburger meat in the pan. "It's hard to give someone a private piece of you when your life is pretty much out there for everyone to pick apart. It's no secret that I can draw. I can't sing to save my life. You've eaten enough of my food to know it's edible, but it's nothing to write home about. It gets the job done, and that's about it. As you've already pointed out, what I can offer in the bedroom is public knowledge. So…I decided to give you something that *no one* alive has ever seen."

"You write?"

"Poetry," he said, bobbing his head without making eye contact. "I've been doing it since I was a teenager. And before

93

you ask, no…Jessica never read anything. She made a joke about it one time, and after that, I kept it from her. I don't think she meant it maliciously, but it bothered me all the same."

"So, you wrote that? On the mirror? When?"

He shrugged, acting too busy to look my way. "An hour or so ago."

"*Brogan…*" It was nothing more than a whisper lost in a steady breeze, yet it was enough to catch his attention.

When he finally met my gaze, his eyes were dark and closed off. "Don't, Mercy. Don't tell me what you think I want to hear. I wanted to share my thoughts, and I couldn't think of any other way to do it than with the one piece of me no one else has."

"I don't…" I swallowed harshly, my words sticking to my dry throat. "I don't know what to say, Brogan. *Thank you* doesn't seem to be enough."

"It probably makes no sense to you. What I wrote, I mean. I was just trying to say—"

"I know what you were trying to say." A single tear slipped free and ran down my cheek. Luckily, I was able to catch it before Brogan glanced up. "I understood what you meant. Which is why any form of gratitude doesn't come close to what I'm feeling right now."

Brogan had intentionally given me a glimpse into himself by expressing his feelings in words he'd never shared with another living soul. But in that moment, when his eyes met mine, he offered me something else.

Likely unaware he'd even done so.

He gave me a piece of his vulnerability. His pain. A sliver of the hidden humiliation that he kept buried beneath a painted canvas. Covered in graffiti. Locked behind years of loss and doubt. It crossed his brow in shallow valleys of hesitation and colored his cheeks in raw insecurity.

He was open. Closed off. Pushing me away while desperately trying to hold me close.

It was too much to process at once, leaving me immobile,

grounded in place. The only thing I could do was open my mouth and give him honesty. "Your words...they make my chest hurt. As I read them, I breathed them in, and they burrowed themselves next to my heart. Took up residence within my lungs. They're powerful enough to keep me safe, yet just as capable of destroying me."

"Mercy..."

"They make my eyes burn. Every vowel, every period. Every syllable you wrote and verse you formed did something to me that I've never experienced. I've never read something so beautiful, something that literally brought tears to my eyes."

"Mercy, that's enough." Beneath the stern tone and harsh shell lay a boy who couldn't accept my praise. "I didn't do it for compliments. You said you didn't know me, so I'm showing you who I am. You think I'm using you to kill time until Jessica comes back, and I'm trying to prove to you that I'm not. I don't need your approval. I need *you*."

Under his intense scrutiny, I became fully aware of my state of undress.

"I'm, uh... I'm going to put on some pants." I took a few steps backward, holding my shirt down in the front.

"Hey, Mercy? Could you do me a favor?"

I stopped and held his stare.

"Next time you hang out with your ex, can you tell him that if he ever contacts me again, he'll wish he'd never learned how to type? Thanks."

"He did what? He texted you?"

He went right back to browning the meat, continuing as if he hadn't just dropped a bomb at my feet. "Email, but yeah. Same thing. I think he got off on telling me that I'm runner-up. I guess you told him that you're waiting to see if he lied about where he was that night? And if he was telling the truth, you plan to get our marriage annulled?"

"He twisted what I said."

"Then I guess it's a good thing I didn't give a shit what he had to say." He moved the pan off the burner. "Although, I don't think he liked it too much when I told him I hoped he enjoyed the taste of my cum, because I fucked your pussy so hard and so deep it'll be a while before it's all out."

I was shocked. And mortified. And incredibly turned on by his possessiveness.

"Did you really?"

His smile became visible in his eyes first, but half a second later, it was drawn across his face. "No. Of course I didn't. I'm not about to warn him of that shit. He can figure that out when he gets there."

"Brogan, we didn't—"

"I don't care."

"But I want—"

"It doesn't matter, Mercy. Now...go get some pants on before I say *fuck it* and prove myself to you in a very different way."

I wanted to stay and call his bluff. But that would've only made things worse.

10

BROGAN

The door to the shop opened, calling my attention away from Indi—who stood in the hallway with me, bullshitting. Like usual. People came in and out regularly, be it to smoke, to check out the shop, look at the merchandise. And clients.

But this time, heaven walked through the door.

"Everyone," I called out, making sure the entire shop heard, "I present to you, Mercy. My wife." My cheeks ached from my smile, but that might've had more to do with the shock and embarrassment on her face as she glanced from side to side at all the people now staring at her.

As soon as she was within reach, I didn't wait for her to say anything. I held the side of her face in one hand, pulled her to me with the other, and claimed those lips. Not caring who watched. I wasn't ashamed of her, and I wanted everyone to know that. Including her.

Mercy pushed against my chest and broke the kiss, though not angrily. Her eyes cut to the side, likely noticing Indi, and then lifted to meet mine. "I'm not interrupting anything, am I?"

"Nope. Just discussing the day with Indi." I pointed to the woman who hadn't left my side, who was also smiling like she

97

knew a secret no one else did. "Mercy, this is Indi. Indi, meet my wife, Mercy."

Mercy didn't seem overly comfortable when she shook Indi's hand.

"It's nice to meet you. I've heard so much about you."

Mercy glared at me for a second before returning her attention to my colleague. "Same here. I've also seen the show—binged it, actually. You do amazing work. It's nice to finally meet the person Brogan spends so much time with."

Watching her claws come out, practically branding me in front of another woman, was insanely hot. It stirred something in my chest...as well as in my pants. And while I would've loved to see how this interaction turned out, I wasn't willing to lose one of my best employees. So, I took Mercy by the hand and led her into a room, closing the door behind us.

"Do I have anything on my leg?" I asked after she sat in the chair in the middle of the room. I lifted my foot so she could see better, and when she shook her head, I hummed with my hands on my hips, confusion exaggerated. "I'm surprised, considering you basically peed on my calf in front of Indi, marking your territory."

She rolled her eyes and dismissed me with a flick of her wrist. "No more than you did when I came in. What was that anyway? Why would you announce that to the whole place?"

"It's part of my strategy, babe." I lowered myself to the stool I used when working and rolled it over to where she sat. To my surprise, she didn't protest when I parted her legs to make room for my body, or when I nudged my way between her thighs. "I'm hoping it'll be harder to walk away from me if the world knows you're mine."

A soft smile curled her lips as she brought her hands to my shoulders. And as though it were instinctual, her fingers began to dance on the sides of my neck. She dropped her forehead to mine, and just like that, we were in our own bubble. Our own world. Where no one could come between us.

It was safe. Comforting.

It was my heaven, and I never wanted to leave it.

"Well, you might want to start keeping that to yourself, because my parents are talking about coming down sometime soon." Her words were spoken softly, but they felt like sledge-hammers with as hard as they hit me in the gut.

"Do they not know about us?"

She pulled away, her attention dancing around the room—which meant she either didn't want to look at me as she answered, or she needed to search for the right words. "No."

"They don't know we're married?"

She shook her head.

"Do they at least know I exist?"

Again, she shook her head, her attention still on everything other than me.

I huffed and pushed away from her, my fingers twisted in my hair as if yanking on the strands would somehow make me feel better. "Then what the fuck have you told them, Mercy? Who do they think you've been living with for the past week and a half?"

She shrugged, and then her eyes finally fell to mine. "A roommate."

At some point, regardless of my feelings for her, no matter what I trusted to be right, I had to harden myself. Lock my emotions down and keep them secure. Refuse the hope that followed me like a shadow. Ignore the dreams. They did nothing but build me up, lift me high. And if I didn't rein them in, I'd come crashing to the ground when Mercy left.

"I told them about Jordan—well, mostly."

"What does that even mean? *Mostly*?"

Mercy huffed and turned her sights to the ceiling. "Just that I had second thoughts about marrying him and called off the wedding. I told them that I stayed in town for the week to contemplate my options, but in the end, I decided to keep the job I was offered and move here regardless of what happens with Jordan."

"Any idea how you plan to explain me when they get here? Or why you're living in my house?" I blew out a sharp, incredulous laugh with a slight shake of my head. "Oh, that's right. I'm your roommate, aren't I?"

"I honestly don't know how to explain any of this to them. I'm hoping I'll have time to sort it out and come up with something before they get here."

I sucked my teeth and finally nodded. "Do you happen to know when that might be? I just received the schedule from the producers—for when they'll start filming again. And I'm pretty sure you don't want your parents to know about that, either."

"This one time, can you please see this from where I'm standing, versus letting your ego get bruised by thinking this has anything to do with you? Keep in mind, they've put down a good amount of money on a wedding I just postponed. And before you say anything, I did that instead of canceling it so everyone wouldn't freak the fuck out."

"But you do plan to cancel it, right?"

"Well, I'm certainly not marrying him, if that's what you're asking. I'm kind of already married."

Damn, I loved it when she got riled up. It was sexy as hell.

"If I'd gone home and told them that, a month before the wedding they've been planning and paying for, I'd run off and married some random guy I'd only known for a week, I doubt it would've gone over so well. I didn't have much choice. It's not about being ashamed of you or finding reasons to leave. It's simply navigating through parental landmines."

I couldn't argue her reasons, considering parental *anything* wasn't familiar territory for me. I'd had Nonna and Uncle Jerry, but I never considered them parents. Had I been raised by my uncle, there was a good chance I'd be in prison next to my cousin. The life Mercy had lived was about as opposite of mine as it could get.

"Okay…so when do you plan on telling them? When they get here and figure it out on their own? Because, I have to be honest with you, babe…I don't know how to keep the camera crew from outing us. Their job is to film drama, and at times, I've seen them stir the pot to cook some up. And once people find out about us…it'll be everywhere."

Mercy huffed and hunched forward, head in hands. Frustration evident in the curve of her slumped shoulders and in each puff of her chest as she took full and deep breaths. "I don't know, Brogan." She dropped her hands and met my stare. "Why don't you tell me how this should go, since you're the one who knows everything."

I pushed myself to my feet and stepped up to her, making her sit straight to see me. With my hands on either side of her head, fingers woven in the silky strands of her hair, I searched her eyes, something I hadn't had many opportunities to do since she'd been back.

"I don't like fighting. Especially with you. Got it?"

Fisting the sides of my shirt, she nodded.

"Now…about your parents. You need to find out when they plan to come down, and I'll look at the filming schedule. The crew won't be here for two more weeks, so if you can get your parents to be here before they show up, that would be best. If not, we'll have to work around it and come up with creative ways to keep them busy."

Suddenly, her eyes grew full and glassy. "I'm not going to be on the show, am I?"

"Not if you don't want to be." I fucking prayed like hell she didn't.

I didn't want to share her with anyone, let alone the entire world.

"But we don't need to worry about that now." I dropped my forehead to hers and closed my eyes. "Damn, Mercy…the things I want to do to you on this chair would make a porn star blush."

She laughed and tried to push me away, but I wouldn't let her. Instead, I covered her smiling lips with mine until the song of pleasure replaced the humor from moments ago. And had someone not knocked on the door when they did…I would've shown her *exactly* what I wanted to do to her on that chair.

"Sorry to kill the mood, Wrong," Indi said from the doorway, a sliver of amusement shining in her dark eyes. "But there's a delivery out back that only you can sign for."

Mercy slipped off the side of the chair, keeping her head down as if in shame. "That works. I was actually on my way to the school to fill out some paperwork and meet a few people. I just stopped in here on my way."

Ignoring Indi's presence, I blocked Mercy's exit with my arm and kissed her one last time. "See you when I get home?"

"Yeah." That one word would get me through the rest of the day.

———

I stood back and watched as Mercy moved around the kitchen. Dinner was almost done by the time I arrived home, and I was torn with how I felt about it. On one hand, the domesticated image made my dick hard. On the other, there was still a very real possibility that she'd leave, and this wasn't something I should get used to.

"Is it your birthday?" I asked, questioning why she chose to make dinner. Suddenly, what had been meant as a joke quickly became a ton of bricks, landing on my head. "Fuck, babe. Is it? I just realized I don't even know when your birthday is."

She giggled and shook her head. "No, it's not. But I'm glad you asked, because I was hoping we could get to know each other over supper. We kind of jumped into this whole marriage thing without going through the normal stages of a relationship. And at the point when we should've been learning about one another, my ex decided to pop in and flip everything upside down. So, I thought this would be a good time to kind of...play twenty questions, if you will."

Hearing her refer to the bastard as her ex made me smile. "I think that's a fantastic idea."

It didn't take us long to get food on our plates and take our seats at the table—across from each other. At first, the silence was uncomfortable, as though neither of us knew how to start the conversation.

"The pasta's really good, babe."

She sucked in a noodle and nodded, acknowledging my compliment.

"September second," I said just before taking a drink of water. "That's my birthday. When's yours?"

"February eighteenth." For someone who wanted to play twenty questions, she certainly wasn't doing a whole lot to make that happen.

"What else do you want to know about me?"

"Do you love me?"

I nearly choked on my food, having to cough several times before I could swallow and speak. "Holy shit, babe. Where the hell did that come from?"

She shrugged, though I knew if I gave her a few moments, she'd verbally respond. "I get that people make rash decisions and run off to get married without fully thinking it through. In fact, I imagine it happens a lot in Vegas. But what I don't understand is...why fight to keep it if you don't love the other person?"

"I never said I don't love you." Being vulnerable made me uncomfortable, but with Mercy, I felt this unexplainable need to give it all to her. To show her every side of me, even the ones I didn't often let others see. "But I guess for me, it's not as simple as that. It doesn't come down to endorphins or deep respect."

"Then what is it? Please, Brogan...explain it to me. Because I don't understand any of this, and the more I try, the crazier I feel."

I'd trusted that the right time would show itself, so I had to believe this was it.

"Do you remember when you asked about Jessica and if I thought she was my soulmate?" I waited for her to nod before I continued. "Well, I guess the only way I can explain it is to say I believe we have many soulmates. But to me, they are nothing more than people who come in and out of our lives for a reason. Everyone has more than one."

"So you don't think there's only one person out there for each of us?"

"I do. Just not the same way you do."

Curiosity brightened her eyes as she leaned forward. "I don't get it."

"Picture a quilt that's made up of a bunch of squares of different patterns—the patchwork kind. Each square represents a *complete* soul, and as a whole, they all become soulmates to each other. One could be a life partner, another a best friend. Some might even be relatives. But the pieces that make up that one blanket are all cut from the same cloth."

Mercy barely blinked while I tried to paint the vast picture for her.

"Now, imagine taking one of those squares and cutting it in half. You've now taken one complete soul and separated it into two. They are each half of the other, a mirrored image. A twin, if you will. And that's the only person who will ever complete you."

Her head bobbed slowly, the information settling in. "I guess I don't understand how that's any different than what the rest of us would call a soulmate."

"I just see it on a bigger scale. I don't think we have only one person made specifically for us in this life. I think that person is the same, life after life after life. They are meant to make us the best possible versions of ourselves, to help us grow as individuals, and in the end, when we come together again, it's solid."

"Interesting theory." She nodded while twirling her fork in the pile of noodles on her plate. "So, to back up a little...you what? Think I'm the other half of your soul or something? How would you even know?"

"You've heard people say, 'when you know, you know,' haven't you? That's exactly how it is. It's the other half of you, a mirror of you. You recognize that person, and it's instant. It doesn't require time to develop feelings or learn to love them. It's innate. It's powerful and unstoppable and more significant than anything you can feel for *anyone* else. The love is there from before you meet; the rest of it is simply falling *in* love."

"This might take some time to wrap my brain around." Her honesty was all I could ask for. "So please, forgive me if I come to you asking a million questions. I want to understand what you believe. Whether I agree or not."

"Feel free to ask as many as you'd like. I'll answer them all the best that I can."

I had assumed there would be a shift between us once I thoroughly explained it to her. I'd worried she would run. Hoped she'd feel the same and it would click for her. But more than that, I was scared shitless that she'd press pause while taking everything into consideration. I didn't want to live in static. I didn't care for the glitches or grey space.

Noise, I could handle.

Silence would kill me.

———

I stood against the far wall of the shop and watched person after person enter, scan the crowd, and then leave once they realized there were no cameras here. It pissed me off, but there was nothing I could do about it.

"You should just put a sign in the front window saying

we're not filming. That way, they won't waste their time." Indi handed me a beer and settled against the wall next to me. "As much as I've appreciated the business the show has brought in, I have to admit, I can't wait for it to be over."

"You and me both." I took a swig of beer and glanced around the room, taking in all the attendees dressed in stripes. I wasn't the kind of guy who cared much for events or fancy functions, but this one was special to me.

"This is the last season, right?"

"Yeah. Though I'm pretty sure they'll be coming back with a new contract."

Indi groaned. "I know the other guys in the shop want to keep going."

"Of course they do. Even Kickstand gets laid." I pointed to the skinny guy leaning against the front desk, talking to some top-heavy blonde. His name was Daryl, though we all called him Kickstand because that kid did nothing but hold up the walls and furniture around here, always leaning on something.

"But you're not gonna sign it, are you?"

"Fuck no. I'm already having a hard enough time convincing Mercy to stay; I don't need to add to her reasons to take off." Just thinking about her leaving made my chest constrict. Then I flicked my eyes to the front door, waiting for her to arrive.

Indi tapped her beer bottle against mine, catching my attention. "She's going to stay. Stop worrying about it. And she's going to show up, so stop watching the door like you're some Secret Service agent or something. She'll be here. I have no doubt."

"I don't doubt it, either. It would just be nice if she'd hurry up and walk through those doors." I had to smile at my own eagerness. I'd always been one who could wait something out. But when it came to Mercy, I didn't have an ounce of patience.

"Well, when you're tired of standing back here by yourself, staring at the door, come join the rest of us. After all, this is *your* event. I'm sure the people writing checks would love to mingle with the man who set this whole thing up."

Laughter bubbled in my chest as I shook my head. "I do this every year, Indi. They don't come to rub elbows with a guy named Wrong. They come to give back to their community. I doubt anyone cares that I'm not mingling."

She waved me off and then walked away. I may have been the one who set this thing up every year, paid for it and made sure it was a success, but Indi played the part of the hostess perfectly. She was beautiful and friendly, and she knew how to work a crowd. I wouldn't doubt it if she was the reason we'd exceeded our goal three years in a row.

While watching her stop and talk to a young couple, my entire body flushed. A layer of intense heat covered me from head to toe, and my heart rate accelerated. I glanced to the front door and caught sight of Mercy coming in, dressed in a pair of black pants, a black-and-white striped shirt, and the same teal heels she'd worn the night we'd met.

She was a candle in a dark room.

Soft and gentle. Yet unmistakable.

A smile crossed her lips as she made her way farther into the shop, silently greeting those around her with a simple nod or shining eyes. I should've gone to her, but I couldn't stop staring long enough to make my way across the room. I was frozen in place, mesmerized by the most incredible sight.

I didn't need to see her mouth to know she wore a grin on her lips. Her eyes gave it away. Real joy shined bright like gold reflecting the sun, and I believed with my whole being that it was meant for me. Only me. I wouldn't be surprised if everyone in the room thought the same—that her smile was aimed at them. But I knew better. In that moment, standing against a wall with an entire room between us, I'd convinced myself that she was aware she had my attention.

And there was no doubt in my mind who she smiled for.

Then she found me. Locked eyes with mine. The sparkle in

those two pools of whiskey made me want to drown in them. Drown in *her*. Dive in and let myself go. Forget everything. And just...*be*. For in that moment, there was no chance she'd leave. There were no obstacles between us. It was only her and me. Me and her. And that smile.

11

MERCY

The way Brogan rested against a graffiti-laden wall, eyes on mine, and his lazy, panty-melting smirk made me swoon. It also made everything infinitely harder. There was no question in my mind how genuine it was. It was aimed at me, meant for me. No one else.

"Hey, babe," he whispered seconds before closing his mouth against mine, as though we were the only two people in the room.

As I parted my lips for him, the noisy chatter and clinking glasses disappeared. His warm tongue touched mine, and the heat that radiated between us hijacked the evening. Nothing else mattered or existed.

I pulled away from the kiss and touched his face, keeping my forehead to his. Never wanting the moment between us to end. "Hey, baby."

"Oh, before I forget...these are for you." He picked up a bouquet of flowers off a small table and handed them to me. "You don't have to carry them around all night. I just wanted to make sure I gave them to you before I got carried away and forgot."

I pulled an open lily to my nose and breathed the fragrance

in, ignoring the question in my head about how he knew what my favorite flower was. It reminded me of all the things Jordan didn't know, regardless of how long we'd been together. Which didn't surprise me, if I were being honest. In order to truly know someone, you had to pay attention to them—or at the very least, talk to them. And considering Jordan had always seemed content going long stretches of time without contact—this last week was proof of that—it would be difficult for him to know much of *anything* about me. However, I didn't want to think about him right now. I wanted to enjoy my time with Brogan.

"I have to be honest," I said after putting the bouquet on the front desk so I wouldn't forget to take them home. "With all the people here, I assumed this was being filmed for the show. I got a little worried when I first walked in, but I was happy to see no cameras around."

Humor rumbled in his chest as he placed his hand on my lower back to lead me around the room. "Nah. They've tried to film it before, but I won't let them. I don't do this for publicity, or for a fucking pat on the back. This is something that means a lot to me, and I refuse to taint it."

"At the risk of sounding dense, why does it mean so much to you?"

He stilled and moved to stand in front of me. "You already know that I didn't grow up with much. But I guess what I didn't tell you is that the people I grew up with had even less. We lived in a very poor part of town, and over the years, I'd witnessed many families leave—and not for something better. I had friends who ended up in the system because their parents were living on the street. A few were there due to addiction, but most were in that situation because of money—not being able to afford the basics in life."

"So what's with the stripes?" I used my question as an excuse to touch his shirt, run my fingers down the vertical blue pinstripes that colored the otherwise pressed, white fabric.

Brogan always dressed well—usually a pair of jeans with a nice fitted tee that showed off his body and accentuated his ink. Or maybe that was just how I saw it. It was rare to see him in a button-down with a collar, though I had to admit, I liked it a lot.

"I do a different theme every year. This year it's *stripe away the hunger*."

"What did you do last year?"

His smile lit a flame in the pit of my stomach and set my entire body ablaze. Little things like that caught me off guard the most. It was as though his dimple or the feathered creases next to his eyes called to me from a long-lost memory. A part of my brain that had been locked away, untouched until Brogan Daniels had come along with the key.

"It was *black tie, big heart*. You should've been here. I wore a penguin suit."

"I would've loved to see you all dressed up."

The spark in his eyes warned me of an idea. The last time I saw that, we got married. "Yeah, well...I'd love to see you all dressed up, too. Maybe we can make that happen by having a real wedding. One where you walk down an aisle to me. Where we actually exchange rings and vows and all the good stuff. What do you think?"

Contemplating my response, I ran my tongue along the sticky gloss that coated my bottom lip and glanced around the shop. It'd been almost a week since our discussion on soul mates, and even though I'd given it a lot of thought since then, that didn't mean I was ready to let go of my fears and jump in with my eyes closed.

Before I could speak and give him any sort of answer, he cupped my jaw and guided my attention to his face. "Your hesitation worries me, Mercy. I guess I assumed you were starting to come around to the idea of us actually being together the way we promised in Savannah. Please don't tell me I was wrong about that. Don't tell me we're not on the same page."

"Brogan..." I huffed and glanced away for a moment,

steeling myself against the pain I'd undoubtedly see in his eyes once I got these words out. "It'll take more than a few conversations about soul mates before we can both be in the same book, let alone on the same page. I'm doing the best that I can with the hand I've been dealt. This isn't an easy situation to be in."

He brought his lips closer to my ear and whispered, "It would be a lot easier if you stopped fighting this and just accepted it the way I have."

It'd been days since he'd expressed his belief and, essentially, told me I'm the other half of his soul. I still couldn't wrap my mind around that one. Especially since he all but refused to say he loved me.

Figure that one out.

While I hadn't given in to Brogan's theory, I hadn't fully dismissed it, either. There were a lot of pieces of the puzzle that made sense, some I'd even experienced firsthand. I couldn't deny that. Albeit, they could've easily been explained as coincidences. Some were so powerful they gave me goose bumps. Others left me scratching my head.

It'd become one more item on the growing list of things I needed to figure out. And I feared I was running out of time. Brogan wouldn't be patient forever, but it would be foolish to dive in without processing it all. Considering everything up until this point could've—and rightfully so—been classified as foolish, I didn't need to add to it.

"Brogan, this isn't the time or place to have this conversation."

It seemed he'd make the time and find the place, because he took me by the hand and led me to one of the rooms in the back. Once he closed the door, we were draped in muted silence, nothing more than soft mumbles reverberating through the walls. But that wasn't what caused my heart to still.

Brogan's thin lips, hard eyes, and furrowed brow had done that.

"Okay, now that we're alone, answer me. Please," he all but begged.

"I don't know what you want me to say. I *have* looked into it. I've read through the books and checked out the websites you told me about. And while it all sounds amazing, I can't ignore the fact that most of it can also be explained away as something else. Coincidence, or the high everyone experiences during the honeymoon phase. You can't say that just because our meeting was random and unconventional, it somehow means anything more than being in the right place at the right time."

"Have you ever been in the honeymoon phase?" His brows pulled together, and what I assumed was rejection darkened his eyes. "Because I have, and I can honestly tell you that this isn't it. This is more. What we have is lightyears beyond that. If you can't see it…" He shook his head and took a step back.

"That's not what I mean."

"Then what *do* you mean? Tell me, because I'm not understanding."

My heart was in my throat. Just the thought of hurting him killed me. Like I could feel every ounce of his pain. "The last thing I want to do is read too much into this. To get my hopes up, only for them to come crashing down on top of me. I'd rather look at this logically so that I'm prepared."

"Prepared for what, Mercy?"

I swear, my every heartbeat was controlled by him, by the organ beating within his chest. Because I had absolutely no power over it. I couldn't slow my heart down or ease the ache. Only he could, and if we continued this conversation for much longer, I'd likely die of heart failure. "I don't want to believe this is what you say it is, and then find out it's not."

"You'll never believe it is if you keep one foot out the door, either."

"I don't have one foot out the door," I argued with tears shredding and burning the backs of my eyes, begging to be released. "I'm here, aren't I?"

"Yeah." He shook his head and took another step away. "You're sleeping in my spare room. You haven't unpacked a single box. And you've yet to make a decision about one goddamn thing. But yes, Mercy…physically, you're here. I guess that'll have to be enough—until you're *not* physically here anymore."

And with that, he walked out.

He'd reached into my chest, grabbed ahold of my heart, and taken it with him. For there wasn't a single detectable beat inside. I was numb. Empty. Lost and confused. I wanted to chase him. I wanted him to come back. I wanted to run and hide…and hold him close.

Instead, I slid down the wall and wrapped my arms around my legs. I tucked my chin to my chest and allowed the hurt and love to battle it out. I prayed for a sign. For something to tell me what to do. I wanted to believe him, believe every word spoken. To feel what it was like to love someone without doubt. To trust in the universe and not question anything.

I took a few deep breaths and calmed myself. Brogan was out there somewhere, and I needed to find him. Preferably, before he lost hope in us. I had seen it in his eyes before he left. He'd pulled away, effectively closing himself off in order to protect his emotions. Which I understood. I couldn't blame him for that; I could only blame myself.

I'd done this.

The gaping hole in my chest was *my* doing.

I had to find him. I had to make this right before I ruined what my heart believed was the best accident that had ever happened to me. I still wasn't a hundred percent sure that this thing between us was what he'd said—fate designed by our souls and carried out by the universe, painted in the sky and sealed by the stars. But that didn't mean I was ready to give up on finding out the truth.

Picking myself up off the floor was the easy part. Walking out of the room proved slightly more difficult. But nothing—

and I mean *nothing*—came close to how hard it was to move through the room, between the bodies, the smiling faces, the laughter and overall happiness, and not find him. He was lost to me. Just as I'd been lost to him. And for the first time, I fully understood how it had made him feel.

"Hey, Indi...do you by chance know where Brogan went?" I stopped the inked bombshell on her way to the bar. "I've looked all over, and I can't find him."

She appeared hesitant at first, which did nothing but make my lungs deflate and choke me. But when her eyes met mine, compassion painted her brow in subtle creases that softened her jawline. "He, uh...he left, honey. I don't know where he went, but he asked me to handle the event just before he walked out."

Right then, something inside me snapped.

I felt disconnected. Like a kite without a string. A boat without an anchor. Disoriented. In that moment, I realized that, without Brogan, I was a compass without direction—nothing more than a dial with no magnetic pull to anything. Lost.

Utterly fucking lost.

"Thanks, Indi." I wasn't sure she'd heard me, but I also didn't care. She wasn't the one who needed my words. She wasn't the person who deserved to hear my voice. My gratitude. My apologies.

Those were reserved for Brogan.

There was only one thing left to do.

I grabbed my keys and the flowers that sat next to them on the reception desk and ran out as fast as my heels would allow.

Sitting behind the steering wheel with my eyes closed, I tried to clear the fear and doubt from my mind. I trusted that if I could just wipe away my own ego, I'd know where to go. I'd know what to do. But the deeper I breathed, the worse it became. The voice in my head grew louder, telling me I'd ruined everything.

Out of all the literature Brogan had given me to read about mirrored souls, the one thing I truly took away from it was the need to separate what I thought *should be* from what *was*. Just letting it happen the way it was meant to.

That wasn't easy. Possibly one of the hardest things to do.

So, I pulled the flowers to my nose and inhaled, hoping that if I had something to actually smell, it might help to distract the negativity, allowing the uncertainty and trepidation to fade and make way for trust. But as I did that, something hard and sharp hit my cheek.

The sign I'd asked for.

A card.

I hadn't noticed it when he gave me the bouquet earlier. Now, I couldn't tear into the envelope fast enough. Couldn't pull the note out quick enough. And once I had it open in front of me, I couldn't read his words slow enough.

"Save me and have me, fix me and I'm yours"
With her words burning in my mind I tried,
I took from me, gave to her and left myself a broken shell,
I stripped all I could spare and more besides
As I emptied myself into Mercy

———

I doubted I'd taken a breath between reading another piece of his heart and pulling down the driveway to the garage. It wasn't until I found his Jeep parked inside that my nerves settled and my stomach unclenched.

There wasn't a single piece of the drive home that I could recall. The lights on the highway had been a blur, the hum of the tires on the road nothing but white noise droning on in the background. I'd raced home, trusting my gut that he'd be there. And he was.

Now…I only had to get to him.

I left my purse and flowers abandoned on the seat beside me. My shoes on the floorboard. And, with the card held tightly in my grasp for fear of someone stealing his words, I climbed the steep steps from the garage to the house.

Once I made it inside, it didn't take me long to find him. I heard his bedroom door close about two seconds after I'd shut the one leading in from the garage. And without worrying about changing my clothes or what I'd say, I went to him.

I didn't knock. Didn't announce my presence. I simply flung open the door and stepped inside. He stood on the other side of the room, in track pants, next to the bed. Shirtless. Looking like a god in inked flesh. The sight alone stopped me just inside the doorway. But even if it hadn't, the way he stared at me with broken eyes would have.

"What are you doing, Mercy?" His voice was empty. Hollow. No longer filled with untold secrets and promises.

I held up the card, as if that somehow meant anything. "I read what you wrote."

"And?"

I'd had a rather long drive from his shop in the city to his house in the boonies, yet I hadn't spent one second of it contemplating what I would say when I reached him. If I had, I might've come up with something better than, "Why is it so easy for you to tell me all this, but you can't even say you love me?"

"What does it matter? Love is a given, Mercy. I've loved you since before I found you on that sidewalk. Just like I don't need to hear you say it, because I know that you've loved me since you took your first breath. Saying it doesn't change anything. If you would stop overthinking it all, you'd realize that you've *felt* my love for you all along."

I stood there, silent and awkward, desperately holding back tears. The need to cry was almost unbearable, as if emotion filled me so full I couldn't contain it all. I'd never, in all my life, felt anything close to this. It was overwhelming, to say the least.

"Listen, Mercy…" He closed his eyes and quickly shook his head. "I've had a long day, and I'm tired. We can discuss this tomorrow. Right now, all I want to do is climb into bed. If you would like to join me, you're more than welcome—but don't forget the rule." He dropped his pants and kicked them to the side, standing completely naked in front of me. He'd said since the first night I'd slept in his bed that clothes weren't optional. "If not, then please close the door on your way out."

Brogan sat on the edge of the mattress with his back to me. While he fiddled with the cords on the nightstand, plugging in his phone, I took in his hunched shoulders and curved spine. I'd somehow taken a man who walked ten feet tall and cut him off at the knees. All because I'd denied him one thing—confirmation that he completed every part of me.

We were playing with fire.

And I wanted to get burned.

To be so consumed with his heat that I couldn't breathe. Couldn't think. Couldn't see or speak or hear or...*live without it*. So, I did the one thing that would guarantee it. I stepped toward the door.

12

BROGAN

The second the door clicked shut, I knew I'd lost her.

I'd expected this, tried to prepare for it, and still, it hurt all the same. If I was right about us, about what we had, then I had to trust she'd come back. I wouldn't know how or when, but she would always come back.

I pulled the chain on the lamp next to me, shrouding the room in darkness, and then slid beneath the covers. The pillows didn't need near as much *fluffing* as I gave them, but it was the only way to expel some of this anguish and madness that surged within me. I'd contemplated going after her, but I couldn't. It wouldn't do any good. It would only exacerbate my hostility, and I couldn't afford much more of that right now. So instead, I lay there, staring at the ceiling and wishing someone would give me answers. Guidance. A fucking flashlight at the very least.

Then I got exactly what I'd asked for.

The covers on the other side of the bed flipped back, and a body slid in beside me. Lavender permeated the air, leaving no doubt whatsoever in my mind as to who was in bed with me. Still, I turned on the lamp, needing to see her to believe it.

With the room bathed in light, I turned to face her, propped on my elbow. Ignoring the undeniable fact that she was naked —or at least topless—beneath the covers, I stared into her eyes and prayed this meant what I hoped it did.

"I'm not playing games, Mercy. If you don't intend to stay in my bed from here on out, then I suggest you go back to your room. I won't share you. If you're in my bed, then you're mine. Not his. No questions. No games. No more doubt or excuses."

My lungs burned as I held my breath. I refused to get excited, knowing how badly it would hurt to have it stripped away. So I waited, feeling the milliseconds drag on for what seemed like hours. Days. Eons upon eons while the silence in the room rang in my ears, my heartbeat creating the bass in this tragic symphony of despair.

She pressed her warm palm against my chest, filling me with heat and hope and fear.

"I'm yours, Brogan. I'm not going anywhere." Her words were lyrics written to my soul.

The dam broke, and I grabbed her waist, pulling her beneath me. "Say that again."

"I'm yours."

I claimed her mouth for the final time, knowing no one would ever touch these lips again. No other man alive would understand what it felt like to kiss heaven, for heaven was mine. And when we both needed to breathe, I gave my attention to the rest of her, starting with her neck.

I'd only needed to trace the spot beneath her ear with my tongue one time to know the whimper it pulled from her. I was fully aware of what it did to her when I kissed along her collarbone to the hollow space in the middle. And how she'd dig her nails into my biceps as I tasted the heated skin just above her breast on my way up to the other side of her neck.

"Brogan. Please." Her plea was raspy and desperate.

Opening my mouth, I raked my teeth along her sensitive flesh down the curve of her shoulder, all while sliding my cock through her slick folds. She was turned on and ready. And hell, so was I. But there was no way I'd hurry this along. Not when I'd waited a lifetime to get her here again. Instead, I squeezed her hip, digging my fingertips into the soft meat of her ass, and hoped that would ground me for now.

"Please what, babe? What do you need?" I rolled my hips, hitting her clit with the silver ball on the underside of my dick, right below the crown. Her moan made me do it again. "Tell me, Mercy…please what?"

"I need you. Now."

I inched myself down her body, just enough to place my mouth between her breasts. With my lips barely meeting her skin, I chuckled—the taunting kind of laughter that would rile her. "Not yet. Not until I'm done admiring what's mine."

Then I turned my head to the left, held her stare, and covered her nipple with my mouth. I smiled when she gasped and threw her head back into the pillow. I never took my eyes off her while flicking the hardening peak with my tongue. Once I had her panting, desperate, hungry for more, I moved to the other side. And when she was needy for more, I pinched her nipple between my teeth, knowing precisely what she would do next.

A cry ripped through her chest as she threaded her fingers into my hair, tugging on the strands until the roots pulled taut at my scalp. Her eyes met mine; her thighs clenched at my sides. Then she rocked her pelvis against me, seeking what she craved most. But I wasn't ready to give in. It didn't matter how hard I was. How eager I was. How badly I wanted to bury myself in her, allow her heat to light me up…I wasn't done appreciating her body. It had been so long, and I'd imagined this moment a thousand times over while she kept me waiting.

Against her protests, I continued my way down her stomach, stopping briefly to trail my tongue around her navel before kissing the soft spot above her trimmed hairline. She bucked her hips, seeking out my mouth. And I smiled. "Not yet, babe."

"We can do all this the next time. I need you, Brogan. Please, baby. Just fuck me." Mercy knew exactly what those words did to me. She was the only woman who had ever been able to make me give in by saying those three words. *Just fuck me*.

But not this time.

I moved my attention to her left leg, starting with her inner thigh while trailing my fingertips along the crease below her ass cheek to the sensitive spot right above the bend in her knee. By the time I made it to her ankle, I had to hold her down with my hand against her pussy to keep her from moving so much. She began to rock herself against my palm. I could feel how wet she was, and how hot her body had become against the heel of my hand. If I didn't hurry this up, she wouldn't wait for me.

There was something intoxicating about that. About knowing she was so hard up for me that she couldn't wait another minute, let alone another second. And as much as I wanted to continue up the other leg, I couldn't.

Taking her by surprise and pulling a yelp from her throat, I hooked my arms beneath her thighs and covered her sex with my mouth, flattening my tongue against her heat to taste her arousal. I could drink her all day. Every day. Get drunk off her juices and never be sober.

My dick throbbed and my balls ached, but I continued. I needed her, probably more than I'd ever needed anything or anyone in my life. I flicked her clit with my tongue, and she reared her hips toward my mouth. She gripped the sides of my head and ground her pussy against my face. When her cries became indecipherable, I knew she was on the edge. The second she tugged on my hair, I didn't bother questioning what she meant. I didn't care to ask questions or drag this out any longer. I pulled myself over her and tasted her lips. Her tongue. Making her taste herself on mine while I ran the crown of my dick through her folds, painting her clit with my precum. And the moment she parted her lips to take a breath, I pushed into her.

As soon as I was buried inside, balls deep, I didn't wait

before I slid almost all the way out and slammed into her again. Over and over. Never letting her catch her breath. Her nails raked over my ribs, digging into my flesh. Likely breaking the skin as she clawed at me. She'd done that before, but I didn't mind. After all, I'd marred her body with bruises from my hands, my fingers, and love bites from my teeth. We'd branded each other and wore the marks with pride. I'd never been with anyone as passionate as I was in the bedroom.

Mercy Wright was my match.

My equal.

And I'd never be able to get enough.

I held her by the nape of her neck and pulled her closer. There was something about making her watch as I moved in and out of her that turned me on. However, not nearly as much as when she grabbed my shoulders to bring her face closer to mine, kissing me as if staking her claim. Marking her territory.

Owning me.

And just when I thought I couldn't handle any more, she pushed against the mattress, throwing me off balance until I rolled over. Then she held herself upright, straddling me, pressing her hands on my chest. Riding me. Her head tilted back. Her neck on display. Her hips rolling, rocking, back and forth as she rode me with wild abandon.

"Fuck, babe." My raspy voice gave away the desperation that ran through me.

But it seemed to spur Mercy on. Rather than speed up her movements, she peered down at me, a wicked grin lining her sexy lips. She knew she had me. And this was her way of informing me that she was in control. "Not yet, baby. Not until I'm done enjoying what's mine."

I grabbed one thigh and flipped her over. I slid off the side to stand next to the bed, pulled her to the edge, and filled her once again. "I'm yours for the next hundred lifetimes, Mercy. You'll have more than enough time to enjoy it. But right now, I need to see you come for me."

With my thumb against her clit, I increased the pace. Skin against skin. Hips against hips. It was all too much, yet not nearly enough. Using her legs around my waist, she pulled me into her, meeting me thrust for thrust. Showing me that she was just as much a part of this as I was. She was in it with me. Right there with me. A participant, a partner in every sense of the word.

"Babe. I can't… I don't know if I can hold on. I need you—" I didn't have to say anything else. Right then, she tightened around me, and her breathing became heavy and ragged. Two seconds later, I followed, emptying myself into her.

Even though I could barely stand, I slipped my arm beneath her back, moved her up the mattress, and then collapsed next to her. As I lay there, tangled in her, I traced the lines of the tattoo I'd put on her ribs, making her squirm.

"Why is your name Mercy?"

She turned her head to the side to look in my eyes. "Why do you think?"

"Because your parents just liked it?"

"Wrong again." She squinted as if studying me and took in a full breath. "Does your nickname not bother you?"

"Not really. Should it?"

She moved her attention to the ceiling, quiet and contemplative. "I just can't imagine going my whole life having people call me something that means incorrect. A mistake. Immoral or sinful." She rolled her head to the side again, meeting my stare once more. "I don't know how you're okay with having a nickname that means corrupt, depraved."

"We can't all be right, can we? We can't all have names that mean correct. Honest. Righteous and moral. But maybe that's the point. Without a right, you don't have a wrong. Without you, I would just…*be*. I'd have no meaning. No purpose." I ran my fingertips along her face, across her brow, around her jawline. "Without you, I'd be without mercy. And I think that's worse than not having a definition."

Her cheeks glowed crimson as her smile took over her face. Then her eyes met mine, and in them, I found confirmation for everything I'd felt since the moment we met. If love had a color, it'd be a deep, rich topaz. If love had a scent, it'd smell like an endless field of lavender.

Love was compassionate, kind, and sympathetic.

By definition...love was Mercy.

———

I had slept next to Mercy for six nights, even though I'd only needed one to know I never wanted to sleep without her again. Then I'd gone to bed alone for the next month—half of that time Mercy was on the other side of the house. But after being tangled up in her all last night, it was as if every lonely evening without her never existed.

And *nothing* beat waking up, rolling over, and wrapping my arms around a naked Mercy first thing in the morning.

She was so responsive to my touch. Always had been. Hell, there were times I only needed to say something the right way and her breathing would change. It'd slow down, become slightly labored. And rather than speak, she'd simply nod and say "yup" or "uh-huh." But when I used my touch instead of words, I got an entirely different reaction.

With my arm around her waist, I dragged her warm back against my bare chest and curled my body around hers. Much like the week I'd woken up next to her, my hand immediately cupped her breast, as though it was instinct. She pushed her ass against my erection, an involuntary moan rumbling in her chest, and with that one move, every day, every hour, minute and second, between then and now vanished.

"Morning, babe," I mumbled against the nape of her neck where I buried my face to breathe her in. "As much as I would love to make this morning even better"—I nudged her with my hard-on to let her know what I meant—"I don't really want to wait another second getting your things into this room and put away where they belong."

I didn't have to see her face to recognize the smile on her lips. It sang in her contented sigh and danced along her skin as she curled into me more. Then she turned, shifted onto her back to meet my gaze, and I wanted to thank the heavens for the ability to witness it. The soft curl of her lips. The spark in her hooded eyes. The proof that I wasn't in this alone.

"Where did you come from?" Exhaustion scratched through her morning voice.

With a smile, I pushed up on my elbow to lean over her, to see her better. "I've been right here, right beside you, this whole time. I haven't gone anywhere, babe."

"No," she whispered with a slow shake of her head. Then she reached up and cupped my cheek, the heat from her palm spreading through me like a wildfire. "That night. In front of the club. When we met for the first time. Where did you come from? Why were you there?"

As much as I wanted to spin an elaborate tale of fate and divine intervention, I settled for a more realistic truth. One she'd understand better than the stars guiding me to her. "I was on my way into Rulebreakers to meet a friend."

"That late?"

"Well…yeah. I was at the shop when Indi called, so I was close by. She'd gone out with her little sister but ended up getting ditched and asked if I could pick her up."

Puzzlement pinched her brow, forcing me to fall onto my back. Yet that didn't stop her from pushing for more. Reversing our positions, she lifted herself with her elbow and leaned over me, seeking answers I didn't care to give. "But you didn't pick her up."

"No, I didn't. I found you instead."

"What happened to her? How'd she get home?"

"Uber, I guess." I shrugged against the pillow beneath me. "It's not like she *needed* a ride. That's what she did—she'd go out with her sister, have too many drinks, and then call me for a ride. Sometimes I picked her up; sometimes I didn't."

Mercy was silent for a moment, although it seemed to be more of a quiet contemplation than doubtful hesitation. "I'm assuming you did more than pick her up and drop her off at her place when you did this?"

"Yeah."

"And yet you chose to drive a stranger all over town, then take her back to your place—all without once making a move on her—instead of getting laid?"

One corner of my mouth curled just enough to create a burning ache in my cheek. "Yeah."

"How'd she take that?"

I lifted the covers and sighed at my deflated erection. "Moby doesn't like it when you spend naked time asking why I didn't sleep with another woman."

"*Moby?*" She pushed away with a smile brightening her entire face, lighting up her eyes until they resembled two shiny pennies. Sitting up, she shook her head and allowed the most infectious giggle to drift through the room like an easy breeze. "You named your penis Moby?"

"What else was I supposed to name him?"

Her laughter didn't let up. "Is it strictly because of Moby *Dick*? Or because he's as big as a whale? Wait…never mind. I don't want to know. Pretend I didn't ask."

"All of the above, babe." There was something about teasing her until her cheeks turned the color of cherries that made my heart speed up. I loved how innocent she acted. Even though we both knew how naughty she was between the sheets.

She'd checked off every last box on my list, and then added more, checking those off as well. And for the life of me, I had no idea how I'd gotten so damn lucky to have found her. All I knew was that I must've done something extraordinary in a past life to have earned a chance to have her in my arms. In my life.

"I can't with you," she said through rumbly humor as she climbed off the bed. "I'm going to start the coffee before you name my lady bits."

"How do you know I haven't?" I hadn't, although admitting that wouldn't have been as much fun.

As she bent over to pull up her panties, I smacked her ass. Hard. Earning a yelp and the most gorgeous grin I'd ever seen. And even though I didn't necessarily want her to get dressed or leave the room, I needed coffee—purely for the energy required to keep her in bed all day.

13

MERCY

It'd taken a few minutes of frantic searching to remember I'd left everything in the car last night—my phone included. And once I'd retrieved it, I wished I hadn't.

Thirteen missed texts.

Seven missed calls.

Don't get me started on the emails or social media notifications.

Two of the messages were from my parents, as well as a phone call and voicemail. The urgent *call us back!* text was enough to move on and save that one for last. Skipping over the little blue dot next to Jordan's name, I tapped Stella's while pulling on a pair of leggings I'd managed to grab before Brogan moved every last piece of my clothing out of the spare room.

The number of unread texts in our thread made me laugh, roll my eyes, worry, and sigh with relief all at once. At least I knew the majority of those thirteen messages had come from my best friend and not my ex.

Message one: *Have you seen the Google News feed??*

Message two: *Well, now that I think about it...I doubt Google chooses the same articles for both of us. Then again, I'm pretty sure you've searched Wrong's name enough times for the bots to assume you'd be interested in them now.*

Message three: *You're not reading your texts, which worries me. Knowing you, you're freaking out and rocking back and forth in a corner somewhere. Should I come and feed you tequila? Binge on chocolate cake in bed?? (Wrong is welcome to join us)*

That was enough to cause my heart to stop. I had no idea what she was talking about. And considering the abundance of notifications that currently littered my screen in the form of annoying red dots—my complete lack of a social life meant I rarely had to deal with them—I had a very bad feeling I wouldn't like it.

Google. News. Freaking out. Wrong.

The combination of those things couldn't have equated to anything good.

Without reading the rest of her texts, I exited out of the message app and tapped the icon with the colorful *G*. Breathing became easier when I scrolled through the generated list of articles—an odd mix of reputable news and trashy gossip—and didn't see anything alarming. Well, aside from a headline about a woman who had a quarter of her ribs removed in order to make her waist smaller.

However, all that changed the moment I typed Brogan's name into the search bar.

"*Wrong Daniels, Star Of The Hit Show 'Wrong Inc,' Is Married.*"

"Women all over are crushed to learn their favorite eligible bachelor, reality star and tattoo artist, Wrong Daniels, is officially off the market."

I shouldn't have been surprised that people had found out—

considering Brogan had no qualms about announcing it to the entire shop anytime I visited. Honestly, I should've been surprised it'd taken *this* long for people to start talking. After all, we'd been married for a month. Had I taken a second to contemplate the whole world talking about his relationship status, I might've expected it sooner. But for some reason, I never thought about it—after all, people in *normal* relationships don't have to worry about their marital status popping up on Google alerts.

I'd just started to think this wasn't as bad as I had initially assumed when another headline caught my attention, stopping me mid-thought. Dead in my tracks. My lungs nothing but two shriveled organs, and my heart ceasing to beat.

"Daniels' New Wife Said 'I Do' While Engaged To Another Man."

I tapped on the link and skimmed the words in search of my name. Halfway through the second paragraph, there it was. *Mercy Wright.* As well as my age and where I was from. I didn't scroll any further. Didn't skim other words. I refused to see what was said about me, knowing I couldn't do a damn thing about it.

"I'm not sure which drawers you want all your clothes in, so I left them folded on the bed in piles." Brogan's voice startled me, which made me gasp, effectively forcing me to take a breath for the first time in far too long.

When I turned to face him, the sight of his bare chest, covered in colored ink, calmed me in a way I hadn't expected. And the way he leaned into the room with his hands gripping the edges of the doorframe filled me with a sense of protection, even from several feet away. Just like that, the anxiety that had riddled my entire body quieted to a slow sizzle, all because of his presence.

It was as though my soul knew he'd keep me safe.

"Oh, that's okay. Thanks, baby." I smiled and prayed he couldn't see the remnants of panic in my eyes. "I'll put them away in a minute."

Brogan regarded me a little longer than usual. Eyes slightly squinted. Lips almost pursed. He'd obviously picked up on the unease that lingered just beneath my ribs. But at least he didn't question it. Rather than point it out, he said, "No worries. Finish up in here, and I'll go pour us some coffee. Meet you in the kitchen when you're done."

I held my breath until he disappeared from the doorway. Once it was safe, I released the longest, heaviest sigh that left me empty, and then went back to Stella's texts. However, the paranoid thoughts wouldn't quiet. Add in the constant fear of Brogan returning, and she might as well have sent me gibberish. So, I took the phone to the bathroom, turned on the faucet to drown out the noise in my head, and sat on the toilet to finish going through Stella's rant.

Message four: *Answer me woman!!!*

Message five: *That's it. I'm getting on a plane.*

Message six: *Disregard that last text. The next available flight is tomorrow morning. I'll be there at noon. Your ass better come pick me up, because I don't know where the hell he lives. < -- That's a discussion for another time.*

Message seven: *Flight is booked. See you tomorrow!*

The sharp smack of my palm against my forehead resounded in the small, tiled room, followed by the low rumble of the groan that slipped past my constricted throat. I loved my best friend. I missed her more than I'd thought possible. And honestly, this was the time I needed her most—right when my entire world was on the cusp of exploding. Or imploding…

depending on how this all played out. But I worried how Brogan would feel about Stella, someone he'd never met, invading his private life with nearly no warning at all.

I quickly typed out a response, explaining that I'd left my phone in the car overnight and had just seen the news. Then I asked if she'd gotten to the airport yet—hoping there was still a chance I could convince her to postpone her trip until *after* this all blew over.

She sent a picture of her sitting at the gate next to a hot guy.

Guess there was no changing her mind now.

There were still four more unread texts, and considering the only name with a blue dot next to it was Jordan's, they were all from him. My only saving grace was that I'd taken off the read receipts for his messages, so he wouldn't know if I'd seen them or not. I wasn't stupid enough to think he'd believe me if I told him I hadn't looked at them, but at this point, I didn't care.

And I *really* didn't care what he believed once I saw what he had to say.

The first one had come in just before eleven the night before. *I miss you.* A part of me felt bad for him. For what I'd done to him—providing he'd been truthful about who he was with that night. But a little over an hour later, at a few minutes after midnight, he'd sent another. *Thanks for making me look like a fool to everyone I know*, which was followed up with *I hope you're happy.*

The last one was at two in the morning, and I could only imagine how much he'd had to drink by that point. *I take it this means you've made up your mind. It really shows what kind of person you are that you didn't bother to tell me and made me find out from other people. I used to think he'd ruin you, but now I think maybe you two are meant for each other. Enjoy your ride to hell.*

If I checked Facebook, I'd probably find pity posts on his profile, or memes meant to garner sympathy. I couldn't handle seeing those. Not because I'd feel bad for him, but because they'd anger me and cause me to respond, and that was the last thing I wanted. So I ignored the red number in the corner of the blue app with the white *f* and opened my voicemail.

This ought to be fun.

Checking the time of each notification aided in figuring out when the news broke. And so far, the earliest timestamp was from my parents' missed call—at a quarter to nine. I couldn't for the life of me recall when I'd arrived at the shop for the fundraiser, or when I'd left. There was a chance I hadn't seen the alert after running out to find Brogan. My mind had been on getting to him, so I could've had a hundred missed calls from the Pope, and I wouldn't have noticed.

"Mercy, honey…what's going on? We got a call from your Aunt Grace, and she said something about you eloping with some guy. We're just wondering what she meant by that. Please call us back when you can. We love you."

Knowing my aunt, she'd called for gossip. She was the kind of lonely old woman who got out of bed every morning to stick her nose in everyone else's business. I was pretty sure the only reason people still spoke to her was the friendly smile she wore while making you feel like she was genuinely interested in what you had to say, somehow leaving you convinced that she only gossiped about others, never you.

Apparently, I was the only one who saw through it.

Considering the urgent, *call us back!* text came almost thirty minutes after the sweet, calm, *please call us back when you can* voicemail, I could only assume that meant they'd received additional information regarding the news. However, without returning their call, I wouldn't know for sure what they'd heard.

And I wasn't in the mood to call them back quite yet.

I'd need coffee for that.

In fact, I would need extreme levels of caffeine to deal with the rest of the notifications that riddled my screen. So I decided to disregard the others in favor of making my way to the kitchen, where Brogan stood—still shirtless, thank God—holding a piping hot cup of coffee in his hand.

"Sorry about that," I rasped as I took the offered mug and brought it to my lips. "I jumped out of the car so fast last night that I left my phone in the front seat. And it just so happened to be the one night everyone and their brother decided to call or text. Or email. Or send me messages on Facebook."

Brogan moved to stand in front of me, so close I could smell his skin, and took my coffee from my hand before I could take the first sip. He placed it on the granite next to his, and then lifted me by my hips to perch me on the edge of the counter. All without saying a single word. Then he stepped forward, sliding between my legs and bringing his face closer to mine. I could see in his eyes that I hadn't pulled one over on him—he more than likely knew something was up before finding me in the spare room earlier.

Being so connected to someone that they could sense things without reason had its downside. Such as right now. All I wanted to do was play it off and pretend a wrecking ball wasn't headed our way. I'd just made it back into his arms, and I worried that everything I'd discovered this morning—the news, my parents' concern, as well as Stella coming for a visit—would ruin it all. I simply wanted to enjoy what little time we had before our world came crashing down around us...but *no*. Brogan wouldn't let me avoid it. Even though we still had so much to learn about each other, this was a piece of him I'd discovered from the beginning.

"You're acting eerily calm, babe." He kept his warm gaze on mine while holding me in place with a firm grip on my thighs. "Either you've gotten really good at hiding your fears, or you've finally accepted this. So, which one is it, Mercy?"

"I have no idea what you're talking about."

He was no fool. Tilting his head to one side, he called my bluff with his raised brows and intense eyes. "Are you trying to tell me it's merely a coincidence that *everyone and their brother* contacted you on the same night the internet blew up with stories of us?"

Ironically, I hadn't once contemplated the idea that he would've already heard about it.

"When did you find out?" I asked in a hesitant, whispered tone. I prayed he wouldn't tell me that he'd seen it last night. Because that would mean he'd kept it from me, knowing how I would've reacted. And I wasn't sure how I felt about that.

"Right after you left to make coffee. I checked my phone and caught the Google alert." Thank God he wasn't a manipulative person. "So tell me, which is it? Have you gotten that good at faking your emotions? Or am I worried for no reason that you're about to freak out and take off?"

I shrugged and glanced over his head, unable to hold the intensity of his stare. "Maybe somewhere in between?"

"Can you at least tell me what you're most concerned about?" He lifted his hand and cupped my cheek, drawing my attention back to his face. With one glance, the trepidation that had resided in my chest ever since reading that first article withered away. His eyes were like two lily pads relaxing beneath the sun's rays. I wanted to feel their warmth and allow them to soothe away every last fear within me.

"My parents. They called…and left a couple messages. I'm not sure what all they've heard. I haven't gotten back with them, so there's no telling how they feel about it. But I'd bet it's not good."

Brogan hated the fact that I still hadn't told my parents about us—or that he even existed. So the flicker of hurt across his face shouldn't have come as a surprise. Yet it did. The only thing that kept me calm was how he never wavered. Not once did he flinch or make even the smallest attempt to back away. His eyes remained on mine. His hands never left my body.

Regardless, I felt compelled to make the unintentional rejection go away.

"I guess they had to find out sooner or later. Right?" Trying to lighten the mood would be easier if he'd smile, though it seemed it would take more than a rhetorical question to make that happen. I sighed and rested my hands on his shoulders, dropping my focus to his chest. "I would've preferred it if they had heard it from me, but I don't really have anyone to blame for that. Had I been honest and just told them from the start rather than keep putting it off for fear they'd disown me, this wouldn't be an issue."

"Babe..." He curled his finger beneath my chin and lifted my attention to his face once more. "Don't do that. There will always be things we could've done to prevent something from happening, but there's no point dwelling on them. It is what it is. You can't change the past; the only thing you can do is focus on dealing with the here and now."

"Great advice. Got any suggestions for fixing it now?"

A smile finally broke free across his arousal-inducing lips, though it was small. And a bit smug. "I'm not sure you can do much without returning their call. That would probably be step one. Then listen to what they have to say, and make sure you answer their questions honestly. You don't have to divulge details if you don't want to, but they deserve the truth."

"I really don't care to listen to their lectures. And I can't handle my dad's disappointment."

"They'll likely be upset, but that's their right, Mercy. Above all else, you're their daughter. And if I try to put myself in their shoes, I imagine I'd be more hurt by not knowing it'd happened to begin with. By not having the option to be there for my daughter on her wedding day."

The way his eyes glowed at the mention of a daughter practically made my ovaries explode. And that realization caused my lady parts to constrict—though I wasn't sure if that was a result of being turned on, or if it was my body's way of trying to close up shop to prevent anything from stretching it out. Nope, definitely not ready for babies.

Luckily, he didn't let me panic for long before he spoke

again, silencing my mental freak-out. "I don't know your parents, but I have a feeling that's where they're coming from—upset over the money spent on a wedding you'll never have, but not as much as knowing they missed seeing their little girl get married."

I nodded, admitting he was right, even though it didn't change anything. Either way, I'd have to listen to a lecture, sit quietly while they listed their concerns and all the ways my decision could blow up in my face. At the end of the day, it didn't matter *why* they were upset, only that they were, and they weren't the kind of people who kept their opinions to themselves. Especially when it came to me and my life. Regardless, there was no way out of it for me…unless I avoided them for the next few years until they got over it. Which, at this point, sounded rather appealing.

But I couldn't argue with him about my parents. There were more pressing issues to discuss. "Do you remember me telling you about my best friend, Stella?"

He regarded me with narrowed eyes and nodded slowly. His confusion was obvious, probably due to the sudden change in topic. Then again, there was a good chance my own apprehension was palpable, increasing the worry between us.

"Well, she took it upon herself to get a plane ticket, and she's on her way here. As in…right now. She'll be here in"—I glanced over his shoulder to the glowing digits on the microwave and huffed out a disheartened sigh—"three hours. I guess she panicked when she couldn't get ahold of me last night and booked a flight. By the time I found out about it, she was already at the airport."

His rumbled laughter made me pause. "Good. That makes me happy to hear. I hate leaving you alone all the time while I go to work, and it's only going to get worse once filming starts again. I'm glad you'll have someone to keep you company—especially now that the crew knows about you. I don't want you around that if you don't have to be."

"You seriously don't care that she invited herself to stay with us?"

He grabbed our mugs, handed me mine, and then leaned against the counter to drink his as if absolutely nothing out of the ordinary had happened this morning. "Not in the slightest. How long will she be here?"

A very large gulp of coffee seemed to be the perfect way to take a bit longer before answering without *looking* like that was what I was doing…until I ended up with a very large gulp of burning liquid in my mouth and down my throat. In the end, I succeeded in taking a while to respond. I also succeeded in singeing my entire esophagus and more than likely searing every last taste bud I had.

After coughing and whining like a puppy who'd accidentally been stepped on, I wiped the tears from my lashes and spoke, too worried about the damage to my mouth than the answer I offered. "I have no idea. She didn't tell me."

That seemed to amuse him and, after the morning I'd walked into, hearing him laugh and seeing his smile was worth the pain and humiliation. It was enough to promise me that everything would be all right, regardless of what lecture my parents gave or how long my best friend decided to hang around. Hell, at this point, I probably could've finished clearing out my notifications without feeling an ounce of anxiety— though I wasn't willing to take that chance.

"Well, she's welcome to stay as long as she'd like. Just keep in mind the cameras are coming to town in ten days. Obviously, I don't know your friend, other than what you've told me, but in the event she'll still be here while they're filming, I don't care for her to drag you down to the shop just to get on TV." His smile faded, though it was still detectable in his eyes. "I don't want you to get caught up in that if I can stop it."

It was yet another aspect of his life I hadn't contemplated.

And it made me wonder how many others would pop up unexpectedly.

Or how many more I'd be able to handle.

"I doubt she'll be here longer than a week. And at the risk of sounding like a heartless bitch, I kind of hope it won't be that long. I miss her. Don't get me wrong. But I woke up this morning to a lot of fires that need to be put out, and I'm not sure how I'll do that with her in town."

Brogan wrapped his fingers around the back of my neck and pulled my forehead to his lips. "Don't worry, babe. The news will die down, and everyone will go back to their own lives. I'll field as much of this as I can, but just know that you aren't alone. This will blow over. And despite the hoopla that's being made about it…it's really not that big of a deal. Everyone's talking about it because it's shocking."

"I know, but thanks, baby. Once my own shock settles, I won't be as jittery."

"I'm sure a lot of those nerves come from the dread of talking to your parents. And I'm confident that once you do, you'll feel a lot better. Think of it as a bandage and rip it off." His hand, which had been idly placed on my thigh, began to move higher, and the gleam in his eyes brightened. "But that can wait. We still have a little time before I have to leave for work and you have to pick up Stella. I can't think of a better way to spend that time than in the shower. Can you?"

After one night together, we'd managed to fall right back into the same routine we had before Savannah. However, much like that week, I couldn't shake the feeling that this was temporary. Not because I wanted it to be.

But because things as good as this never last.

14

BROGAN

When I first woke up, I contemplated staying home. Staying in bed with Mercy. All day. And after seeing her reaction to our relationship being plastered all over the internet, there was no way I'd leave her for work. Then she told me that her best friend was on her way to town, and I felt better about heading to the shop—just for a little while.

As much as I wanted to be everything she needed, I knew that wasn't—and never would be—the case. Stella could offer her things I couldn't, and I was okay with that. Which was why I felt confident giving them time to themselves to deal with whatever I couldn't help with.

Not to mention, I had my own agenda to deal with. *Someone* had tipped somebody off about our relationship, and for their sakes, it better not have been anyone from my shop. I'd spoken to everyone who worked for me about the need to keep it private. I hadn't explained *why* that was important—Mercy still had a lot to deal with as a result of our getting married—but the reason shouldn't have mattered.

And if anyone from the shop *did* open their mouth, there'd be hell to pay.

As I walked in, I glanced at Indi, and without exchanging a

single word, she followed me to the storage room in the back. Out of everyone here, she was my right hand. I wouldn't be able to keep up with this place if it weren't for her. Which meant I *really* hoped she hadn't been the one who'd leaked anything to the press. I didn't think she was, but that didn't stop the nagging voice in the back of my head—which sounded a lot like a jealous Mercy—that told me she might've been in love with me, and this was her way of reacting to the heartbreak.

It was a ridiculous thought; nevertheless, I had to confront it before I could dismiss it.

"I realize marriages are a matter of public record, so before I ask this, I understand that I don't necessarily have a reason to be upset. But someone leaked my relationship to the media last night." I leaned back in the chair and regarded Indi as she perched herself on the edge of the desk a few feet away. "The only people who knew about it are her best friend and you guys here at the shop. I'm just trying to find out who spoke out, so I figured I'd come to you and see what you thought."

The shock across her face was genuine. I felt confident about that. It was enough to assure me that she hadn't been the one who'd done this. But there was still hope she'd know who had, or at the very least, help me go through the possibilities before confronting anyone else.

"Well, you said yourself that it's public record. Are you sure someone called it in versus a reporter finding out on their own?"

That had been a possibility at first, though I'd had enough time between the alert this morning and getting here to think it through, and I decided that couldn't have been the case. "It would be an impressive coincidence for so many sites to have all discovered it on their own at the same time."

This wasn't my first rodeo with having my personal information smeared all over the internet. The one thing I'd learned throughout this process was that when *multiple* websites break news at the same time, it's because someone called around with the intention of spreading the word—or seeking the highest bidder. If it'd been an accidental discovery of information, then *one* site would report it, and the others would follow within a couple of hours. Last night, three main entertainment media pages had published the news within fifteen minutes. It took less than an hour for the rest to have their own articles posted.

"So you think it's someone from the shop?" Concern darkened her eyes, likely at the thought of one of our brothers being capable of betraying either of us. Because, realistically speaking, if they were willing to stab me in the back—their boss, the one who paid them, who'd given them the chance to be on a television show—then they'd have no issue doing the same to her. "Who could it be?"

Feeling slightly more hopeless than when I first sat down, I shrugged with a huff. "I don't know, Indi. I was hoping you could tell me. Whoever it was said some really horrible things about Mercy, though. If it'd only been about me, I'd let it go. Maybe speak to him and let him know I won't stand for it again. But it's about her. Anyone who could spread this kind of filth about Mercy deserves much worse."

"Honestly, Wrong...this is the first I've heard of it. I don't even know what was said."

I pulled up the Google search page filled with all the articles from last night and this morning and handed her my phone. There was too much to read, so while she skimmed and scrolled, I filled her in on the main points that were given. "They've accused her of being with me for the fame and fortune. Said she married me while still engaged to her ex, and that this happened while they were in the middle of planning their dream wedding."

"Who here even knows that, though? You've told me, but who else have you talked to about that part of it? I don't think you even told them how you met her in the first place. Just that you did and then married her. End of story." She wasn't entirely wrong about that, which only confused me more as to who it could've been.

The longer this went on, the more frustrated I became. There was a chance I'd never find out who'd done this. And it was the not knowing that made it worse. All it did was leave me with more questions and a nagging doubt that there might've been someone working for me who was capable of hurting Mercy. That was a thought that didn't sit well with me, and one I didn't care to let carry on longer than needed if I could do anything about it.

"Like, here… It says she used her ex to get closer to you, going as far as getting a job in town to increase her odds of running into you. And has even come to see you for a tattoo on a few occasions." She glanced up from the phone, meeting my stare with a furrowed brow. "I thought she lived in another state, so if I didn't even know she had a job here, then how the hell would any of the other guys? Maybe I don't give them enough credit, but I just can't imagine they'd pay *that* much attention to her to have this kind of information."

I scrubbed my hands over my face and dropped my head back. "A lot of what was written is nothing but lies—or extreme stretches of the truth to make it sound worse than it is. Which is what makes this so hard. Clearly, anyone can make something up and sell it to a drama-hungry media site. But there are aspects that hold *some* truth, and other parts that are completely authentic."

"So she doesn't have a job in town?"

"She does, but she hasn't started yet. And she got it because her ex lives here. They decided to wait until she graduated college to get married, and since he already has a job in town, the plan was for her to move here to be with him. She didn't even know I existed until the night we met, so her moving here to get closer to me is absolute bullshit. And that part about her coming in several times for ink? She has *one* tattoo—the one I gave her that week she stayed with me. It's like someone knew just enough to make the story legit, and then added a bunch of shit to make it worse. And *that's* what enrages me."

"How's she doing? I take it she knows about this?" Indi asked while returning my cell.

"She's acting fine for the most part, except I think that's a front. There's no way she's this calm about it. I mean, I know she's freaking out about her parents because, until last night, they didn't know anything. She hadn't told them about me at all, and now she has to explain not only how she ended up married to someone other than her fiancé, but also why she's kept it from them. I'm pretty sure if it were up to her, she'd just avoid her parents for the rest of her life."

"Well, that's understandable—being nervous to talk to your parents about that sort of thing. But if she's acting fine, then maybe you should do the same. I get that you're pissed, and I wholeheartedly agree that, if you find out one of the guys was responsible for leaking the news, they should get their ass kicked. However, if she can sense you're bothered by it, then she'll think there's something to be bothered by, and therefore, no longer be okay. And in the event she's only *acting* fine, seeing your nonchalant reaction might calm her down."

I exhaled, though it came out as much more of an exhausted sigh. Indi was right...again. Nevertheless, I wasn't about to tell her that. Instead, I chose a more genuine approach. "You really are a good friend. I've been twisted up all morning over this, and after a few minutes with you, I'm already feeling better. Thank you, Indi."

A small smile curled her lips, but I only got a glimpse of it before she tucked her chin to her chest. When she glanced up again, it was like she'd pulled a mask over her face. Hidden her emotions from me. There was a reason she fit in so well with the guys. And that was because she could protect her feelings better than any woman I'd ever met.

"If I find out anything, I'll let you know." She slid off the desk and turned toward the door. "Oh, and before I forget...is it okay if Kickstand closes up tonight? Johnny's on the schedule, but he has strep throat, so he won't be in. I've been here since this morning, Craig has plans, Lenny won't answer the phone, and Brent's wife could go into labor at any minute. Which leaves you and Kickstand. Your call."

I groaned inwardly and shook my head. Shit like this didn't happen often; when it did, I'd rather be in charge of locking up at night. To me, that level of trust needed to be earned, and while I trusted my guys—for now, at least—a few of them had a little more to prove before I handed them the keys to my shop. Since Stella was coming into town today, and after this morning's surprise, not to mention the fact that I'd finally gotten Mercy back, this was *not* the night to stay late.

"Yeah, go ahead and have him close up. I'll run through the checklist with him before I leave to make sure he doesn't forget anything."

"Got it." She opened the door, then paused before leaving. "Everything will be okay, Wrong. Trust that. I realize I don't know Mercy all that well, but I'm pretty good at reading people, and she seems like a tough girl. It'll take a lot more than this to break her."

"Yeah, she's a lot stronger than she gives herself credit for."

After one more simple grin, Indi left me in the back room with my thoughts.

15

MERCY

I'd arrived at the airport early, circled it a few times to make sure I knew where to go, and then pulled into the cell lot to wait for Stella to text me that she was ready to be picked up. Which meant I sat there, staring at my phone while it burned a hole in my hand.

I still hadn't called my parents, and even though I knew I needed to—especially before I had company—the fear prevented me from following through every time I pulled up their number. On top of that, there was the issue of Jordan sending me message after message until I finally put him on mute, unable to deal with the constant chime of his incoming texts.

After glancing at the clock on the dash, I decided it was now or never to return my parents' call. It would give me roughly five to ten minutes of listening to them condemn me for eloping with a stranger and then keeping it from them for over a month before I'd have to cut them off to pick up my friend. And knowing my mom as well as I did, there was no way she'd carry on a conversation that involved the family while in the company of others.

"What's going on, Mercy?" Mom answered the phone,

sounding frantic and on the verge of a full-fledged panic attack. It was enough to make me feel bad for avoiding this call for so long—she rarely sounded rattled, even when she was.

I cleared my throat and set my attention on a tree in the distance, hoping it'd distract me long enough to speak without sounding affected by her worry. "Nothing, Mom. Everything's fine. I didn't have my phone on me last night, and I've had a busy morning. Stella is coming to visit, so I had to get things organized."

Technically, moving all my belongings into Brogan's bedroom had nothing to do with Stella's arrival, though the timing of it all worked out rather well. Granted, she didn't need to know that. I had no intention of telling her *everything*. After all, if I had any hope of getting their approval—not that it would change anything if I didn't—informing her of my doubts and fears would ensure I'd never get it.

There was a bit of rustling over the line, then my mom's muffled voice, and after a few seconds, my dad's deep baritone came through the speaker. "Hey, honey. Are you all right? Is everything okay?"

I closed my eyes while releasing a long, exasperated breath. "Really, guys…there's nothing to worry about. I don't know who told you what, but you're all riled up for no reason. I'm fine."

"Are you really, Mercy?" There was more animosity in my dad's tone than concern, which struck me harder than I'd expected. "What in the world is going on with you? You left for a week, and when you came back, you told us to postpone the wedding, that you and Jordan had a few things to work out before you could follow through with marrying him. Now we learn that you're married to someone else?"

For some reason, I figured my mom would've been the one flying off the deep end. Not him. But I couldn't back out now. I had to see this conversation through to the end—or at least until Stella arrived.

"It's a messy situation. One I didn't care to divulge to you guys when I got home. I had a lot to think about, a lot to figure out, and none of it was anything either of you could help me with. I know you guys, and I knew you'd want to help—whether by offering advice or taking action—and this was something I had to do on my own." That was a lot harder to get out than I'd assumed.

My dad sighed, giving Mom a chance to speak. "I think what we are most confused about is who this guy is? And why would you marry him before you worked things out with Jordan?"

"Well, for starters, his name is Brogan Daniels."

"Just tell us one thing." Apparently, Dad didn't care to hear the rest of my explanation. "Is he in a gang or something? He's covered in tattoos like a thug, and from what we've read and heard, his nickname is *Wrong*."

I couldn't say I was surprised by my father's assessment of Brogan. It was more or less the biggest reason I hadn't wanted to deal with this. "No, Dad. He's not in a gang. He's a tattoo artist, and he owns his own business. He does very well for himself. In fact, I think you two could really get along if you'd ignore the stereotypes and preconceived judgment. You're both successful business owners who have created a life for yourself from nothing."

Granted, my dad built, sold, and installed doors, while Brogan drew pictures on skin. So technically, the *only* thing they had in common was owning their own businesses. That should've been enough to form a solid foundation for a great relationship.

If that wasn't a delusional thought, I didn't know what was.

"I have to tell you, Mercy…we've spoken to Jordan." That wasn't surprising; Mom had always favored him. "We called him earlier today when we couldn't get ahold of you, and his heart is breaking. You really hurt him with this stunt. I'm not sure how you'll fix the damage you've caused to your relationship with him."

After a few moments of concentrated breathing to keep from speaking too harshly, I cleared my throat so I could get this over with. "It's complicated. I would love to fill you guys in on what happened and why I chose to run off and get married to someone else, but it'll take longer than a ten-minute phone call, and honestly, it's not something I feel comfortable explaining to my parents."

"That's understandable." Based on his tone, it was clear as day that my dad did not, in fact, understand it. But at least he wasn't pushing for more information. "We're in the dark over here. That's all. We're simply trying to wrap our heads around your decision, and it's difficult to do when we have no idea why you'd choose to run off and marry the guy. And more than that…why you've kept it from us."

"To be fair, I haven't told anyone." *Other than Stella.* "I won't lie; we got married on a whim. We didn't talk about it ahead of time. It wasn't planned, and I'll be the first to admit that it wasn't the most responsible thing I could've done. I can't go back and change it, and if I'm being truthful, I don't really think I want to."

Dad's sigh of disapproval was capable of causing physical harm—no girl wanted to disappoint her father, and I was no exception. "This just isn't like you, honey. You've always approached everything in life with caution and rational thinking. So why is this time, this guy, different?"

There really wasn't any logical way to explain this without sounding like a crazy person, and to my parents, that was the last thing I wanted to come across as. Unfortunately, I couldn't avoid answering *all* of their questions, no matter how uncomfortable this whole thing was. "For the first time in my life, I did something for me, without obsessing over the outcome or implications."

"And how'd that work out for you, Mercy?"

Brogan had told me I needed to answer their questions honestly, and that was what I tried to do. Except, this was one of the times I couldn't bear the absolute truth—not because it would prove them right, but because I would end up making myself sound less sure of the choices I'd made. And that couldn't be further from the truth.

"So far, it's worked out rather well, Dad. Thanks for asking."

"Your father doesn't deserve that kind of attitude, young lady."

She was right, which forced me to lower my guard a little bit. "I'm sorry. I guess I'm just tired of defending my decision to be with Brogan—to Jordan, to you guys, to the whole world who has decided to attack me for things they know nothing about. I just want everyone to take a step back and trust me on this."

"How are we supposed to trust you when you can't even tell us why you did it to begin with?" Dad was on a roll, and if I didn't give him what he wanted, I worried this would all blow up in flames.

So, I took a deep breath and tried my best to ease their worry. "You know me; you've said it yourself—I don't make any decision without thoroughly thinking it through. And while I fully understand how this looks to everyone, like I was impulsive and careless, I need you both to know that in my heart of hearts, deep in my gut, at the center of my being...I believe that my choices regarding this are right. I won't say it's been easy, because it hasn't. Trust me when I say I'm not wearing rose-tinted glasses. I'm not living in fantasy land. I am well aware of what marrying him means for the bigger picture. I don't, for one second, regret it."

"Mercy"—Mom huffed—"do you even know anything about this boy?"

"I know enough. The rest will come with time—just like with any other relationship. But I've chosen to stay and see this through, which has nothing to do with Jordan. So if possible, could you two please leave him out of it and let me handle things with him?"

Through my dad's frustrated groan, Mom spoke up. "I don't want to say that this is all right with us, because it's not. There are still so many issues we need to discuss—mainly about why you never told us, and if you had planned to ever let us know. But we can talk about that later when you're more open and willing to give us more of the story than these cryptic bread-crumbs. Right now, I would like to know what you plan to do about this wedding and all the money we've put down. Had we known from the start, we might've been able to look into getting the deposits back, but since the original date is only a few days away, I don't see that happening. Especially since we've already contacted the vendors about changing the date."

As annoyed as I was that my mother seemed more concerned about the financial aspect than anything else, I couldn't blame her. My irritation was nothing more than mani-fested guilt over my part in her potentially losing her deposit for the venue. So, I had to choke down the waves of irrational—and immature—frustration and let her voice her concern.

"I guess I need to cancel it, huh?" My question was barely a whisper.

"Yeah, I'd say that's the right thing to do. No sense in stringing along an entire guest list. It's bad enough you changed the plans at the last minute, keeping everyone in the dark as to what's going on. I wouldn't be surprised if most of them have already purchased a gift for you. And they've just been holding on to it, waiting for you to set a new date. I'd say you need to get on that and contact everyone *personally* so they might be able to return what they bought. Dresses and shoes for weddings aren't cheap."

"I know, Mom. Not being honest with everyone up front was a cowardly thing to do. I guess I was worried about the ridicule or criticism I'd get."

This time, when she sighed, it was a sign that she had softened a bit. "I understand, honey. Trust me…I get it. But you're an adult now. You're out of college and *married*. It's time you start taking responsibility for yourself."

The phone buzzed in my hand, Stella's text flashing across the screen, and I'd never felt more relieved to see a message in my life. I closed my eyes, gritted my teeth, and exhaled every last ounce of air from my lungs.

I wasn't angry with them, even though I probably sounded like it. The truth was, I was pissed at myself for all the reasons they'd pointed out, which were all the things I knew they'd say. Apparently, I needed to hear it from them to force me to face the consequences of my actions. And maybe that was why I'd avoided it for so long.

"Stella's here, so I'll have to let you guys go. I'm sorry for keeping this from you, and I'm sorry about the money. I didn't mean to let you down; I was scared and didn't want to say or do anything until I knew for sure what was going on. But I promise I will take care of the guest list, and I'll make sure nothing comes back on you or Dad…or Jordan. This is my mess, and I'll clean it up."

I put the car in reverse and backed out of the parking space while they said their piece.

It was no surprise that Mom went first. "We're always here for you, honey. Don't ever forget that. It worries me that you're so far away. I was okay with it when I thought you were with Jordan, but now that we know you're with some strange guy we've never met, it makes me uneasy."

"Mom, you're more than welcome to come down and stay for a while. Meet him and see where my life is now. I've talked to him about you guys visiting, and he's excited to meet you. We both know this wasn't ideal, and it'll take a lot of adjusting for everyone, but he makes me happy, and that's all that should matter."

"You're right," my dad admitted quietly, as if his emotions had settled around his voice box. "Your happiness is important, but we're thinking of your safety. That's what matters most to your mother and me. Go pick up your friend, and we'll finish this conversation later. In the meantime, do you think you could send us some info on this kid? His age? Address? Anything that might make us feel a little more secure with where you're at?"

I couldn't fault him for his concern, so I gave him what he wanted. "Yes, Dad. I'll email it all to you as soon as I get back to the house. I love you. Both of you. And again, I'm sorry for everything."

A couple of minutes later, I pulled beneath the overhang and squeezed my way into the far-right lane where passengers loaded their luggage into trunks and back seats. I said goodbye and disconnected that call three seconds before Stella opened the rear door and tossed her backpack inside.

"Where's your suitcase?" I asked once she took the seat next to me.

With her thumb hitched over her shoulder, she said, "Right there."

"That's a backpack."

"What's your point? I was able to fit enough stuff in there to last me a couple of months."

"Do you have something against checked luggage?"

She blinked at me with a level of dramatic flair only Stella could pull off and then rolled her eyes. "Bitch, please. Do you have any idea how much these pocket pickers charge for luggage? It's highway robbery. Especially when you consider how much you've already spent on a seat that a four-year-old couldn't comfortably sit in. Hungry?" She stuck her hand in the front pocket of her jacket and pulled out approximately six bags of peanuts.

That was what I needed—my best friend and her uncanny ability to make me laugh.

While Brogan eased my fears and cleared my doubts, Stella made me forget what the problem was to begin with. I had a feeling that spending time around the two of them would be exactly what the doctor ordered.

————

Rather than take Stella to see Brogan after leaving the airport like she'd wanted me to, I brought her to the house to get settled. Not to mention, the *last* place I wanted to be was at Brogan's shop—especially after last night.

"Are you almost caught up yet?" While I finished making the bed in the spare room for Stella, she sat on the floor with her legs crossed beneath her, reading through the obscene number of texts I'd received from Jordan over the last twelve hours.

"Almost," she said from the other side of the room, her back flat against the wall and attention glued to my phone in her hands. "I told Wrong that we're gonna spend the afternoon in the pool, which means I—*meaning you*—won't be able to cook. He said he'll bring home something for dinner. He's a keeper."

My eyes rolled involuntarily. "Why are you even talking to him?"

"He texted me."

"*No...*" I tossed the last pillow against the headboard and faced her with my hands on my hips. "It's my phone, which means he texted *me*."

"Tomato, to-*mah*-to. Don't worry, Best Friend, I pretended to be you, so it's all good."

I wasn't sure what the worst part was—her pretending to be me, or the fact she was in the middle of a conversion with my husband, *pretending to be me*. Then I contemplated all the things he might be saying while under the impression I was the one on the other end of those texts. That man had the ability to be filthy when he wanted, which was most of the time. "Oh, God...he thinks he's talking to me?"

Stella waved me off without taking her eyes off the screen. "Unfortunately, no. He figured it out after my first text. We're

155

getting to know each other now. You know…since you refused to introduce us when I got to town."

"What the hell did you say to him that made it so obvious it wasn't me?"

"Nothing special. He asked if you'd picked me up yet, and I said yes, that we were at the house because *'I refused to take Stella to meet you.'* Then he came back with…" She scrolled up a bit, leaving me a little worried about how long this conversation between them was, and read, *"'Doesn't surprise me. I didn't figure she'd bring you up here on your first day in town.'* And then he added a winky face."

Perplexed, I grabbed the phone out of her hand to read the texts for myself, unsure how he could've possibly known he wasn't speaking to me based on that one sentence. But right there in front of me, in blue and white message bubbles, were the exact words she'd read aloud, followed by her questioning how he knew. His reply was simple: *I know my woman.*

There were many other messages that came after, going back and forth between them, though I wasn't interested in going through them all. I trusted them both, so I didn't have to worry about what was said—considering it was *my* phone, which meant I could read their conversation later if I wanted. I was just surprised Brogan had recognized something in that one written reply that told him he wasn't speaking to me.

"Come on, Mercy…give me the phone. I'm not done yet."

With a slight shake of my head in feigned exasperation, I handed it back. "I thought we were going to get in the pool. We can't do that if you spend all afternoon chatting with my husband. You do realize he lives here, right? You can meet him in a few hours when he gets home, and then you'll have all night to interrogate him."

"Oh, his client came in. We aren't talking at the moment."

"Then what in the hell do you need my phone for?"

She peered up at me without tilting her head back, her

brows arched and pulled tighter in the middle of her forehead. "I'm talking to Jordan."

"For crying out loud, Stella." I plopped onto the edge of the bed and fell back onto the mattress with my arms stretched out above me. "I thought you were just reading what he said, not entertaining his ridiculous rants."

"Oh, I'm not entertaining him. Don't worry your pretty little head about that. I'm setting him straight. He needs to understand that there are boundaries he shouldn't cross, so I'm informing him. Well, I mean *you* are informing him."

I sat up and stared at her, though she never glanced up from the phone to look at me. "Are you pretending to be me to everyone you're texting?"

"It's from your phone. It'd be a little weird if they knew they were talking to me." She didn't need to add *duh* to her statement; it was implied by the tone. "Not to mention, in order for him to cut his crap, he needs to think this is coming from *you*. It wouldn't do any good if he knew I was the one putting him in his place."

My mind raced and swirled for a moment before I could form enough words to make sense. "Wait…so he actually thinks that's me texting him? But Brogan knew immediately it wasn't me—by nothing more than a basic sentence that answered his question?"

"Yup. Crazy, huh? Guess this just goes to show who knows you better."

The longer I sat there, comparing the two men and everything that came with that, the more confused I became. And scared. However, I didn't understand that emotion. Which only fueled the confusion that did nothing but make the room feel like it was closing in on me. Finally, unwilling to lose myself in the chaotic thoughts that typically led my fight mentality to cower and my flight mentality to take center stage, I stood and moved to the doorway.

"Put on your bathing suit…let's go swimming." I exited the

room, leaving Stella sitting on the floor with my phone in her hand, furiously tapping out a message to Jordan—at least, I assumed and *hoped* it was to him.

Going to Brogan's dresser to get my bikini made me smile. The thought of my things taking up space next to his covered me in a warming sense of peace. Like this was where I belonged. Unfortunately, that thought wasn't enough to stop the worry from overshadowing my happiness while I slipped into my swimsuit.

I knew how I felt about Brogan. I could question it every second of every day, yet it wouldn't change the bone-deep certainty that he was it for me. There wasn't an ounce of my being or my soul that questioned if this was real. In a way, I'd recognized it the first time I heard his voice. The first time I felt his presence. The very first time I ever looked him in his eyes.

Nevertheless, the gloomy cloud of dread would never leave. It hovered, following me, assuring me that my time with Brogan was temporary. Reminding me that I needed to enjoy this while I had it, because at some point in the near to near-distant future, it'd be gone.

Shaking off the negative waves that threatened to drown me in sorrow, I grabbed a towel from the hall closet and met Stella on the back patio. All I needed was a little vitamin D and laughter to get me out of this ill-timed funk. Things had been going so well, especially since climbing into Brogan's bed last night and waking up in his arms this morning. Concentrating on the *possibility* of losing him would only ruin the one thing I wanted to hold on to forever.

They say you get back what you put into the universe.

I couldn't expect positive things if I only focused on negative scenarios.

"You never finished telling me what happened last night with Wrong." Stella leaned against the side of the pool, the water cascading off the ledge around her crossed arms. "Did you two finally say the *L* word?"

My heart constricted as I stared off into the distance, setting my sights just over the tops of the trees in front of us. "No. But I mentioned it—the fact that he hasn't said it. By now, it kind of feels like he's refusing to say it, except I don't understand why."

"No wonder I'm single. I finally get it now."

"What do you mean?"

She turned her head to the side to regard me. My reflection shone back at me in the lenses in her aviator sunglasses, which prevented me from seeing her eyes, yet I didn't necessarily need to. Her tone was enough when she said, "I've been doing this relationship thing all wrong. I've dated in the hopes of getting married. But I see now that I should've gotten married first, and *then* dated the guy. I've told ex-boyfriends that I love them, and they've said the same to me. Had I known, I would've waited until after the fourth or fifth child to say it. If more people found out about this, there might not be a need for divorce lawyers."

I rolled my eyes and shook my head at her sarcasm.

"But in all seriousness..." She wasn't capable of that, so I wasn't sure why she wasted her breath saying it. "...do you think this is the real deal? You and Wrong, I mean? You were with Jordan for years, the picture-perfect couple to everyone. Are you sure you didn't choose Wrong because you got cold feet or anything?"

"We both know I married him to spite Jordan. Which I'm aware was irresponsible and immature. And reckless. But no, I don't believe he played any part in my decision to stay with Brogan. I never had cold feet when it came to Jordan. Maybe I'm wrong, though; maybe I subconsciously freaked out and threw a match on our relationship. Seeing him at the club, grinding on that woman...it killed me. So I guess it's possible I've done all this to keep him from hurting me again."

"Do you think you chose Wrong because you don't believe he'll hurt you the same way Jordan did? If you don't love the guy, it's kinda hard to get your heart broken by him." Every now and then, Stella would make me realize something I'd refused to see for myself.

This was not one of those times.

"No. I didn't choose him because I believe he can't hurt me. Quite the contrary. If I'm being honest, I'm convinced he's capable of hurting me more than anyone." This wasn't new to me. I'd contemplated this a lot lately—the unfathomable power he had to demolish me without even realizing it. Divulging that to someone else made it more real. Gave it more weight. And took it from a possibility to a certainty.

"How in the world can he do that if you don't love him?"

"I never said I don't love him. We've just never admitted it… if that makes sense."

"So you *do* love him?"

I had to look away before she caught a glimpse of something I wasn't ready to open up about. Squinting at the sun, I sighed and then answered her as truthfully as I could. "I feel something for him. But I'm not entirely sure what it is. It's different than any love I've ever had for anyone else."

"Then why can't you tell him that?"

"Because sometimes I wonder if it's infatuation, though it doesn't seem to be. Then I question if I'm simply blinded by how different he is than Jordan, how different he makes me feel." I glanced at her again and confessed, "The only thing I can do is wait it out and see."

"At the risk of Jordan being the one and losing him in the process?"

"No matter what happens between Brogan and me, Jordan and I are over. I accepted that last night when I chased after Brogan, and oddly enough, I'm content with that."

Stella's lips pursed in thought, which was never a good thing at a time like this. "If I were to take a guess, I'd say you've had your mind made up from day one. What I don't get is why it took so long for you to see it. Because, if you ask me, you've always *seen* it, but for some reason, you've fought against it this whole time. You could've made things so much easier if you had been honest from the beginning."

"Don't you think I know that? It's easy to sit back and judge me for dragging this out."

"No." She pointed at me, finger less than two inches from my face, splashing water on me in the process. All the while, she kept a straight face. "I'm not judging you, so don't think that. And if I was, I can guarantee it's not about how long you've dragged this out. It's for being so damn wishy-washy you've given everyone around you motion sickness."

If I couldn't count on my best friend to tell it like it was, then nobody would. "Again, Stella…it's easy to say that while being on the outside. Put yourself in my shoes for five minutes and then tell me you'd handle it *so* much better. If Jordan had cheated on me, this wouldn't even be an issue. But since he swears he didn't—and honestly, I don't even know what to believe anymore—choosing Brogan over the life we spent two years planning would only hurt him. Regardless of how I feel about Brogan, I still love Jordan. Hurting him hurts me. I'm not a heartless person."

"I know you're not." She offered a small smile, comforting me in ways only she could.

"And then there's the fear. What if I'm making a mistake? What if Brogan didn't show up that night as some message from the heavens that I'm supposed to be with him? What if he was sent to me to test my relationship with Jordan, and by choosing Brogan, I failed? This isn't which candy to get at the theater or what to make for dinner. This is my *life*. And such decisions can't be made lightly."

"I'm not saying that at all, Mercy. Trust me, you know I'll go round and round with you for as long as you need me to. I'll be your sounding board, your advice columnist, a good slap across the face when you need it. Just as long as you can admit that by *not* doing this sooner, you haven't spared anyone. Jordan was still hurt in the end."

"Yes, I'm aware. And I can admit that. I guess I thought that, if I stalled, maybe he'd make the decision to walk away and spare me from being the bad guy—selfish, I know, but I'm human. Sue me. Or maybe I hoped the truth about that night would come out and prove that he was the guy I saw on the dance floor, and therefore, I wouldn't have to worry about breaking his heart. And to top it off, there's the whole situation with the wedding. I've been terrified of how everyone will react when I cancel it."

"Oh, yeah…you have to call all those people, don't you?"

The mere thought of explaining it to one person, let alone over a hundred people, left my stomach twisted in knots. "Since you're so good at pretending to be me, you should do it. At this point, I've already assumed my throne and title of the biggest piece of shit on the planet, so I guess it doesn't matter how you tell them. Maybe a mass email would be better."

"Don't worry, Best Friend. I've got your back. I'll make Jordan handle it," she said with a giggle and quick flick of her wrist.

My smile burned my cheeks, along with the intense heat of the sun overhead. "The one thing I wish I could change about this entire situation is you. It'd be so much better if you lived here."

Stella peered over her shoulder at the house behind us. "Yeah, I think you're right. I'd love it here. Give me a few days, and I can have the rest of my crap shipped here. I'll only need to know the address."

Even though I nearly choked on my laughter and splashed her in the face, I had to admit that the idea of having her this close would be a godsend. I had a feeling that when the rug got swept out from beneath me, I'd need Stella more than ever before. And being hundreds of miles away from her would only make things worse.

16

BROGAN

I'd never admit it to Mercy, but meeting Stella made me more nervous than the thought of meeting her parents. Granted, my anxiety over it had nothing to do with her friend—or her parents. From everything I'd heard and learned about her, she seemed like someone I'd want to hang out with. Fun and entertaining. But she was Mercy's *best* friend, which meant her opinion carried a lot of weight. Not to mention, she was a fan of the show.

There was a good chance she expected to meet *Wrong*.

And with Mercy, I was Brogan.

The real me—the side of myself I didn't offer many people.

If that were the case, she'd possibly be disappointed. Not that I cared what she thought of me, per se. But I wasn't stupid when it came to women. They talked. And I wasn't entirely sure how much influence she had over Mercy.

Whereas, if her parents didn't care for me, I doubted Mercy would give it much thought.

Which was why I had planned to bring home the best food in town, no matter how much I had to pay for it. If Stella wanted surf and turf, then she'd get it. Lucky for me, she'd requested KFC and a bottle of whiskey.

"Why did her parents name her Mercy?" I figured if Mercy wouldn't tell me, I'd ask her best friend. There were always other means to get the information I sought.

Stella laughed and shook her head at my wife. "You still haven't told him?"

"No. It's a stupid story, and it's gone on for so long that he probably has this amazing reason built up in his head. If I tell him now, he'll be let down." Hearing her explanation only made me want the answer even more.

"Trust me, babe…I'm not expecting anything mind-blowing. Especially after you said that."

"It doesn't matter, because I'm not telling."

Stella leaned across the kitchen table where we all sat and shared a few drinks together, getting to know each other, and placed her hand on my arm. The twinkle in her eye made me wonder if she was about to fuck with me, but if there was a chance—no matter how small—that she'd tell me the truth, then I'd take it.

"She was such a big baby that they had to give her mom a bunch of drugs." Not once did Stella look away or even crack a smile. "The nurse happened to come in right as the meds were wearing off and the pain was coming back. She was really out of it with all the pills they'd given her. Anyway, the nurse asked what the baby's name was, but her mom thought she was there to give her more morphine or something, so she kept mumbling, 'mercy.' The nurse thought that was the name and marked it down."

I glanced between the two women, wondering how much truth that story held. Once I stopped and took stock of the entire situation, I realized there couldn't have been an ounce of truth in it. "I know you're lying; want to hear how? Because that one right there"—I pointed to Mercy without taking my eyes off Stella—"didn't object once while you spoke. And with as adamant as she's been about keeping me from finding out the reason behind her name, there's no way she would've let you say more than three words if any of them were true."

Stella sat back and shrugged—the kind that says, *believe what you want.*

"Don't worry, babe. I'll figure it out one day."

Mercy smirked and raised her brows. "Doubt it."

"We have the rest of our lives together, so I'd say the odds are in my favor." I winked at her and then pulled myself to my feet. "Well, ladies. I think I'm going to call it a day. I have a feeling I'll need a full night's sleep to deal with the two of you."

It'd been a long day at the shop, most of it spent hunched over, and it was already nearing midnight. It also didn't help that I hadn't gotten much sleep the night before with Mercy in my bed, but there was no way in hell I'd complain about that.

"Night, babe." I leaned down to kiss the top of Mercy's head, but at the last second, she tilted her chin up and met my lips with hers. I had no idea why that one simple, easy gesture affected me so much, but it did. It made my heart beat faster and my smile spread wider.

"Night, baby," she whispered, increasing the high she'd just given me with her kiss.

"Good night, Wrong. I'll be in bed shortly."

Stella had made several teasing comments throughout the evening that seemed borderline inappropriate. I had allowed them because the look on Mercy's face—even knowing her best friend was only kidding—was both entertaining and encouraging.

Laughing them off, I turned and headed for my room. While I wasn't excited to fall asleep alone, the thought of waking up to Mercy crawling beneath the covers, naked, thrilled me.

————

The sun hadn't even met the sky when my phone woke me. I strained against the light on the screen with one eye closed and noticed it was a few minutes before five in the morning. Normally, I would've ignored it, but it was Indi, and she knew better than to call me this early if it wasn't an emergency.

Three words in, and I was out of bed, reaching blindly in the dark for something to put on so I could meet her at the shop. Someone had broken in and smashed the place. I didn't waste time asking why the alarm company had called her instead of me. That was shit I could find out once I got there. I just needed to get there.

The thought of leaving Mercy to wake up alone gutted me; however, I didn't have a choice. So I quietly went to her side of the bed and leaned down to kiss her goodbye. Even in the dark, I found her lips. I never needed light to know exactly where to touch or lick or kiss. I'd know her body blindfolded, like I'd spent hundreds of lifetimes worshiping every curve. Every dimple. Every line and pore and hair on her head.

It was instinctual.

I headed into town with that thought running through my mind—how being with her never felt like a choice. I hadn't been given an option. Not that I needed one. I wouldn't have even wasted my time contemplating it. Because the truth was…as soon as I saw her on the sidewalk that night, I had found what I never knew was missing.

She was the answer to a question I never realized I had asked.

The tourniquet I wasn't aware I needed.

Mercy made me feel on top of the world. Unbeatable. Unbreakable.

Fearless.

But the most amazing part about all that was how I used to believe I was all those things. Prior to meeting her, I was confident—not arrogant or egotistical, merely secure with who I was and what I was capable of. It was what made me good at what I did. And anyone who knew me would've agreed. Then I met her, and everything changed.

Without knowing it, Mercy had opened my eyes. Made me see that what I'd assumed was confidence was really one step below it. It was a truth I never would've uncovered without having her by my side. She'd saved me, long before I understood how badly I needed it. And I truly believed that, had she not come along, had I not run into her that night, I would've continued slowly dying inside.

In fact, it was the life she'd breathed into me that kept me sane as I walked through the front door of Wrong Inc, as I assessed the damage that only seemed to get worse the farther into the shop I went. It was the promise of a solid future she'd instilled in me that stopped me from losing hope. Stopped me from breaking down over the destruction of something I'd built from the ground up with my blood, sweat, and tears.

As I stared at the back room—at the shelves that had been ripped off the walls, the supplies that littered the floor and striations of vibrant ink splattered about—I had to remind myself that *this* wasn't my future.

This wasn't the sum of my worth.

This wasn't what got me out of bed anymore.

No. I could walk away from this if I chose to. I could move on from this place and still be the man Nonna had raised me to be. All I needed was Mercy. Her love and support. Her laughter and kisses. So I held on to the knowledge that I had everything I needed. Everything I wanted. And I began to sort through the wreckage that no longer defined me.

"You might want to take a second look, but I don't think anything was stolen." Indi came into the back room, wearing leggings and a ratty T-shirt. It was clear she'd been dragged out of bed to deal with this as well.

There were so many questions running through my head, but while standing in the midst of this mess, only one came to mind. "Why'd the alarm company call you instead of me?"

"It seems we never switched the primary number back to yours after your last vacation."

I'd taken the week off right after meeting Mercy, leaving Indi in charge of the shop in my absence. It wasn't until now that I even remembered having the alarm company list her number before mine. Now that I thought about it, it made the most sense—she lived much closer than I did.

"Looks like that worked out in our favor." I crossed my arms, unsure if I was allowed to touch anything. "What all have the cops done?"

Indi rolled her neck, exhaustion evident in her shoulders. "They went around assessing the damage while I started taking inventory. Like I said, as far as I can tell, nothing's missing. And if the bastard did steal something, it wasn't anything important."

"What about the register?"

"Wasn't touched. He came in through there, hitting this area first."

I followed her finger to the door that led outside from the storage room. From what I could see, there didn't seem to be any damage to the frame. In fact, it didn't look like it had been messed with at all. "How'd he get in?"

She dropped her head—the universal sign for bad news. "The only thing I can think of is Kickstand forgot to lock the door. And for some reason, he only set the silent alert part of the security system."

"Had he fucking set it the way I showed him, the asshole would've taken off as soon as the alarm started blaring. Then again, he probably wouldn't have made it that far if he'd locked the fucking door." Knowing I'd allowed Kickstand to close up shop so I could be home with Mercy and Stella had me fuming with myself—as well as the irresponsible bastard who might not have a job after this.

"It could've been worse, Wrong."

I silenced her with narrowed eyes and a tight jaw. "Worse? It looks pretty fucking bad. How in the hell can you say it could've been worse while I'm standing in the middle of this?"

"Well, it appears he went from here to the studios and ransacked those, but only the first two were thoroughly smashed."

The shop only had four studio spaces, two on each side of the hallway that led from the front of the building to the back. Indi and I had our own, while the rest of the guys shared the others, depending on how much privacy their clients needed. Beyond those, there were a couple of additional stations, sectioned off by half walls with no doors on either side of the front desk.

"Based on the CCTV feed," she continued, "he got spooked and split. That's why most of the damage is back here. Looks like he went to trash the front, but after a couple of minutes, something outside sent him running. We're not sure what it was, though."

"Do we have good enough footage to find out who did this?" I prayed the asshole wasn't wearing anything to obscure his face.

Her nod filled me with hope. "The dumbass assumed that just because the lights weren't on, it meant he couldn't be seen. Thank God for stupidity...and cameras that don't need light. I made a disk for the cops with the entire footage, as well as several stills and close-ups of his face."

"That's great, except without an identity, all we have is a face and a fucked-up shop."

Her lips split into the faintest, most hesitant grin I think I'd ever seen on her. "I know who he is...I'm just waiting for my sister to call me back so I can give the cops his name." Without prompting, she answered the question that burned the tip of my tongue. "He's some guy she hooked up with a month or so ago —the one she would always ditch me for whenever we'd go out."

"When you get his name...I want it."

"Only if you swear to let the police handle this." Her raised brows were more than a scary threat, and enough to make me agree.

One of the officers came to the doorway and asked to speak with me. And for the next hour or so, we moved from one room to the next, noting damage while we chatted about the shop, ink, and the show. Apparently, he was a big fan. Go figure.

By the time we finished that, it was late enough to call Mercy without worry I'd wake her. I'd left a note near the coffee pot, as well as a text telling her about the shop and that I'd call as soon as I could. I imagined her sitting in the kitchen, phone in hand, frantically waiting for it to ring, and I refused to make her wait any longer.

Luckily, she remained quiet while I explained what I could, which allowed me to get it all out as quickly as possible. But the second I had her caught up with my morning so far, the questions began, flying through the earpiece one right after the other.

"Listen, babe…there's still a lot to do here, so we'll have to finish this later. Is that okay?"

Her sigh felt like a punch in the gut. "I'm sorry, Brogan. I didn't mean to keep you."

"Don't apologize. I want you to keep me."

"Good. That makes two of us." The happiness in her tone put a smile on my face. "Do you have any idea what time you might get home tonight?"

Just then, Indi came into the room and handed me her phone, the screen unlocked and opened to a text conversation. As I tried to understand what she wanted me to see, I said, "Not a clue, but I assume it'll be late."

"Well, Stella and I can come by and help any way we can. There's something I need to deal with first, but hopefully, that won't take too long." Mercy continued to talk in my ear, though her words began to fade once I figured out the texts in my hand were from Indi's sister—with the information about the guy who had destroyed my shop. As soon as I read his name, Mercy's voice returned. "…so I can put Jordan behind me."

"Jordan…" I repeated. "What's his last name?"

"Hamilton. Why?"

My chest constricted to the point I became concerned my ribs would snap. "I'm sorry, babe, but I have to take care of something."

"Okay, but before you go, is it all right if Stella and I come to help? I don't want to get in your way, but we want to give you a hand if you need it." Damn…it was as though she knew exactly what I needed before I realized it.

"I can't think of anything better than having you here with me."

I couldn't take my eyes off Indi's phone. Off the text from her sister.

Off his name.

Jordan Hamilton.

My heart thumped vigorously against my ribcage as I waited for Jordan to meet me in the lobby of his office building. Even though he believed we'd spoken yesterday through texts, I hadn't actually held a single conversation with him since my life blew up all over the internet. Not to mention, this would be the first time we'd seen each other face to face in a month.

When he came down the hall, he walked with his head bowed. Meaning, I noticed him first. And when he glanced up, catching the sight of me in the lobby, the surprise on his face told me he wasn't expecting to find me there. It left me to wonder what the receptionist had told him when she called him down here.

"Hey," I said while taking a few steps toward him. "Do you have a minute or two to talk?"

Jordan glanced around the empty space, as if looking for someone. His narrowed gaze and creased brow only worsened once he returned his attention to me. "Why are you here?"

"I, um…" At least I hadn't expected this to go well. "I was hoping we could talk."

"Did *he* send you?"

Confused, it was my turn to search the room for someone

else. "Uh, no. It was my choice to come. I figured it would be best if we had this conversation sooner rather than later. And as much as I would've rather done this somewhere other than your office, it would be best if we take care of it now."

Defeat painted his expression as he nodded and glanced at his feet. With his hands in his pockets, resignation weighing down his shoulders, he tipped his head toward the exit. "Probably best if we speak outside then."

This whole situation was becoming weirder by the second.

All I'd come for was to address the issue to his face. I'd chosen Brogan without explaining anything to Jordan, and while I understood it wasn't feasible to have left Brogan's bedroom to call my ex and let him in on what was happening, it didn't change anything in Jordan's mind. All he could focus on was being the last to know.

"Listen, Mercy…" He waited until we were around the side of the building before speaking, which prevented anyone from overhearing our conversation. It would've been easier to have done this in his office, but if this was the way he wanted to do it, I couldn't complain. "I'm sorry. Okay?"

Well, that certainly threw me for a loop. I hadn't expected him to apologize.

Stunned silent, I couldn't manage much beyond blinking, mouth agape, which gave him ample opportunity to continue surprising me. "I've had a hard time with this—with you and him. I realize I haven't handled it very well, but I guess I've held on to hope that you'd come back and we'd figure everything out together. And I know…I should've expected it. I should've seen it coming. But I couldn't seem to let go of the dream we started, or the promises we made. So when I heard that you had made your choice, and it wasn't me—and I hadn't heard anything from you—I lashed out."

"Jordan…" My voice was so low and airy I doubted he heard me.

"I've had a shitty couple of days, and I know I shouldn't

have done what I did. I shouldn't have stooped so low, but I was so hurt by losing you that I couldn't think straight. Trust me; I wish I could take it back. All of it. It was stupid of me to think I wouldn't get caught." He ran his fingers through his hair and met my stare. The amount of regret that pooled in his eyes made my chest ache with sympathy. "He's going to press charges, isn't he?"

"Um…I'm not sure." My mind continued to swirl with utter confusion.

Until he said, "It was dark, so I couldn't really see what I was doing, but I'm sure I did a lot of damage. And I assume it'll cost a lot to replace everything. But I'll pay him back. I'll do what I have to for the money—but please, Mercy, don't let him press charges. You know me. I'm not a bad guy. I've just been in a horrible place since you left, and I guess I took it out on him. I shouldn't have. But it's so hard not to blame him when he's the one you left me for."

In my muddled brain, it seemed like he was admitting to being the one who'd destroyed Brogan's shop. In fact, I couldn't imagine he'd meant anything else. Yet I couldn't very well ask if that was what he meant, because it would prove that I hadn't known prior to coming here. Which I hadn't. And if he realized I hadn't known ahead of time, I ran the risk of him clamming up and not giving me anything else.

I had to play my cards right.

Unfortunately, I *sucked* at poker.

"Why, Jordan? I don't understand why you'd do something like that."

His eyes closed, and a long, broken exhale seeped past his dry lips. The same lips I used to kiss. The same ones that used to caress parts of my body. At one point in time, my whole world had revolved around him. I'd loved him—hell, I still did, only in a different capacity. The last thing I wanted for him was to be in pain. But he was the only one who could change that.

Until he could snuff out the flame he still carried for me, he'd never understand the blessing this tragedy offered.

After all, the stars can't shine without darkness.

"I was hurt." His words croaked out as his gaze landed on mine, feeding me the raw emotion within him. "I'm not excusing my behavior, so please don't think that. I admit it was wrong, and if I could go back in time and stop myself from going to his shop, I would."

"I get that…but why were you even there to begin with?"

He gave a pitiful shrug. "I guess I wanted to see what he has that I don't. It sounds ridiculous, but I've struggled to understand why you'd choose him. It took you six months to tell me you love me. A year into our relationship, you told Stella you wouldn't say yes if I asked you to marry me. And when I finally did ask, and you said yes, I felt like I had to beg you to start planning the wedding—even though you'll deny that's how it was. So excuse me if I can't comprehend how someone who seemed so scared of marriage would jump into it with a stranger…and then refuse to get it annulled."

This was where my own guilt reared its ugly head. I'd avoided him for the last month, claiming there was nothing he could do or say that would help me sort through the mess I'd found myself in. And maybe that was true, but I never considered that there might've been something I could've done or said to help him find peace with this.

Nothing tasted worse than the bitter realization of selfishness.

After a deep inhale followed by a long, heavy sigh, I steeled myself to give him the truth. "I can't tell you why I decided to marry him when I did. I've spent a lot of time analyzing that decision, picking it apart, questioning everything. I was hurt by what I saw in the club that night. In a way, it felt worse than betrayal. From the moment I had my flight switched to the second I walked into that club, I was practically jumping up and down at the thought of surprising you. I had imagined all the ways you'd react—that goofy grin, sparkling eyes, your arms around my waist as you lifted me off my feet. And in a split second, my balloon popped. My mirror shattered. Everything came crashing down around me, and all I wanted to do was close my eyes, cover my ears, and sing a ridiculous song until the picture of you with that woman stopped playing in my head."

"*It wasn't me,*" he argued—the same argument he made every time this came up.

"I know. But it doesn't change what I saw. What I felt. The heartache and emptiness I left that club with was real, whether what I saw was you or not. Listen, Jordan...I don't expect you to get it. I was there, and even I don't understand; maybe we aren't meant to. Maybe this all happened for a reason, and when the time's right, we'll see what it was. Until then, arguing about it, obsessing over it, and questioning every little thing is only dragging it out. We need to make peace with it and move on."

"That's easy for you to say. You aren't the one who lost everything over an assumption. The least you can do is be honest with me. I've already lost you. The future we planned together is gone. There's no need to sugarcoat anything anymore, so you might as well tell me the ugly truth. We both know you wouldn't have chosen to stay with him without a list of pros and cons."

The lump in my throat grew larger until I could no longer swallow without feeling like I was about to choke. "I don't know how to talk to you about this."

"Have you always had a problem talking to me about things?"

A horn honked in the distance, pulling my attention to the parking lot while his gaze remained on me. His intense stare made it clear he wouldn't let me avoid this. Jordan deserved answers. He deserved the truth. As well as my parents and everyone who had been invited to the wedding. The only problem was, I was terrified to speak the words aloud.

"No, Jordan," I whispered slowly, closing my eyes and shaking my head. "But this is different. We're not discussing vacation plans or how my day was. No matter what I say, it'll hurt you, and I don't want to do that."

His incredulous laughter boomed around us. "You ran off and married someone else without informing me that we had broken up. I told you I didn't care, that we could figure it out together. I was willing to move past it. I was willing to still marry you and spend the rest of my life with you. But instead of getting the marriage annulled, you moved in with him. And still, I stuck around like a fool. I had to find out that you'd made up your mind from the internet. You couldn't even show me enough respect to let me know you weren't ever coming back. So excuse me for laughing, but I don't see how you can look me in the eyes and tell me you don't want to hurt me, when you've already left me gutted and filled with salt."

Arguing with him would be futile. He'd never let it go until he got what he wanted, and right now, he wanted answers, even if they'd hurt him. He was right—it wasn't my place to spare him the pain after causing so much already.

As difficult as it was to look at him, I refused to turn away while giving him what he'd asked for. "You're right, Jordan…it took me six months to say I love you because I wanted to make sure I meant it first. The reason it took so long is because anytime you uttered those words to me, it freaked me out. And after a while, I felt like you were getting irritated that I still hadn't said it back."

"So you told me you love me because you *assumed* I was irritated?"

I'd gotten this far; no point in turning back now. "A person can only profess their love to another for so long without hearing it back before they start to question it. You used those words on our one-month anniversary. So for five months, you told me you loved me, and I hadn't returned the sentiment. Admit it, Jordan. You were growing impatient."

"There's a difference between wanting to know I wasn't alone in my feelings and needing validation so badly I'd resort to pressuring you into it. Are you telling me that you said it just because you thought I was getting pissed?"

"Not pissed, no. But impatient, yes."

"So you didn't mean it at all?"

My throat closed, and my chest tightened. Tears stung the backs of my eyes as I formed the words on my tongue—the words I'd only ever thought to myself with no intention of lending them a voice. "I remember lying in bed one night after getting off the phone with you and staring at the ceiling for, like, an hour. I didn't understand why it freaked me out so much when I'd hear you tell me you love me. I assumed that because I didn't get butterflies when I heard it, that meant I didn't feel the same. I never got excited. I never got the urge to call up everyone in my contacts to tell them you love me. But I knew I didn't want to lose you. I knew I *cared* about you, so while I stared at the ceiling, I convinced myself that I did love you, and the reason I didn't feel all those other things was because this love was different. The real kind. The next day was the first time I repeated it."

"Did you ever love me?"

"Of course I love you, Jordan." A large part of me wanted to reach out and touch him, though I refrained, knowing it wouldn't comfort him the way I would've intended. "I don't believe you can be with someone as long as we were together without love being a part of it."

His gaze shifted all around, occasionally landing on me for only a split second before darting off to something else. It made me a little uneasy. Then again, everything about this situation was uncomfortable and awkward.

The only way to end it was to keep going. Get it over with. "I told Stella that I didn't want you to propose because I needed to focus on school and get my degree. I truly believed that was my hang-up. It made sense to me—get through school, *and then* worry about the future. I never saw it as hesitation, but more of a responsible decision."

"Let me guess…since you'd already graduated, you didn't have a problem saying yes to him?"

My hands fisted at my sides. It became increasingly more difficult to control my anger, and I wasn't sure how much longer I could put up with his digs before I lost my temper. "You really want to know why I married him? Why I didn't think twice about it or get it annulled after I came back?"

"Yes, Mercy. I would like you to tell me why."

"Because when he asked, I felt something. And the entire time I was with you, I felt nothing. Is that what you want to hear? Do you feel better now?"

Jordan took a step back, his jaw ticcing as if I'd slapped him. "What did you feel? *Butterflies*? You married a complete stranger, chose him over the guy you've been with for years, all because of a nervous stomach?"

As much as I wanted to yell, I had to keep my composure. So I released a steady breath and waited a couple of seconds before responding. "No. My chest ached, like my heart had grown too big to fit in my ribcage. I became lightheaded; not dizzy, though. And my entire body grew so warm it felt like I stood beneath the sun on the hottest day of the year. I had this insane urge to cry, and for the life of me, I couldn't fathom why. I wasn't sad—quite the opposite, really. It also wasn't a happy cry…at least, not the kind most people are used to. The tears never came, never burned my eyes, never even *moistened* them."

"Wow, Mercy." He shook his head, exasperation glittering in his rolling eyes. "We had something solid, real, and safe. Too bad I didn't know all of this before. If I had, I could've given you panic attacks all the time. Maybe if I'd done that, you would've married me instead."

Nothing I could say would change his mind. He was angry, and he had every right to be. I'd broken his heart. I'd stolen his dreams and his future, and the only explanation I had to offer was that I had never been in love with him. I had no right to strip him of his feelings over what I'd done to him.

"While I get why you don't like him, your issue should really be with me. You went after the wrong person last night, Jordan. He didn't *make* me marry him. He never forced me to move into his house, nor did he pressure me into staying. I chose to do all of those things. Yet you went after him instead."

His disposition changed again, shifting from ire to sorrow to guilt in the blink of an eye. "Like I said…I wasn't thinking. In my head, he had to have something over you. There had to be a reason you wanted him instead of me. I needed to see with my own eyes what he has that I don't."

"Did you find what you were looking for? Did destroying everything make you feel better?"

"No. Not at all. It made me feel worse. Once the blinding hatred wore off, I realized what I had done, and I ran. I wouldn't blame him for pressing charges, but if you can convince him to let me pay him back…" Jordan shook his head without finishing his sentence. It almost sounded as if he wanted to say I owed him that much yet stopped himself.

In all honesty, I did owe him. I'd caused him so much pain, and if this would make it up to him, prove to him how sorry I was, then I had to do it. "I'll talk to him. But you have to promise to pay it all back by the time you say you will. Screwing him over won't hurt me, so it won't do you any good to make this agreement and then back out after he calls off the guards."

"I have no intention of screwing him over."

"Okay. I'll see what I can do. Go back to work and stop worrying. I'll text you later."

With a curt nod, he took a few steps backward, and then turned to head inside. Meanwhile, I needed a couple of extra minutes to collect my emotions off the ground. I'd expected his anger. His hurt. His accusations and insults. However, in all the scenarios I'd played out in my head on the drive to his office, I never assumed I'd be leaving here to defend him to Brogan.

I really began to miss my uncomplicated life.

18

BROGAN

"I have entirely too much going on right now to continue this conversation." I opened the door, and then leaned against the glass with my arms crossed over my chest. "If you have any hope of keeping your job, I suggest you leave and let me cool off. Trust me…you don't want me making a decision about your employment anytime soon."

"I understand," Kickstand mumbled with his hands in his pockets.

I didn't bother to move as he shuffled past me, squeezing between my body and the doorframe. "And if I find out you had any part in this—planned it, agreed to it, got paid for it—then I hope for your sake you can afford a good attorney."

Kickstand glanced over his shoulder and met my stare with wide eyes, fear burning bright in their depths. "I swear, boss. I didn't know anything about it. It was a mistake."

"A rather costly mistake, if you ask me." Honestly, I believed the kid. I felt I'd known him long enough to see through his bullshit, but I wasn't about to let him off the hook that easily. I was still too pissed off for that. Not to mention, a little fear might do him good—it was the only way to ensure he'd learned his lesson. However, I had no intention of giving him the keys to close up the shop again.

Without moving from my position in the doorway, I grabbed my cell from my pocket and checked the screen. Mercy had called almost two hours ago, asking if I wanted her help, yet she hadn't shown up. While that wasn't overly concerning in and of itself, considering I assumed it would've taken her and Stella time to get dressed and drive into town, she also hadn't answered any of my calls or texts.

I pulled up our message thread to see if she'd even read the last one I had sent, but before I could do anything else, I caught a glimpse of her car out of my peripheral vision. Instantly, my posture softened, and my lungs returned to normal working order. I wasn't sure I'd ever stop worrying so much about her wellbeing. And while I realized that wasn't a bad thing, the potential heart attack begged to differ.

"Where have you been? I've called and texted. Why didn't you answer?" I asked while she approached me, Stella following close behind.

Mercy tilted her head back and met my lips with hers. It was a quick kiss—we'd learned a while ago that if our lips touched for too long, clothes came off—followed by her sliding her hand into mine. "Let's go talk."

"That's never good." It was meant to be a joke, except her somber expression killed the humor. I followed her to my studio room, which was mostly cleaned up by now, and closed the door behind me. "What's going on, babe? You're worrying me."

Without anywhere to sit—boxes of trash occupied the table she normally sat on when in here—she leaned against the side wall with her shoulder and glanced around the room. "Do you know who did this?"

"We have his face on video."

She nodded slowly, as if mulling over my answer in her head. "Are you planning to press charges?"

I tensed against the door at the notion she knew more than she was letting on. "Why wouldn't I? Not only am I out the money for all the supplies that are destroyed, which need to be replaced, but I'm also losing out on at least two days' worth of business until I can get the shop up and running again. This asshole has cost me a lot of money, time, and grief."

"What if he's willing to pay you back?"

"It doesn't matter because I'll press charges, and then he'll be forced to pay me back."

Her eyes closed and head fell forward. If I didn't know better, I would've thought I was looking at the culprit. A guilt-ridden sigh escaped her downturned lips, and when she lifted her gaze, my heart stopped.

"What aren't you telling me, Mercy?"

"When I saw Jordan, he told me what he did."

On top of my heart not beating properly, my lungs decided to shrink, making full breaths nearly impossible. "Where did you see him?"

"I went to his office before coming here. I told you that's what I was doing."

My mouth opened and closed while I replayed our earlier conversation in my head. There was a large piece missing, which coincided with Indi handing me her phone, so there was no telling if she had or hadn't told me. "Sorry, I must not have heard that part. Anyway…what did he say?"

"I don't know how to tell you this, Brogan, but Jordan's the one who broke in last night. He must've thought you knew and told me, and that's why I was there. I'm not sure. But he confessed immediately, and I truly believe he's remorseful." Her throat dipped with her harsh swallow right before she added, "I don't think you should press charges."

I saw red, though not at her. At the bastard who put her in the middle of his war. "And why do you think that?"

"Because he said he'll pay you back. And he realizes he fucked up. Listen, I get it. He's my ex, and he hasn't made things easy for either of us over the past month. Taking the high road isn't the easiest choice to make, but please do it for me?"

"I don't understand why you'd want me to after what he's done."

She shuffled her feet along the floor until she stood directly in front of me. With her hands on my chest, calming my erratic heart rate, she lifted her chin and looked me in the eyes. "I feel like I have some blame in this, too. He's hurt and angry, and after seeing him today, I can honestly say he's lost. I did that to him."

As much as I wanted to give in and let her have her way, I couldn't. Not yet. "I don't care how he feels about us, that doesn't give him the right to fuck my shit up. He's got a broken heart; so what? Can he not control himself? Does he not take responsibility for his own actions, or does he have the mentality that it's always someone else's fault because they hurt his feelings? Hell no, Mercy. I'm sorry, but I can't condone vandalizing someone's property—*their business*—simply because the woman he cheated on married someone else. That's his own problem."

"He didn't cheat on me," she said, resignation heavy in her soft tone.

From the moment Mercy first told me that he had denied being in that club with another woman, I didn't buy it. He might've been convincing enough to make her question what she saw, but I never contemplated the possibility that she'd actually doubt it. At the end of the day, she slept in *my* bed, so it shouldn't have mattered what she believed. However, hearing her defend him sent my pulse racing and my blood pressure through the roof.

She fisted the front of my shirt and relaxed against me. "Everything happened the way it was supposed to. I trust that. Except it doesn't ease the guilt I feel for what I put him through. Can't you take a day or two and think about it before making a decision?"

"He clearly didn't take the time to think through his before ransacking my shop."

"No, but here's your chance to be the bigger person. We can't continue playing the eye-for-an-eye game. Someone will get seriously hurt." She was right, and the thought of that someone being her made me sick to my stomach. "You have the chance to put an end to it now. There's really no point in keeping this war going."

"I won't wave the white flag."

"You have me, so you're already the winner. Want to know what he has? A broken heart. Guilty conscience. Regret that probably won't go away anytime soon, especially if he has to make payments to you—the one who's sleeping next to the woman he wants. If anyone's surrendering, it's him. He's at your mercy, groveling at your feet, begging for leniency. Can't you at least give him that?"

Damn…in less than ten minutes, Mercy proved she could get whatever she wanted from me. I only hoped she wouldn't ask for the world. Because I'd die trying to give it to her.

"Okay, fine. I won't press charges. But if he fucks up again, don't bother asking me to take the high road, because I won't. This is his first and last chance. I'll do this for you, this one time, but if he even *thinks* of acting out again, he'll wish he decided to play in traffic instead."

A slow smile of approval curled her lips while pride glistened in her eyes. "Thank you, baby. I know this isn't what you want, and you're only doing it to please me. I can't tell you how much that means to me. And if he messes this up, he's all yours. After this, my debt to him will be paid in full."

I cradled her face in my hands and brought her mouth to mine.

Mercy Wright had a way of making me a better man.

And for that, *my* debt to *her* could never be paid off.

———

It took close to a week to get the shop back in order. Luckily, Mercy had Stella to keep her entertained while I spent long days dealing with the aftermath of her ex's childish tantrum.

Even though it wouldn't have been my choice to take it easy on him, I had to admit that I felt a certain amount of satisfaction at the thought of handing him a bill for all the damage he'd caused. I also looked forward to witnessing the pain in his eyes when I gave him the legal document detailing the stipulations of our agreement.

Now, Stella had gone home, and the shop was back in business.

Just in time for the camera crew to arrive and create yet another headache.

There were still three more days before filming began, and after that, Mercy would start her new job at the small private school in town. In two and a half weeks, our schedules would become chaotic. Between her early mornings and my late nights, I worried we wouldn't have much time together. Mercy didn't seem concerned. As she so eloquently put it...*there's always the middle of the night*.

The thought of having her naked body next to mine made me impatient to get home.

My knee bobbed as I sat in the lobby of Jordan's office building, waiting for him to acknowledge I was there. Granted, I didn't blame the idiot for taking his time. This wasn't the kind of meeting that would leave him with a smile on his face. But if he kept me much longer, I'd make sure he understood the reason for my impatience. And no man wanted to imagine the woman he loved being loved by someone else—especially if that image was as detailed as I'd make it.

"Mr. Daniels," the receptionist called as she made her way toward me. "Mr. Hamilton is ready for you. If you'll follow me, I'll take you to him." Fucker couldn't even get off his ass to come get me. Shouldn't have surprised me, yet it did.

I kept one step behind the blonde, who made it a point to

dramatically swing her hips with every step. It very well might've been her normal gait, though I doubted it. I'd seen women completely change their entire demeanor—and tone—in front of me. But if she thought I'd pay attention to it, it was a waste of her time and energy.

Halfway down a long hallway, she turned toward me with a smile and said, "Here you are." She knocked once and, without waiting for a reply, opened the solid door. "Have a nice day, Mr. Daniels."

"You too." I had no idea what her name was, and I didn't really care.

I stepped into Jordan's office, disregarding the fact that he hadn't greeted me, or even glanced up from his computer screen to acknowledge my presence. If this was how he planned to treat me throughout the entire meeting, he'd wish I had pressed charges.

"Jordan," I greeted him as I took a seat in front of his desk—in a chair he hadn't offered because he still hadn't looked at me.

Finally, he pushed his keyboard to the side and turned his seat to face me. "How would you like to be addressed? As Wrong? Or Brogan?"

I could've had a little fun with him, but I chose to keep this as simple and painless—for me—as possible. "Either one is fine."

He nodded, yet he refrained from choosing a name, and instead, said nothing.

"Here's a copy of the final bill for all the repairs and items that needed to be replaced." I slid a few pieces of paper across the desk to him. "And here's the agreement I need you to sign. It simply states the terms you've discussed with Mercy as well as what will happen if you don't follow through. Feel free to take your time going through the itemized receipt, because once this is signed, you can't contest any of the charges."

While he scanned the papers lined with dollar amounts, I leaned back in the chair, my legs stretched out in front of me with my ankles crossed. I almost locked my hands behind my head, but I figured that might've been too much. Being an asshole wasn't as much fun when the douche who deserved it acted more like a frightened housecat than the lion he pretended to be while destroying my shop.

Once he finished going through the itemized list, he moved on to the contract. He might've been a fast reader, though it seemed more likely that he simply wanted to get this over with. In a way, it made me believe Mercy when she said he was genuinely remorseful for what he'd done. I was even more convinced when he signed the last page and then slid it across his desk to me, avoiding eye contact.

Pussy.

"Thanks. I'll get a copy made and send it to you. Would you prefer if I emailed it? Or would it be better if I dropped off a hard copy?" Damn…playing nice wasn't as easy as it looked.

"Email is fine," he answered and then went back to his computer.

I stood from the seat, but before moving away from his desk, I decided to get as much information as I could. "She's never coming back. You know that, right?" That got his attention, his narrowed eyes swinging my way. "Why not tell her the truth? That's what I don't understand. You're so angry with her, and apparently, with me as well, so why keep up with the lie? We both know that was you she saw in the club."

"You don't know what you're talking about."

"Oh, I don't? How do you think I knew it was you who trashed my shop? We've never met. In fact, I've never seen a picture of you. All I had was a face on camera, so how could I have known it was you?" When he didn't respond, I pressed my hands flat against the top of his desk and leaned forward, towering over him. "I know who you were with that night."

His face turned beet-red as the muscles in his jaw danced to the cadence of his fury.

"Let me ask you again, Jordan. Why continue to lie?"

"I don't see why you care. Believing I hadn't cheated on her didn't stop her from choosing you. So what does it matter if I tell the truth or not?" He was millimeters away from snapping, and it made me pause to question if it would be worth it or not.

Then I decided I didn't give a shit. "Because she deserves to know."

"She broke my heart. She deserves to feel at least some guilt for that."

I pushed away from his desk and glared at him. "Are you kidding me right now? You cheated on her, and she caught you. The only person you have to be mad at is yourself. The only person who should be feeling any sort of guilt is you. *You* fucked up. Own it."

The bastard must've found his balls, because he stood up and squared his shoulders. "I'm not proud of what I did behind her back. I hate myself for it. But that doesn't really matter, does it? Because I wasn't given the opportunity to make it right, or to prove how sorry I am. I've given her everything, and she couldn't even give me a chance to prove to her how much I love her."

"You can't say you gave her everything. You didn't give her respect. You didn't give her any loyalty. You took advantage of her trust and played roulette with her love. And guess what? You lost. Game over. You can't be upset with her for choosing someone who treats her better than you ever did—and that's even without her knowing all you've done behind her back."

"Just give it time." His tone held a bite of bitterness, as well as a heaping of resentment. "You've only been with her for a few weeks. It's easy to stand here and act all high and mighty. How about in two years you come back and see me. I'll treat you to a beer while you try to tell me how much better you are than me."

I should've left. Walked out. But for some unexplainable reason, my feet remained rooted to the carpet and my eyes steady on his. "Two years. Ten. Fifty. It doesn't matter how long

I'm with her, I'll always be better than you. I'll never treat her the way you did, no matter how many anniversaries we celebrate."

"You say that now. But sooner or later, her act will eat at you. You'll no longer find it cute or endearing. It'll get to you, and before you know it, you'll be lying in bed, Mercy curled up on the other side as far away as she can get, and you'll think about the woman who touched your arm while laughing at your joke. You'll remember the way she smelled when she leaned closer, or as she flipped her hair over her shoulder. And without realizing it, you're fantasizing about *her*."

I clenched my jaw and fisted my hands, fighting the urge to explain just how pathetic he was. If these were his thoughts as he slept next to Mercy, then he had more issues than I'd initially thought. "You're assuming everyone's as stupid as you. Well, guess what? Only a moron would think of another woman while lying next to someone as amazing as Mercy."

"You're absolutely right. Maybe her insecurities won't ever get to you. Maybe you'll spend the rest of your life content with having sex in the dark. And on the rare occasion she lets you keep the light on, it's possible you won't mind that she doesn't take off her shirt. Always under the covers as if sex is something to be ashamed of."

I lost the ability to speak. There was no way he was talking about Mercy.

"And as long as you don't mind always being the initiator, then yeah…I guess it's possible you wouldn't think of other women while lying next to her. But if you're like every other living, breathing man, you'll reach a point when you start to recall the feeling of having someone touch you because *they* wanted to, without you having to make the first move. What it was like to sit on the couch next to your girl and have her move closer to curl into you rather than shift on the cushion to give you more room. And then there will be nights when you can't stop thinking about that one girl who just couldn't get enough of you. That's when you'll turn to the side and realize you'll never have that again."

"Then why the fuck are you so broken up over losing her? If that's how you truly feel, you should be thanking me. Not vandalizing my shop. Not giving Mercy a hard time for leaving you. Not continuing to lie to her about what she saw just so she'll feel guilty for hurting you."

"Because I love her." The emotion in his tone was raw, proving that somewhere inside, likely deep within his black heart, he truly did love her in some way. Unfortunately, that didn't make up for how poorly he'd treated her.

"I guess it's easy to overlook what you perceive as downfalls in the relationship when you're getting it somewhere else. Is that what you planned to do for the next sixty or so years? Sleep around while taking advantage of everything else she had to offer?"

As his defensiveness waned, his shoulders drooped, and the hard lines of his expression began to fade away. "It was just until she moved in with me. I told myself that once she got here, once we were no longer in two different states, but under the same roof as husband and wife, I'd put a stop to seeking affection elsewhere. It was selfish. I know. In my head, I told myself she'd never find out—what she didn't know wouldn't hurt her. That it was nothing more than a man on the cusp of marriage sowing a few last-minute wild oats."

"Well, I'm sure you don't need this pointed out, but I'd say that didn't work out quite like you planned, huh?" I backed away from his desk until my heels met the door on the other side of the room, not once dropping my stare from his. "Like I said, Jordan...you don't have anyone to blame but yourself. Hopefully, paying off your debt will be a constant reminder that you're the reason you lost everything—not me. And certainly not Mercy."

I didn't bother to wait around for a response.

He didn't deserve any more of my time.

19

MERCY

I was standing at the island with a knife in one hand and a tomato in the other when I heard the Jeep coming down the driveway. I'd been on pins and needles ever since he left the shop to finalize his agreement with Jordan. It wasn't that I was scared of anything happening, considering Brogan trusted me and anything my ex could say about me would be water off his back, but that didn't stop the nerves from eating away at me for the last two hours.

Hearing the door from the garage open and close, I scooped the diced tomato into the salad bowl and then hurried to rinse off my hands. I had a feeling I'd need to feel his arms around me, and that wouldn't happen if I had tomato juice all over the place. And as if I'd timed it perfectly, Brogan stepped into the kitchen just as I finished drying my hands.

He took one look at me and stilled between the laundry room and the kitchen island I stood behind. Even with a giant slab of granite—as well as the mess left over from preparing dinner—hiding half my body from view, it didn't stop him from practically stripping me with his heated stare. And once he brought his attention back to my face, there was no denying the thoughts that ran through his filthy mind.

I might've seen his smile with my eyes...but I felt it between my legs.

Brogan didn't waste another second getting to me. He rounded the counter, turned me in his arms, and lifted me off my feet while owning my mouth with his tongue. It was intense and passionate. Then he set me on the edge of the counter next to the sink, his body positioned between my legs. His hands frantically drawing my hips closer to his.

And there wasn't a damn thing I could think of other than feeling him inside me.

Following his lead, I tugged at the hem of his shirt until he leaned away long enough to slip it over his head. However, he didn't allow me time to explore the colors and lines on his chest like normal. I'd only ever seen him this impatient when he was in a mood, irritated at something he couldn't control. Except this time was different. It wasn't anger or frustration that coursed through him, but something else. Something I couldn't recognize. Right now, it wasn't important enough to make me stop and question it.

His need fueled my need.

His desire fed mine.

We stripped each other naked, my bare bottom on the hard, cold granite. His warm body between my thighs. And without the typical foreplay that Brogan enjoyed so much, he was inside me. Filling me. Stretching me. Bringing me to the edge like a freight train barreling toward an unfinished bridge.

I anchored myself to him with my legs around his waist while using my arms as leverage, pulling myself closer to bury my face in the crook of his neck. And at the sound of my name clawing its way past his clenched jaw, raspy and rugged, I sank my teeth into the top of his shoulder and whimpered through the kind of intense orgasm only Brogan could give me.

It was a miracle he hadn't followed me off that cliff, though it wouldn't be long. His movements had become a bit stiff, and his hold on me grew tighter than before. There was some reason he'd held himself back, and as soon as I pulled my head away, I understood what he waited for.

Cradling the side of my face in one hand, the other still digging into my hip and ass cheek, he consumed my mouth in the most eager, fervent, borderline violent kiss he'd ever given me. And I never wanted it to stop. Never wanted *him* to stop. My entire body burned with what he did to me—the warmth of his orgasm, the brutality of his kiss, the eager yet gentle way he possessed me with his hands.

Brogan Daniels did things to me.

Amazing and wild and addictive things.

When the hedonistic fog cleared from my brain, I was able to concentrate enough to ask, "Where did that come from?"

I'd been the willing recipient during his moods, and even though it was a rare occasion, it was enough to know this wasn't brought about by a negative emotion. And I'd woken up to his insatiable appetite enough times to understand that this wasn't a reaction to his uncontrollable desire for me. However, recognizing what it *wasn't* didn't do much to tell me what it was.

"Have I ever told you how much I love your reaction to me?"

I stared into his vibrant green eyes, the color they always were after we were intimate, and tried to read his unspoken words in the juniper-colored striations. Still, I had a hard time translating it all, too lost in the adoration that nearly blinded me. "What does that mean?"

He traced my brow with the pad of his thumb, a lazy grin playing on his lips. "I feel like there's a switch inside me, and you're the only one who's ever found it. It could be a look, the way you say something, your hair, your clothes. You can turn a certain way, move a certain way, and in an instant, I need you like I've never needed anyone else. It's nothing you do on purpose, and I doubt you even realize it, which makes it even more powerful. But the best part is that when you flip that switch and I come to you, it doesn't matter what you're in the middle of doing, it's like you need me, too."

"What can I say? I guess you just do it for me." Probably not the most eloquent response I could've come up with, yet it was the best I could offer, considering the circumstances. If he wanted something more sincere, then he'd have to try again when I wasn't flooded with post-orgasm endorphins.

"That's just it, Mercy. It's more than sex. It's the connection. The intimacy. It doesn't matter how or when or where we do it, the intensity of being with you feels powerful enough to bring me back to life." He closed his eyes and pulled in a deep breath. "I can't explain it."

"You don't have to, because I understand what you're saying." I smiled when his surprised eyes found mine again. "I feel it too, Brogan. It's like you've awakened a part of me I never knew existed. And I'm convinced you're the only person capable of finding it."

The words *I love you* echoed in my head. Burned my tongue. Begged to be released. And even though I recognized the same sentiment in his eyes, I couldn't bring myself to utter it aloud. Fear kept that admission under lock and key. Nevertheless, the closer we grew to one another, and the deeper our relationship became, the harder it was to refrain from telling him how I felt.

I needed to be sure this time. For reasons I couldn't comprehend, I refused to give him that part of me until I knew, without a doubt, this was love. I felt that it was, believed it was, and when I thought about it, I couldn't imagine it being anything else. However, that didn't stop the fear from taking over anytime I found myself at the cusp of saying those three little yet powerful words. It was as though my soul recognized the risk this time—not because of anything that had happened in my past, but because of who he was.

Before anything else could be said between us, the oven timer sounded.

"I should get that out before it burns." I glanced between my legs. "And considering we prepare food on this counter, I should probably clean that up, too. As well as put my clothes back on."

Brogan pressed a kiss to my forehead and stepped away. After grabbing our discarded clothes off the floor, he handed me my panties and his T-shirt. I had a feeling that if he could dress me however he wanted, I'd wear nothing but underwear and his shirts—and, obviously, nothing to bed at night.

"I'll clean up our mess over here while you deal with the dinner in the oven," he said as he helped me off the counter. And with an easy smack to my bare ass, we once again fell into our comfortable routine, moving about with familiarity, as if we'd spent countless lifetimes dancing in sync with one another.

———

"Were you planning to tell me about your meeting with Jordan? Or did you just hope you could distract me with *amazing* kitchen-counter sex?" I asked while mindlessly pushing a piece of chicken around the plate with my fork.

Brogan set down his knife, except he didn't say anything. I glanced up, and the moment my eyes met his, I realized he was waiting for my undivided attention before answering my question. So I abandoned the chicken hockey and focused solely on the man across the table.

"The *amazing* kitchen-counter sex wasn't a diversion. I came home, saw you, and couldn't help myself." His brows jumped, and a slightly devious grin toyed with one corner of his lips. "With that being said...I haven't mentioned Jordan because it was uneventful. I gave him the receipt and agreement; he signed it, and I left."

Something felt off, though I didn't have a reason to doubt him. Chalking it up to paranoia over the thought of Jordan and

Brogan in the same room together, I nodded and dropped the worry. "Well, that's good. At least it's all over, right?"

"Yeah." Again, his reaction seemed like there was more, yet he chose to keep it to himself. Finally, after a few long seconds of silence and staring, he took a deep breath and asked, "What was your relationship with Jordan like?"

That meant more had happened beyond Brogan giving him the papers and Jordan signing them. I could question it, or I could answer him and hope that, through his inquiries, I'd learn where his curiosity came from. I chose to give him what he wanted. "Um...normal, I guess. Nothing exciting. It was what I assumed most relationships were like."

"Would you say it's different than ours?"

"It's night and day," I said with a smile.

"Were you as..." He hesitated for a moment and then pointed to the counter behind me. "...eager? Open? Sexually, I mean. You're just so into it with me, and I guess I'm wondering if you've always been that way."

As much as I wanted to look away, I couldn't. His eyes held mine captive, and they begged for the truth. So, I dismissed my need to hide, choosing honesty instead. "I wouldn't use those words."

"Then how would you have described it?"

"Willing."

His lips split into an infectious grin, a rush of airy humor seeped out, and he dropped his head forward—his signature move when something funny struck him at a time he least expected it. "Well, let's hope so, babe. But other than that, how would you portray it?"

"Brogan...this is a really uncomfortable conversation to have. Can you at least tell me where this is coming from? Maybe then I can understand what info you're actually looking for rather than detailing my sex life with my ex when you're asking for something else."

"Fair enough." He ran his hand over his hair as if smoothing errant strands. "He might've made a comment or two about how you are in bed, and the person he described didn't sound anything like the one I sleep with every night."

My stomach twisted to the point I had to push my plate away.

"He wasn't saying anything...*negative*, per se. It was more or less his way of trying to pop my bubble or make me doubt what we have. It didn't work, so don't let it bother you. Like I said, it made me wonder if he was lying, or if you're simply a different person with me—and if so, why."

While I understood his concern, that didn't make it easier to explain.

"The person he described sounded insecure, which isn't a word I would use for you. Without *saying* it, he implied you were a little prudish—or maybe that was just how I interpreted it. But again, that's the complete opposite of who I know you to be."

"I told you that how we are together versus how I was with him is night and day. And I meant it. There's a comfort level with you that I *never* felt with him. He never made me *un*comfortable or anything. I guess the best way I can think of to describe it is that I felt like I was having sex with a childhood friend." This couldn't have been more awkward.

That was a lie...because a second later, it did, in fact, become more awkward.

"Why would you agree to marry him, then? If that's how you felt?"

"I didn't have anything to compare it to. In my head, that was the way it was supposed to feel. I've always heard my parents talk about how they were so lucky because they married their best friend. So to me, that was exactly what I was doing as well. I loved him—I knew that much. I enjoyed being around him and spending time with him. We had a lot of fun together. But I always knew that we lacked something in the intimacy department, and apparently, he felt it, too. He never said anything about it, so I thought I was overthinking it or something."

Brogan's eyes softened, the color changing to a warm shade of green—the color of a mint leaf. "And it's different with me." It wasn't a question. He wasn't seeking clarification. It was as though he understood that statement on a personal level.

"Exactly." I reached across the table and intertwined my fingers with his. "When I'm with you, I don't have other thoughts racing through my head. You keep me grounded to you. It was never like that with him."

He squeezed my hand in reassurance—except I couldn't tell if it was to assure him or me. "It's crazy how you can think you're happy, truly believe it doesn't get better than this, and then you meet that one person who proves you wrong in all the right ways."

Even though it shouldn't have surprised me, it did. The way he seemed to just *get* me. See me. Feel me in ways no one else ever had. Rather than it terrifying me, it calmed me. Soothed me. It electrified and excited me.

For the first time since we left Savannah, I felt eager for tomorrow.

With Brogan by my side, there wasn't anything I couldn't face.

20

BROGAN

With filming about to start, I'd decided to take the last two days off to spend with Mercy. This turned out to be a good thing, considering we'd stayed up late talking about anything and everything. She'd told me about her past relationships, and in turn, I had shared with her all the ugly and wonderful times I'd been through.

It was nice to actually know things about each other, rather than simply *feel* like we did. Aside from Jess, I'd never had anyone in my life I could open up to like that. Sure, I had Indi, and while I trusted her, she only knew what I'd allowed her to know. And with my life plastered on the internet and in the pages of trashy gossip magazines, it was a good feeling to be able to share my stories with someone without them already knowing.

I'd stopped wondering where Mercy had come from.

I no longer cared.

All that mattered was that she was here. And she was mine.

Shortly after getting out of bed, she'd received a call from the school, requesting a meeting with her. Since this was her first year teaching, the call didn't come as a surprise. And as much as I would've wanted to spend the *whole* day with her, having her out of the house had given me time to do something nice for her.

What I hadn't expected was for everything to fall apart when she got home.

When the door leading out to the garage opened and then closed, I pulled myself off the couch to meet her. I wanted to find out how her meeting went since she hadn't called me when she left. Then I wanted to share the surprise with her. But as soon as she saw me, she tucked her chin and tried to make a beeline for the bedroom.

I wasn't about to let her hide from me, not after last night. Not after sharing ourselves with one another on a level I never imagined possible. So I moved to stand in front of her, blocking her hasty retreat, and then lifted her chin with my finger to see her face. "What the hell happened, babe?"

Inky trails ran down Mercy's cheeks, reminding me of the first night we'd met. Although this time, the slight wobble in her steps hadn't come from alcohol. And the hurt in her eyes wasn't heartache. It enraged me. Saddened me. Made me want to hold her and attack whoever had done this to her at the same time.

"It's nothing, Brogan." The use of my full name didn't bother me as much as the tears that filled her eyes, tarnishing the spools of gold that glistened with sorrow. "They decided they no longer need me."

"Who? The school? Why?" Nothing made sense, which might've had something to do with the influx of incomplete questions and thoughts that flooded my mind. This had come out of nowhere.

She shrugged and glanced away. It had been a while since I'd last seen her need to search a room before responding. And the fact that she had to now gutted me. However, what pained me the most was how she couldn't even look at me while she answered. "They, um…they don't feel I'm a good fit for them anymore."

Refusing to let her continue to turn away from me, I cupped her face with both hands and forced her attention on me. "What changed, babe? How could they hire you, and then decide less than three weeks before you're supposed to start that they don't want you anymore?"

Mercy didn't need to say anything. Her eyes told me everything I needed to know…and then some. The fact that she couldn't even utter the words held nearly as much weight on my chest as the reason for her losing her job before she even started.

"It's because of me, isn't it?"

Her short, jerky nod might've answered my question, but it didn't explain anything. Then again, I wasn't sure I cared what excuses they'd given her. Thanks to the show that allowed me the life I lived, I was considered a public figure. And while I hadn't actually *seen* a single episode, I wasn't blind to the way I was portrayed. So it made sense if I took a step back and looked at it all—my life, the drama surrounding my name, the rumors and assumptions that never seemed to die, all connected to the woman they'd hired to teach young children.

Except to me, she wasn't just a woman they'd hired.

She was Mercy. My wife.

And I refused to let her go long enough to take a step back and look at anything other than the fact she was hurting. That was all that mattered to me. Their reasons be damned. Their feelings toward me or my job be damned.

"I'll fix this, babe. I promise. It's not right what they did to you."

She placed her hand on my chest with enough pressure that her need to push me away was obvious. "No. Don't do anything, Brogan. It'll only make things worse. They don't have anything against me or you right now, and if you go down there and start something, you'll only be reaffirming their decision. Just drop it; let it go."

I put one foot behind the other and took a step back, my

arms dropping to my sides as I stared at her tear-stained face. "Okay. You're right. I won't do anything about it. You don't need that job anyway. Hell, I make enough money that you don't even have to work if you don't want to."

"That's not what I want." Her nose scrunched, and her forehead creased, right as the pain in her eyes swelled then rolled over her lower lids. Cascading down her cheeks. Falling from her quivering chin. "I didn't go to school for nothing. I didn't bust my ass to sit around the house or be taken care of by someone else."

"I'm not just *someone else*, Mercy. I'm your husband. It's my duty to take care of you."

"It's your duty to *support* me. To share your life with me—not your bank account. That makes me feel like you bought me, and I don't enjoy that feeling. I want to contribute. I want to use the degree I spent four years to get. I didn't choose teaching for the amazing hours or lack of stress. I chose it because it's what I've always wanted to do."

Part of me thought it'd be best if I simply stopped talking, knowing I'd only continue to put my foot in my mouth. But as long as she was crying, I wouldn't stop trying to make it right for her. "Okay…there are other schools in the area. You may not get the same offer for the same position, but at least it'll be a start. Right?"

"It doesn't work like that." Defeat had taken over her voice until it was a hoarse whisper. "I don't have an in-state teaching certificate, which takes time to get. The only reason I was able to get a job there was because it's a private school, and they can basically do whatever they want."

"There have to be other private schools in the area."

"None that would take me."

I shoved my hands into my pockets and nodded while desperately forming new ideas in my head. "What if you got something part-time, just to hold you over until you can get the certificate or whatever it is you need to get hired at a school?"

"I appreciate the effort, but really, I have too much on my mind right now to run through my options. But as soon as things settle, I promise, we'll sit down and figure it out. I'm just in too much shock right now for that." Her shoulders fell forward like a cartoon of someone giving up.

And as much as I wanted to hold her here, wrap my arms around her and convince her that there was nothing to worry about, I couldn't. If the time she'd spent in the spare room after moving in with me had taught me anything, it was that she was the type of person who needed a moment to come to things on her own. I had to trust she'd do the same with this.

My only hope was that it wouldn't take as long as it had taken for her to come back to me. If so, I'd deal with it. But since this wasn't as difficult a situation, I had to hold out hope that it'd be a few hours at the most before she'd let me in again.

"Maybe take a shower," I suggested, trying to come up with something to offer that wouldn't push her away. "Or I could run you a bath if that would be better."

Her smile was pitiful—granted, it showed she tried. "Thanks, but I think a shower might be best. I appreciate the thought, though."

All I could do was stand there and watch her escape into the bedroom. And for the first time since she'd crawled beneath my covers after the fundraiser, I got the feeling that she didn't want me there.

There wasn't a feeling worse than not being wanted by the *only* person you wanted.

———

When Mercy finally met me in the living room, the surprise I'd wanted to give her earlier was long forgotten. The only thing I'd been able to focus on was the information I'd received a few hours ago, shortly after she'd closed herself off behind our bedroom door.

Indi had called to share her theory about who she believed had been responsible for this shitstorm. None of this would've happened had the media not exploded with news of my marital status, painting Mercy in an unflattering light. So after hearing Indi's take on who the culprit was—which appeared to have been primarily based on facts rather than assumptions—the surprise I'd planned for Mercy had taken a back seat to the hatred that ran through my veins.

Without making eye contact, Mercy sat on the couch and stared at her phone that she held in her lap. The fact that she wouldn't look at me didn't bode well, yet I couldn't complain. Her avoidance kept her ignorant of the murderous rage I harbored toward the person who'd initiated this whole thing.

Disregarding the pang in my chest, I turned to face her. "What's going on?"

"I just got off the phone with my parents." Then she stopped talking, as if I'd be able to assume the rest.

"What did they have to say?"

"They think I should come home and regroup."

It took me a moment to gather the strength to ask, "And what did you tell them?"

"That I'd think about it."

When I'd discovered Jessica's indiscretions, it devastated me. At least, I assumed so at the time. But now, after hearing that there was a possibility of Mercy leaving, I realized what true devastation was. Like a bomb had exploded in my chest. Leaving nothing behind. Wreaking havoc on every cell in my body until my lungs were devoid of even an ounce of oxygen. Until my brain refused to tell my limbs what to do or send words to my tongue.

She finally gave me her attention, and the amount of pain in her eyes could've suffocated me. She could drown me in the fear that flooded her face. And when she opened her mouth to speak, the quiver in her lips shook me to my core. "Losing my job wasn't part of the plan, Brogan."

The fact that she had used my full name ever since coming home was enough to pull me off death's doorstep. However, it hadn't breathed life into me. Instead, it acted more like a ventilator—prolonging the inevitable. "Nothing we've done since the moment we met has been part of the plan. Coming home with me that night. Staying with me for the week. Getting married and moving in. *None* of it. Why is this any different?"

"That first week was temporary." Those words cut deep. "Everything after that seemed to work into the plan. I already had the job, already intended to move here. It didn't interfere with the path I'd already paved. The job *was* that path, and now I feel like I'm wandering aimlessly without a purpose."

While I understood where she was coming from, it didn't make it hurt any less to hear. "Why can't I be your purpose? Why can't *we* be your reason to stay? Change the path. Make your own. You're not alone here, Mercy. You have me. Why can't that be enough?"

Her tears seemed to come from nowhere, drenching her cheeks with the agony that poured from her eyes. "It has nothing to do with you not being enough. That's not it at all. If anything, I'm the one who feels insufficient."

"How? Why? I don't understand, babe. Explain it to me."

She reached out and covered my hand with hers, which managed to pull me back from the ledge. "I don't want to be the person those articles said I was. I refuse to live off your money. It's not who I am."

The mere mention of those articles had my mind racing back to what I'd discovered over the last few hours. And it took everything I had in me to rein in the anger. This was about Mercy, her job, and where we'd go from here. I couldn't risk her catching something in my expression and sidetracking our conversation.

I took a deep breath to control my emotions before continuing. "That's just it, though. I'm not asking you to live off me forever. I also have no issue with it if that's what you decide to do. If you want to work, I'm not stopping you. If you want to take some time to go after your teaching certificate, I'll support you one hundred percent. But I guess I don't understand the importance of *what* you bring to the table, just as long as you're there at that table next to me."

"Why can't you understand that?"

"Because what you offer is invaluable. What you give me can't be matched with a salary or material things. It's *you*, Mercy. Don't you see? All I care about is *you*. Nothing else. I'd be perfectly happy living in a cardboard box as long as you were with me."

Mercy wiped her cheek with the back of her hand, her eyes once again scouring the room rather than settling on mine. "Being equal contributors isn't my concern. I'll never make what you make. And I'm okay with that. All I want is to know I'm a partner here…not a wife with her husband's credit card."

I slid off the cushion and knelt in front of her, taking her hands until she dropped her attention to my face. "Babe…I get that having a job is important to you. I understand your desire to use your degree and do what you love. I'm all about that. But please, don't bail on me simply because the first school that hired you changed their mind. Can't you just allow me to support you while you figure out how to have what you want? How can you possibly find a job around here if you're in Ohio?"

"I didn't say I was going home." Regardless of the confusion that creased her brow, that was the first glimpse of hope she'd given me since returning from her meeting at the school. "My parents suggested it, and I told them I'd think about it to get them off my back."

A sigh of relief escaped as I dropped my forehead to our joined hands. "So you're not leaving? You're staying here and figuring it all out with me?" I peered up at her and held my breath while waiting for an answer. Pleading with my eyes for the right response. One that would end the disruptive chaos currently taking up residence in my chest.

"No, baby," she said while tracing my jawline with her fingertip. "I'm not looking for a reason to leave you. All I want is a job where I can instill values and morals into young children with the hope they'll grow up to be bright, productive adults."

My cheeks strained beneath the weight of my growing smile.

Which fell flat upon her next words.

"And if that opportunity doesn't exist here, then I'll have to explore my options and see what makes the most sense." Her mouth snapped shut and eyes opened wide when I pushed to my feet in front of her, effectively putting a stop to what she was saying.

Staring at her, I took a step back and fought to control my breathing. My chest heaved with the exertion of each inhale. Every exhale. Practically coming and going at the same time. Panic close to setting in.

"At some point, you'll have to stop running, Mercy."

"W-what are you talking about?"

"You're the runner. You get freaked out or confused, and your first reaction is to flee. I'm the chaser. *My* first reaction will always be to go after you. Beg you to come back. And when you do, I wait on the edge of my seat, anticipating the next time you'll take off. I can't live like that."

She climbed to her feet but didn't come toward me. Instead, she remained in place with her heels against the bottom of the couch, looking up at me with bewilderment glistening in her eyes.

"Brogan—"

"No, *Mercy*." I shouldn't have spat her name like that. It simply came out on its own, filled with frustration. Heavy with the rejection I felt each and every time she uttered my name without any hint of the love song that usually accompanied it.

Hearing it stung like being attacked by a dozen swarms of bees.

"I'm well aware that every time I chase after you and beg you to stay, you do it to please me. To give me what I want. I have no one to blame but myself for the fear I live with—the fear that you'll run off again. And the only way to put an end to that cycle is to let you go and hope you choose to return on your own. To me. To *us*. I don't want to let you go, to watch you walk away. But I also don't know how much longer I can do this."

Her mouth opened and closed a few times while she mindlessly studied the center of my chest. Finally, when the words came to her, she asked, "What does that even mean?"

"If you leave, I won't follow. But that doesn't mean I don't want to. It only means I've chosen to stay here and wait for your return. Wait for you to find your way to me again. I have to trust that what we have was forged in the stars countless lifetimes ago, and if that's true, then I have no doubt in my mind you'll come back." I hadn't intended to say half of that, yet once I started, I couldn't stop, leaving my hands tied in the event she left.

Mercy licked her lips and scanned the room, twisting at the waist to turn in half circles. She appeared to be searching for an exit, though I began to question that the longer she remained in place. But if an escape wasn't what she sought, I was lost as to what she was looking for.

Finally, she faced me again and straightened her spine. Her shoulders were pulled back, squared, eyes steadily on mine. "I didn't say I was leaving."

"You said you'd have to explore your options."

Her tears were now nothing more than dried tracks lining her face. Determination had replaced the unease from moments ago, almost as if she was prepared for battle. However, her eyes spoke of peace, soothing the unsettled rhythm in my chest. "Yeah, I did say that, as in my options for employment. Which could be a bank teller or dog walker...*here*. I'm sorry, baby. I didn't mean to make you think I was talking about finding opportunities that would lead me away from you. I've had a hell of a day, and I guess it's affected my ability to communicate properly."

As much as I wanted to take back all I'd said, I couldn't. Whether she intended to stay or not was on her. All that mattered was that she now knew where I stood. It hadn't been meant as a threat to keep her from leaving, but more of a promise that I'd be here waiting in the event fear chased her away.

Rather than say anything, I closed the gap between us, took her face in my hands, and covered her mouth with mine, saying everything I needed to with my lips and tongue—minus the words.

We'd figure this out.

I had to believe we would.

21

MERCY

I seriously began to wonder if my life would ever go back to being uncomplicated.

Doubtful.

Ever since getting on that plane to surprise Jordan, nothing had been simple. I wound up married to a stranger, had my relationship status broadcasted all over the internet, and lost my job before I had even started. However, the most impressive part was that this all took place in less than sixty days.

At this point, I wouldn't be greedy; I'd take *less* complicated.

And to make matters worse, Brogan had invited me along to take part in their pre-filming ritual. Otherwise known as going to a bar and drinking the night before production started. While I'd done this sort of thing with him before—joining him for trivia and drinks with a few of his friends—tonight was different. It felt a bit like I was intruding. After all, I had no clue what it was like to have cameras in my face while I tried to work or carry on conversations with friends.

So, while they all chatted among themselves about previous seasons and their thoughts on most of the production crew, I sat there in silence. Even though I'd seen the show, there wasn't much I could comment on, since very little of what they talked about had made it past editing. And what I'd found to be interesting nearly two hours ago, now made me feel like an outcast.

Indi came up beside me and took the vacant chair to my left. At least she didn't come emptyhanded. Even if the shot glass she set in front of me seemed more like a peace offering than a kind gesture, it was better than nothing.

"If you can make it through the next six weeks, you're as good as gold, girl," she said before holding up her tiny glass between us. Apparently, that had been meant as a toast, not a few words of wisdom imparted to me by my husband's old lover.

It could've also been a passive-aggressive threat.

Knowing where my mind was at, and realizing the guys didn't seem anywhere close to being ready to call it a night, I didn't hesitate before lifting my glass, tapping it against the rim of Indi's, and shooting it back.

Tequila.

It'd given me yet another reason to be thankful I didn't have to worry about a camera crew following me around tomorrow. Honestly, I had no idea how these guys—or Indi—would get out of bed in the morning, let alone function enough to offer anything of use to the show.

"Wrong told me about your job." If this was her version of small talk, then either I'd been lied to my whole life, or no one had taught her the art of idle chitchat.

"That was nice of him."

"It wasn't like that," she said with a hand on my arm. "He only mentioned it to see if I had any pull with the schools in this area. My aunt used to teach at Lincoln High, so he thought she might be able to suggest something."

I glanced around the table to make sure I didn't keep anyone's attention. Then I faced her once more and decided to ask what had been playing on my mind for a while. "Are you in love with Brogan?"

Alcohol had a tendency to shut down the filter between my brain and my mouth.

Shock ran across her face for a split second, then a smile formed on her lips. "No, Mercy. I'm not. He told me you've thought that before, but I swear, you have nothing to worry about."

"I just don't understand why you'd stick around while he…*did what he did* with other women if you aren't in love with him. Or why you'd keep it going for so long. And I've seen the way you look at him—well, on the show, I mean."

She took a deep breath and turned in her chair to face me. "I care about him a lot. That's no secret. But my feelings don't come anywhere close to love. The only reason I *stuck around* was because of my situation."

I regarded her without speaking, hoping she'd offer the answers to the questions flittering about in my mind. The ones I didn't feel I had a right to ask no matter how much I had to drink.

"About a year before he and Jess split, I lost the love of my life in a motorcycle accident. And when Wrong left Jess, we both found ourselves in a very vulnerable situation, which was what led to us hooking up. I never cared that he was seeing other people. That wasn't what our relationship was, so it didn't bother me. I didn't want to seek comfort from others. Having one person to help me out from time to time was enough for me. And when he told me about you…I couldn't have been happier for him."

Needing a glimpse of Brogan, I glanced to the side and took him in. I could see why she would've been happy finding comfort in him without needing to search elsewhere. But at the same time, I didn't understand why he hadn't simply told me that when I'd questioned it from the start.

"Whatever's going through your mind right now, Mercy, please don't think he told me about your job for any other reason than to help. You're his entire world." *Says a woman who knows my husband intimately.*

I shook off that thought, refusing to obsess over a relationship I didn't understand and couldn't change—even if I'd wanted to. Indi wasn't a bad person, so I hated it when I naturally fell into this jealous role. Especially when I wasn't a jealous person.

"Let me guess...your aunt couldn't help." I quickly grabbed an abandoned drink from the center of the table, not at all caring whose it was. Even though I didn't need more alcohol, it was the closest thing I could find that might keep my mouth occupied so I didn't continue to obsess over the things she and Brogan had done with one another.

I wasn't sure what was in the drink, but it tasted like tea.

There was a very small chance that's what it was, but I didn't care.

"Unfortunately. She retired close to ten years ago, and most of the staff she worked with back then are all gone. Not to mention, Wrong said you can't teach in public schools until you take the state tests, so even if she did have active connections, they wouldn't be of much use."

This entire situation concerned me, except I couldn't pinpoint why. Yes, it bothered me that Brogan had discussed my personal business with the woman he used to sleep with, although I wasn't convinced that was the cause for my concern.

Rather than continue to question it, I swallowed another gulp of whatever this concoction was and said, "It's all right. Thanks for the help. I'm sure I can figure something out, and if I can't, it's not the end of the world."

"How can you be so calm about this? If my ex obliterated my whole world, I'd be livid."

I stared at her for a moment, ignoring the slight blur of her features while analyzing what she'd said. Because I had to have heard her wrong. "He might've messed up the shop, but he can't be blamed for this. They chose to let me go because of the inappropriate attention Brogan's show would bring to the school by employing me."

Indi's head slowly bobbed up and down—the kind of nod that implied she was thinking rather than responding to anything. "Oh, I'm sorry. I guess I assumed he was behind both."

"No. He might be mad at me, but he'd never put my job in jeopardy. I'm sure he holds enough guilt over what he did to the shop to keep him from causing any more problems. And if he does, he knows Brogan won't be nice the next time."

Again, she nodded, but rather than continue the conversation, she blinked a few times and pulled herself out of the chair. "Listen, I'm going to run to the bar for another drink; would you like something?"

I did, but my thoughts were going too fast to do anything other than shake my head. And as I watched her walk away from the table, my paranoia spiked. She knew something but didn't say it. Which only made me wonder *what* she knew and *why* she hadn't told me.

Between the liquor that sloshed inside my head and the confusion that left me impaired—maybe that was also the alcohol, but that was neither here nor there—I couldn't concentrate hard enough on what we had talked about to even consider what she could've been keeping from me. Jordan, my job, Brogan, his shop…there was a chance we'd discussed something else, but I couldn't remember what it was.

Regardless, whatever had sent her running to the bar must've been bad.

And I needed to know.

So, I pulled myself to my feet and followed Color-by-Numbers Barbie for answers. I focused on the back of her head as I put one foot in front of the other to keep myself from falling on my face in front of everyone. While I'd had a lot to drink, the assumption that Indi was keeping something from me—and what it could be—had weakened my knees. The combination was disastrous, though not enough to stop me from going after her.

When I sidled up next to Indi, she turned her head, noticed me, and offered a gentle smile, soft enough to make me question if I'd fabricated her secretive demeanor from a moment ago. "I told you I'd get you something if you wanted it. You didn't have to leave the group."

"What aren't you telling me?" While the words sounded harsh, my desperate tone set the record straight. It left no doubt to my state of mind.

"Nothing. Why would you think that?"

"Because you got all weird when we were talking, and then you quickly left."

Her smile would've fooled me had I not recognized it as fake—not as wide or flashy, the kind of expression a person gave when playing a part. "Oh, no. I just didn't realize your ex was the one who'd broken into the shop."

I hesitated, because I could've sworn she had been the one who brought him up in the first place. Then again, she'd had me so twisted around I no longer knew my right from my left. My brow pinched, burned with the strain of my narrowed concentration, when I asked, "Brogan didn't tell you?"

"No, and now, I wish he would have. It might've made this less awkward."

"Made *what* less awkward?"

"Never mind. If Wrong hasn't mentioned it, then it's not my place to."

The room began to spin as I fought to collect myself without falling over. "Tell me, Indi. Please. If you know something, just tell me."

She huffed after accepting the drink from the bartender. But before offering me an explanation, she took advantage of the cold glass in her hand and gulped a third of its contents down. "The person your ex was cheating on you with is my sister. That's how I was able to recognize him from the security feed.

I'm the one who told Wrong his name. He never explained to me that he was *also* your ex."

There was so much to say. So much to ask. Yet the only thing I managed to utter was, "Y-your *sister*?"

"Yeah, but listen, I can guarantee she didn't know about you. She might be a bit of a free spirit, but she'd *never* be with another woman's man." The pity that stared back at me made me sick to my stomach. "Wrong had told me that you caught your ex with someone else the night you guys met. Well, that was my sister. I was with her that night, and then he showed up —your ex. I had called Wrong for a ride, which was why he was there. I didn't connect the dots until a few minutes ago when you said he's the one who broke into the shop."

I was speechless, but I wasn't sure if it was due to the shocking news or the bile that ate away at the base of my throat. Then my lip began to quiver. If I didn't get ahold on my emotions, I'd never be able to show my face in this bar again— not that I would've cared. But I didn't wish to be forever known as the woman who cried while vomiting on herself, incoherently mumbling things like "there's no place like home."

Indi hadn't let me take more than two steps toward the bathroom before hooking her arm with mine to escort me away from the crowd. She made it hard to hate her. And by the time she had me in front of the sink in the large, handicap stall of the ladies' room, I kind of wanted her to be my best friend.

"Nothing is making sense right now," I muttered while letting her pat my forehead with a damp paper towel. "If you didn't know that Jordan was the one who trashed the shop, then how can you be so sure he was cheating on me with your sister?"

Her ministrations stopped for a moment. But when I peered at her through the mirror, she quickly shook it off, playing off the hesitation as needing to rewet the paper towel. "I'm the one who recognized him on the CCTV footage as being the guy my sister was seeing for a couple of months not too long ago."

I had to force myself to refrain from mental calculations of time so I could focus on what she had to say.

"I'd been around him on a few occasions, but I mostly remember him from the night you and Wrong met, because she had ditched me for him, and it ended up causing a huge fight between us. I know that was the same night Wrong found you outside the club, because he had originally told me he'd come get me and later sent a text saying he couldn't. I found out a few days after that it was because he'd met someone. That someone being you."

The night was so clear in my head—but not the way most memories were. I'd had a lot to drink by the time I'd stumbled outside, and while Brogan's presence on that sidewalk had been sobering, it hadn't reversed the effects of the alcohol I'd consumed. However, when I replayed the events in my mind, turning around and finding him standing there in jeans and a white T-shirt, there was no haze around the memory. It was as if that was the moment I'd woken up from a coma I hadn't known I'd been in.

"Then why did you bring Jordan up? At the table...you suggested he was the reason I lost my job. If you didn't know he was the one who broke into Wrong Inc, why assume he had anything to do with the school situation?"

"Wrong explained the reasons behind their decision to let you go, and since this all happened a week or so after the news broke that you two had gotten married, I naturally assumed that had been the catalyst. Without the internet buzzing with gossip about you, I doubt the school would've ever known and, therefore, wouldn't have had a reason to fire you before giving you a chance to prove yourself."

I turned to the side to see her without having to look at her reflection while we spoke. "Okay, but again, how does that go back to Jordan? You just said yourself that the most logical conclusion would be the school saw the news online. Where does Jordan come into any of that?"

Her brows drew together, creating a valley of concern between them. And the more she narrowed her eyes, staring relentlessly at me, the darker they became. "I guess I don't see how you can't blame him—considering he's the one who sold the story."

My heart stopped.

My throat pinched closed.

And my brain checked out like a worker at the end of their shift.

"He... He did *what*?" I wanted to call her a liar, accuse her of making this all up, yet I couldn't look her in the eyes and *not* trust everything she was saying. Not to mention, she had nothing to gain from making me believe these things.

Indi dropped her chin to her chest with a groan and clenched the damp paper towel in her fist. After tossing it into the wastebasket, she pressed her back against the tile wall, shoulders slumped. Resignation flashed in her eyes as she stared at me. And with the way her thick swallow made her throat bob, I imagined that she was discovering the taste of her foot in her mouth.

We might've been standing in a restroom stall, but the distance between us could very well have been the size of Texas. Neither of us spoke, only regarded the other with undeclared pleas—mine begged her to give me answers, while hers implored me to give this up.

Finally, she caved first—likely due to the fact that alcohol had fried the wires that connected my brain to my mouth, preventing me from forming words in a timely manner. Whatever the reason, I didn't care, because in the end, I got what I wanted.

At least, what I had *thought* I wanted.

"Wrong had asked me for my help to see if any of the guys at work had been responsible for the leak. He said there were pieces of information in the articles that no one could've guessed, and he worried someone at the shop had sold him down the river. Considering I work with these guys as well, I wanted the truth as much as he did—only for different reasons. The thought of working side by side with someone willing to sell their soul for the almighty dollar made me uncomfortable, so I started digging."

I licked my chapped lips, suddenly realizing the invisible cotton that filled my mouth had left my throat dry and voice hoarse. "But if Jordan was the one who pushed the news, then how'd you find out? He doesn't work for Brogan."

"Once I felt confident that it hadn't been anyone from the shop, I couldn't let it go. By that point, I was far too interested in uncovering the truth to drop it. A friend of mine—more like a client I speak to once a year when she comes in to have a new daisy added to her back piece—works at the local news station. They don't run the same types of stories as those trash sites, but I figured it was worth a shot to see what she could find out. Without getting a name, she managed to get enough to piece together that the source was someone close to you—who lived in town."

"That still doesn't prove it was Jordan."

"No, it doesn't. So I called Wrong, told him what I'd learned, and he handled the rest. When I asked him about it this morning, all he said was that he'd confirmed it was your ex. We didn't get a chance to discuss it in detail, so that's pretty much all I know."

My heart thumped wildly, the intensity of each beat increasing at a dangerous rate. I had no way of making it slow. It grew worse with every new piece of information, but I couldn't stop until I had all the missing pieces of a puzzle I had no idea existed in the first place. "When did all this happen? Hearing from your friend and calling Brogan with the information."

"I called her at the beginning of the week. She finally got back with me yesterday, and as soon as I got off the phone with her, I got ahold of Wrong. It was early afternoon. Right after everything that happened at the school—that's when he talked to me about it." It was obvious she wasn't overly comfortable with our bonding time in the ladies' room. The pity on her face said it all.

"Thanks, Indi. I appreciate your honesty."

With a weak smile, she said, "You're welcome. Just whatever you do, don't take this out on Wrong. Okay? If he hasn't said anything to you about it, there's a reason. It doesn't mean he intends to keep it from you forever. Give him the benefit of the doubt...please."

Nodding was about all I could do, because while I wanted to assure her that I'd sit back and wait for him to fill me in, that wasn't something I could promise. With everything that had taken place over the last two weeks—one crisis after another—I wasn't sure how much more I could handle before the weight of it all crushed me.

Indi left the restroom to grab us both a drink from the bar. I had to freshen up, so we'd agreed to meet at the table when we were done. After blotting my face with a damp paper towel, I exited the restroom with my head held high.

That was...until I spotted our group around the table in the center of the room.

I didn't see Indi, which meant she was probably still waiting on our drinks. However, that wasn't what made me stop. That wasn't what caused my feet to turn to cinderblocks and cement themselves to the floor. No. My entire body came to a screeching halt when I noticed Brogan standing a few feet away from the table, talking intimately with a blonde.

He glanced around, as if searching for me, and when he didn't spot me, he placed his hand on her lower back and escorted her through the front door. It wasn't until they made it outside that I recognized who she was.

The one who got away.

22

BROGAN

I'd often wondered how I would feel if I ever saw Jessica again.

At times, I'd assumed it would bring back old feelings, or break my heart all over again. Other times, mostly since meeting Mercy, I questioned if I'd feel anything at all. Oddly enough, the emotions that hit me when I caught her walking toward me from across the bar had taken me by surprise.

"I must say, Jess...you were the last person I expected to run into tonight," I said as soon as we made it outside, away from the noise and drunken chatter.

Her smile hadn't changed. Hell, from the looks of it, nothing about her had changed since I'd last seen her. I realized it'd only been a couple of years, though that didn't mean I expected her to look exactly the same as when we were married.

"Any particular reason you're here?" Standing in front of me. At the bar around the corner from my shop. In town. She had her pick of which *here* she wanted to answer. At this point, an explanation as to why she was in the state would've sufficed.

She tilted her head to the side and gave me the same smirk she'd always used when trying to be cute, though for the first time, it felt friendly. "Lena's getting married tomorrow, so I flew in for the wedding."

Lena was Jessica's childhood best friend—who had acted like I didn't exist after the divorce.

"I saw you took the plunge again?" She studied me with deep interest as I nodded in response. "That makes me happy, Brogan. I was convinced you'd never put yourself out there again, so to hear you ran off and got married was a very pleasant surprise."

"That means a lot, Jess. Thank you."

"Well, I mean it. You deserve to be happy."

Unsure of how to react, I stuffed my hands into my pockets and hoped she didn't notice how uncomfortable I was. "So did you just happen to walk into the bar and spot me? Or is there some other reason you're here?"

"To be honest, I wanted to see you while I was in town. Things between us fell apart so quickly and ended so badly that I thought now might be a good time for us both to gain a little bit of closure. I don't know about you, but I've harbored a lot of emotions over the years in regard to you, our marriage, and my part in how it ended. I never thought we'd have the opportunity to heal from it all...until I heard your good news."

"I won't lie, Jess...I have mixed feelings about this. Not about gaining closure or seeing you. But about being out here with you while my wife's inside. It feels like I've snuck off to see you behind her back. I'd love to put our past to rest, but not like this." Just the thought of Mercy looking for me while I stood outside with my ex-wife left my stomach in knots.

Her brows arched high, surprise widening her eyes. "Oh, shit. I'm sorry, Brogan. That's not how I—"

"I know, Jessica. I don't have a problem clearing the air with you, just not without her knowing about it. She doesn't deserve that. If you don't mind waiting a minute or two, I can let her know what's going on and come back. But if she wants to be here while we talk, I won't deny her that. And while I realize that might be uncomfortable for you, it's her comfort that's my priority."

Her lips spread into an unexpected show of happiness. "Of course, Brogan. And if she wants to be involved in this, I don't really have any say in it, do I? In all fairness, I called Drew when I spotted your Jeep. I asked him if he would mind if I stopped and tried to have a conversation with you. So I get it. It wouldn't be right that I'd let my husband know yet expect you to keep it from your wife."

I nearly choked. "Husband? Wow…I didn't know you were remarried. Congrats."

It wasn't the news of her being married to someone else that I found the most surprising, considering she'd always been the wife type. What came as more of a shock was how I'd managed to never know. Granted, she'd cut all ties with me when she left, but with all the people in town who knew her, I assumed I would've at least heard about it.

The door opened behind me, interrupting our conversation. And when I glanced over my shoulder, the sight of Indi's frantic eyes flicking between Jess and me left my breath stale in my lungs. To make matters worse, the panic written on her face didn't appear to have been caused by the sight of us…but rather the cause of her coming out here in the first place.

Ignoring Jessica's presence, she locked eyes with me and said, "Mercy's sick."

The world around me might've stopped moving, but my feet didn't skip a beat. I was at the open door, in front of Indi, before I even realized I'd left Jessica behind. Without turning around—not interested in wasting the time—I peered over my shoulder and said, "I'm sorry, Jess."

"Don't apologize. Go. We can finish this another time; I'll be here all weekend."

Not another word was spoken. I nodded at my ex, and then I pushed Indi inside, silently begging her to take me to Mercy. With as worried as she appeared when she found me outside, my mind instantly went to everything that could've happened…starting with the worst possible scenario.

"What's she doing here?" Indi asked with wide eyes, not moving fast enough from the entrance to the bar.

"It's not important. Where's Mercy? What happened? What's wrong with her?"

She hitched her thumb over her shoulder in the direction of the restrooms, but before I took off to find my wife, Indi touched my arm, preventing me from leaving. "I'm sorry, Wrong. I think I might've made everything worse for you."

Now, I was torn between getting to Mercy and finding out what she meant by that. "What'd you do?"

"You never told me that Jordan was her ex. And you never told her about him and my sister—or that you discovered he was the one who'd leaked your relationship to the press." She took a deep breath, probably to calm down. Meanwhile, my heart rate skyrocketed. With a softer tone, she continued. "It came up in conversation, and by the time I realized she didn't know anything, it was too late. I never meant to say anything. Had I known you hadn't told her about any of it, I never would've brought it up."

"We can talk about this later. Right now, I *need* to find Mercy."

That got Indi moving, leading me toward the ladies' room in the back. "She had a lot to drink, and I think her emotional state after our conversation might've made it worse. We were supposed to meet back at the table, but after I grabbed us drinks from the bar and realized she hadn't come out yet, I went looking for her."

She pushed open the door, and I walked in, disregarding the stares and gasps coming from the other women in the small room. They could've been naked, and I wouldn't have noticed. Because I didn't pay them a single bit of attention. The second I recognized Mercy's feet beneath the stall door, nothing and no one else mattered.

"Mercy...babe, open up," I pleaded while bumping the side of my fist against the door. The longer it took for her to disengage the latch, the more impatient my knocks became. And the more demanding my voice grew. If I had to tear the door off its hinges to get to her, then so be it.

Luckily, I didn't have to. Eventually, she slid the lock to the side, and the door swung open. Before me stood a weak, heavily intoxicated version of my wife. While I'd seen her drunk before—hell, she was drunk when I first met her—I'd never witnessed her in this bad of a shape.

"Come on, babe. Let's get you home." I wrapped my arm around her to help keep her steady. As much as I wanted to pick her up and carry her out of this place, I knew she'd never let me. If anything, that would only make things worse.

To my surprise, she clung to me. Both arms around my waist. Hands fisted in my shirt. Then she pressed the side of her face against my chest, leaning against me for support. It was enough to prove that no matter what Indi had told her, she still trusted me.

With a little help from Indi, I managed to get Mercy buckled into the Jeep. But before I could walk around to get in myself, a hand on my chest and a concerned voice halted my exit. "Why was Jessica here?"

Meeting my friend's gaze in the light from the parking lot, I lowered my voice to keep Mercy from hearing—if she was even awake enough to comprehend anything—and said, "She saw my Jeep and stopped in to congratulate me. After all this time, I think we're ready to find peace with what happened and close that chapter of our lives."

Indi nodded, though she didn't seem completely convinced. "Are you going to tell Mercy?"

"Listen, I appreciate your concern where Mercy's involved, but just know that I've never intended to keep *anything* from my wife. I planned to tell her about Jordan when the time was right. The last thing I wanted to do was make her question my motives. But to ease your mind, yes...I'll tell her about Jess showing up. Not tonight, clearly." I pointed to the Wrangler to indicate Mercy's state of mind. "But the first chance I have to sit down and explain it all, I will."

That seemed to be enough for her. And the fact that she seemed so concerned for Mercy was enough for me. With a simple nod and tight grin, she stepped out of my way so I could take my wife home. To our bed. Where I'd hold her all night while she slept off the alcohol and battered emotions.

When I slid in behind the steering wheel, I glanced at Mercy, who leaned against the door with her head resting against the window. Her eyes were closed, though I could tell from her breathing that she wasn't asleep. If anything, she was in that stage of intoxication where she was semi-conscious, yet the rest of her was comatose. So I placed my hand on her thigh and took a moment to appreciate her, even if she wasn't aware of it.

The desire to tell her how much I loved her came over me out of nowhere. Like a tsunami. Sweeping me away. Pulling me under. Drowning me in the need to let her know how I felt. We might've done everything completely backward, but sitting there with my hand on her leg, her warmth radiating through her jeans against my palm, I realized I'd always known how I felt about her.

But this wasn't the time to give her those words. Not while she was drunk or half asleep. Not outside of a bar. Not on the night my ex-wife showed up, or shortly after she'd learned of the things I'd kept from her. There was a time and a place to tell her how much I love her. To *show* her how much I meant it.

And that time wasn't now.

As much as I wanted to sit in this parking lot all night watching her, I had to get her to bed. So, I pulled my hand away to shift the Jeep into gear and headed home, spending the entire drive contemplating when I'd fallen in love with her.

But it wasn't until I had her in bed next to me, her back to my chest, my arm around her waist, that I finally understood. I hadn't *fallen* in love with her. Somehow, I'd always *been* in love with her.

I'd known from the very first time I laid eyes on her that she was different. It was more than a feeling. It was an instinct. Just like I knew the grass was green. The sky was blue. The earth was a sphere and rotated around the sun. Mercy was *my* one and only.

My once in a lifetime.

Lying with Mercy in my arms, I thought back to that first night. When I found her on the sidewalk outside Rulebreakers. And I finally understood what I had felt in that moment. The moment when my soul recognized hers and declared: *there you are; I've been looking everywhere for you.*

I'd decided right then and there that, come tomorrow, after we wrapped up our first day of filming, I would share all of this with her. She'd asked numerous times if I loved her, and while I had never denied it, I hadn't been able to admit it, either. I knew in my gut that she was it for me, the only one I'd ever want. Now I understood where that instinct had been rooted.

In my soul.

In my heart.

I loved Mercy Wright.

———

Morning came too early.

I didn't want to get out of bed for *many* reasons. The biggest being Mercy. Seeing her curled up beneath the covers, occasionally groaning at the light as she turned from side to side, made it difficult to get dressed. All I wanted to do was crawl back in bed and help her through this hangover. In the end, I waited until the last possible second to leave, and then kissed her forehead before heading to the shop to get this day over with.

"Does this mean everything's good with you guys?" Indi asked while cleaning up the new tattoo she'd given me. "I assumed she would've been too drunk last night to hold a coherent conversation."

Staring at the fresh ink, I smiled. "Nah. We haven't talked yet. She passed out as soon as I got her in bed, and I let her sleep in this morning. I'm hoping she won't be as hung over when I get home. Either way, I'm definitely going to talk to her after work today."

"So she has no idea you were doing this? What if she hates it?"

"No. She has no clue, and she won't hate it." I coated the small patch of raw skin with ointment before going to the closed door of Indi's studio space. "Thanks again for last night—for coming to get me, I mean."

"How about you hold off on thanking me until after you've talked to her about the beans I spilled in the bathroom of a bar." Her laughter filled the room. "No one can say we're not a classy group of people."

With a smile and jumping shoulders, I shook my head and walked out, leaving Indi and her laughter behind. I should've known a camera would be waiting for me on the other side of the door, especially since I hadn't allowed them in the room while Indi branded me with Mercy's name. I figured that was a private moment I didn't want to be shared with the world. And even though they complied, it didn't mean they wouldn't do everything they could to capture something.

I shoved past the cameraman and headed to the front desk. That was where most of the show was filmed—open space, more room to move around, and it was near the front door. Perfect place to catch all the drama they organized.

However, as I made it to the desk, the last person I ever expected to see in the shop pushed through the front door. My first thought was that production had somehow set this up. But with the way they scrambled at the sight of her, as well as her large, surprised eyes, I realized that wasn't the case.

Thirty seconds after permanently marking my left ring finger with my future, my past showed up. Again. In the very shop she wanted nothing to do with. Standing next to the man she'd left it all behind for.

The motherfucking irony.

"Oh, I'm sorry. I didn't realize they were shooting today." She shook her head while an impish grin played on her lips. "That was about the stupidest thing I could've said. I have no idea what your schedule looks like anymore. I guess it's been so long since I've paid any attention to the show, I wasn't thinking about this side of your job."

"That's okay. Did you want to go in the back and talk?"

She glanced at her husband, who wore a nice suit, and shrugged.

I led her to the supply closet in the back while she followed. Along the way, I glared at the cameramen, warning them to keep their distance. I knew it would be too much to ask that they not use any of this in the show, but as long as they gave me privacy, I couldn't complain. Luckily, Indi noticed what was going on and gave me a short nod, assuring me that she would make sure they kept their distance.

"Is your husband not coming?" I asked, realizing she had come alone as I held the door open for her to pass.

Jessica moved across the room to stand in front of the light-box, and as soon as I closed the door, she said, "We're on our way to the wedding, so we don't have a lot of time. I just wanted to finish our conversation from last night. He knows this is something I have to do on my own."

I leaned against the door with my shoulder, forcing myself not to cross my arms. The last thing I wanted was to come across as closed off. This conversation was long overdue, and the only way we could get through it without leaving anything behind was by being as open and honest as possible.

"Listen, Brogan…" For years, she had been the only one who used my real name. Yet now, it seemed *wrong*. As if it belonged to Mercy, and hearing anyone else use it—including Jessica—

made it feel like a betrayal. But I didn't say anything and let her continue. "I never meant to hurt you. I never went looking for anyone when I found Drew. He came out of nowhere, just like my feelings for him. I need you to know that."

Oddly enough, I understood that more than she would ever know. "It worked out for the best. For both of us. So really, you don't have anything to explain. I get it."

"I never thought I'd hear you say that." Her lips curled, causing her cheeks to grow rounder.

Now was the time to get everything out in the open. Put all our cards on the table. So, I took a deep breath and went for it. "I'm a firm believer that everything happens for a reason. You know that about me. That doesn't mean it's always easy to accept—especially when it hurts. We were good together. I loved you with my whole heart and wanted to spend forever with you. Your thing with Drew seemed to come out of nowhere, which is what hurt so bad. I was confused why you'd go to a complete stranger for support, rather than turning to me."

"That's just it, Brogan. I *did* go to you. About a lot of it. But you were so busy with the shop and the show that it was like you didn't hear me. Or you didn't have enough time to give. At the beginning, I was actually talking to you both about the same things...and it was his support and understanding that made it easier to talk to him instead of you."

I'd expected this to hurt more than it did. So it surprised me when I didn't feel anything other than understanding and relief. I paid attention to everything she said, hoping I could prevent the same thing from happening again, only this time, with Mercy. Because I couldn't lose her.

"I wish I could explain what it was about him—what it *is* about him. I did love you, and I still do. But I've learned that love isn't always enough."

"Jess...it's okay. I get it. Trust me. I've thought a lot about this ever since I met Mercy. You were a ten. Perfect in every way. I never thought there was anyone else out there better suited for me. Anyone I could love more than I loved you. Then Mercy came along. She's my eleven." Just thinking of her made me smile. "It helped me see that, while you were perfect, she's my match. It's taken meeting Mercy to understand everything you tried to tell me back then."

I could practically hear her words from two years ago, as if she spoke them now. *This was never about you. I didn't fall in love with Drew because I fell out of love with you. And it doesn't mean I feel any less for you now than I did before I met him. I know this is hard to hear, because it's probably one of the hardest things I've ever had to say, but he's taught me that there's more. I didn't realize I wanted more until it was too late, and by then, it began to feel like staying here would be settling. I can't explain it. It's just a feeling. And one of these days, you'll find someone who makes you feel this way, too.*

At the time, I'd dismissed her claims. Called her a cheater and a liar. Argued her every point just to prove how selfish she was. If she wasn't happy, then she should've left *before* finding someone else. It didn't matter that they had never been intimate. I didn't care that he had never touched her. My wife had committed adultery. Emotional cheating was still cheating, and I had refused to look past that.

Now, after finding the very thing she had tried to explain, I was able to see things differently. She hadn't planned to meet Drew. But she did. And from everything she'd told me back then, he was nothing more than a friend. A stranger willing to listen. Willing to offer an unbiased opinion—which apparently, had often been in my defense. It wasn't that she was unhappy, just lonely. And by the time she realized how she felt about him, it was too late. She'd already fallen in love with him.

"I know you didn't believe me at the time, but I swear to you, I had told him that I couldn't speak to him anymore. I was married, and carrying on a relationship of *any* kind with someone I had feelings for was unfair to you."

For whatever reason, I believed her now. Maybe it was because she had no reason to lie, whereas before, I thought she'd only said that so she wouldn't look as guilty. But now, I actually believed that she had been telling the truth all along.

"I had no intention of leaving you for him or continuing to talk to him. I had ended things with Drew, because I'd vowed to be with you. That's when you noticed a change in me. I was heartbroken, more than I ever thought possible. Which is how you ended up finding out about him. I know it doesn't matter now, but I needed you to know that." Her pleading eyes held my attention until all the doubt I'd held on to over the years had vanished.

"I believe you, Jess. The whole thing hurt. I can't lie about that. But the one thing I can say is that if you never did that, if I had never found out and practically pushed you into his arms, then I never would've met Mercy. Fate works in mysterious ways, and I think a lot of times, it pops up at the most inopportune time. Like it's testing us or something. Seeing how badly we want it." I shrugged and added, "We could've worked things out and been perfectly happy. Nothing wrong with that. But if that was the path we chose, then neither of us would've had...*this*. You made me happy, Jess. But Mercy makes me excited. You made me smile, but she makes me giddy as fuck."

Her grin started slow, but eventually, it took over her entire face. "You have no idea how happy I am for you. I'd hoped and prayed that, in the end, we would *both* be in good places. Better places than we had been in together. And while none of this excuses my betrayal, it is a good feeling to know it all worked out for the best."

"I guess it's true what they say, huh? You only need to wait for the sun to shine after a storm to see the purpose in the rain." That was one of Nonna's favorite quotes, and reciting it now made it feel like she was here with us.

Jess moved closer. "If I may give you a little word of advice...don't let all this"—she circled her hand in the air, meaning the shop and the show—"get in the way of what you have with her. Unless you've lowered your standards for women, I'm willing to bet none of this means anything to her, and quite possibly, intimidates her. And if she's telling you how she feels about *anything*, listen. Don't try to change her mind or make her see things your way. Just listen."

As much as I hated to admit it, I appreciated her concern. "Thanks, Jess."

Hugging her had to be the most surreal moment of the whole thing. It felt natural, calming, without any of the emotion I'd ever felt for her. While I still loved her on some level, and always would, having her in my arms again seemed no different than hugging Indi. Except, this embrace held an air of finality to it.

It was our way of putting our past to rest.

I glanced at my left ring finger. At my future. And I felt at peace.

That was enough to carry me through the rest of the day. When filming wrapped, I didn't stay late. Their time was up, so I grabbed my things and left the shop. If the others wanted to hang around and film their downtime, that was on them.

I had a woman to get home to.

I'd sent Mercy a few texts throughout the day, but she hadn't responded to the last one—which had been shortly after two in the afternoon. I assumed she had fallen back to sleep or possibly been in the shower. So I sent her another message after I left the shop, to see if she needed me to grab anything on the way home.

Her silence was deafening.

It was also a premonition.

One I should've paid attention to.

Because as I pulled down the drive and opened the garage door, her car wasn't there. And when I walked inside, the house was empty. However, nothing was worse than when I ran into our room and found that her drawers had been emptied. Her side of the sink sat bare. Hangers hung lifelessly from one half of the closet.

Meanwhile, I dropped to the edge of the mattress feeling it all.

Empty.

Bare.

Lifeless.

Without a word. Without a sound. Mercy had left. She'd taken my heart. My soul. My *everything*…and ran. And I'd promised that I wouldn't chase after her. I'd wait for her to return. So that was what I had to do.

Wait.

23

MERCY

I'd made it nearly four hours into my ten-hour drive before Brogan called the first time. I should've answered, but considering it was hard enough to hold back my emotions as it was, talking to him would've only made it worse. I needed to get to Ohio, get to Stella, before I could brave a conversation with him.

He didn't deserve to be left like that. I realized that, but I knew if I stayed and talked to him face to face, he never would've let me go. And in all honesty, I didn't want him to let me go. However, this was the only way for us to know for sure if we belonged together. My only hope was that he'd agree so that we could see where we ended up.

I finally made it to Stella's apartment at two in the morning. After a long hug, we both climbed into bed, where I cried until the sun came up, and she pretended not to notice while gently rubbing my back from time to time.

"Are you ever going to tell me what happened?" She set a cup of coffee on the nightstand before perching herself on the side of the bed.

I pushed up until I sat with my back against the headboard, a pillow against my chest, and a hot mug in my hand. "I don't even know what happened, Stella. That's just it. Over the last two weeks, it's been one thing after another, and I guess I needed to get away before anything else fell apart. I believe we can still come back from this...but if one more thing had gone wrong, it would've been the absolute end of us."

"Let me get this straight." Stella tucked her legs beneath her, looking every bit the yoga goddess she was. "You *left* him because you want to stay with him? Surely you can see how confusing that is."

I huffed and dropped my head back, the impact of my skull against the headboard resulting in a resounding thud. "It's not if you take into consideration all I've lost over the last several weeks. My dignity, thanks to the media running my name through the mud. My job, because, apparently, being the *wife* of a reality TV star is frowned upon. My parents barely speak to me anymore. Anyone I've met through Jordan—be it his family or friends—whom I actually cared for want nothing to do with me. And to top it all off, it turns out that the one person who was supposed to have my back has been keeping things from me."

"I haven't kept anything from you," she argued with a straight face.

"Not you. Brogan."

"Well, you said *the one person*...so I wanted to point out that I've had your back this whole time."

"Fine. One of two people. Better?"

"For now." She shrugged, somehow not breaking a smile. "Carry on."

I fiddled with the mug in my hand, enjoying the warmth it offered through the ceramic walls. "His ex-wife showed up Friday night. We were all hanging out—some tradition they have for the night before filming starts—and when I came out of the bathroom, I caught them walking outside. I waited and waited for him to say something to me about it, but he never did."

"Did you ask?"

I met her stare and shook my head. "I shouldn't have to."

"You can't be upset with him if you don't even know what happened."

"So I shouldn't be upset with Jordan for not telling me about the woman he was seeing behind my back because I didn't ask if he was cheating on me?" I waited for her response, though it was obvious she didn't have a retort for that. "The point is… he's kept a lot from me lately. Maybe he has his reasons. Maybe he doesn't. Even so, there's a reason he didn't tell me."

"Which may very well be a completely logical one."

"You're absolutely right. It could be. But it's not my job to ask him why he's keeping secrets. He shouldn't be keeping them in the first place. First Jordan, now Brogan. And with Jessica coming back into the picture—"

"That's not fair. You don't know that she's back in the picture. Maybe they simply ran into each other, and a bar isn't the best place to have a conversation. Haven't you learned by now that you should never jump to conclusions?"

"Why not? That's what I did the night I saw Jordan at the club. Then he spun his web and convinced me I was wrong about what I saw. He had me so twisted up in it all that I started to think I was crazy. Somehow, he'd convinced me that I was mistaken until I questioned every memory from that night. And guess what, Stella? It turns out that the original conclusion I jumped to was right. So what lesson should I have learned?"

She rolled her eyes and blew out a huff of exasperation. "We're not talking about the douchebag right now. This is about Wrong and your inability to accept that maybe you overreacted."

"I barely know him."

"If that's not a total crock of steaming horseshit, then I don't know what is. But okay, sure…let's go with that for argument's sake. How can you be so sure his ex is back for him, or that he's keeping things from you with malicious intent, if you *barely* know him? You can't have it both ways; you can't say you're familiar with him enough to understand his motives while practically calling him a stranger in the next breath."

"News broke that he's married, and then his ex pops up out of nowhere." I didn't understand how she couldn't see this the way I did. "Ever since the internet decided to take interest in my relationship, Brogan's shop was destroyed, I lost my job, and now, his ex-wife is back. Why else would she be there?"

Stella shrugged, showing a complete lack of concern over my fears—rational or not. "Maybe she wanted to bring him a wedding present. Or maybe she ran into him in a public place and wanted to congratulate him in person."

I set the mug down and flung the covers off my legs. "You're not getting it, Stella. It doesn't matter what led them to meet up or why she was there. The problem is…she's *Jessica*. The one he and his buddies have always referred to as *the one who got away*. And if there's any chance of them working things out, I'd rather know that now instead of way on down the road when I have far more invested in the relationship."

"Are you seriously telling me that you left to give them a chance to work things out?"

"Not entirely."

"There's more?"

After slipping off the bed, I went to my backpack and pulled out a piece of paper. "When I woke up yesterday morning, I decided to do a little investigating. Basically, I cyberstalked Jordan until I found a picture on Instagram of him in a shirt just like the one he'd left at my house. The same one I saw him wearing the night I showed up to surprise him. You know…his whole reason why it couldn't have possibly been him with that girl."

"I don't understand. Why does it matter? I thought you already had confirmation that you were right. Why look for proof? And what the hell does this have to do with you leaving Brogan?"

This was the problem with being so emotional that I'd ended up giving Stella pieces of the whole story in no particular order, fully expecting to fill her in once I'd gotten to her apartment.

"I wanted to confront him—Jordan—but I knew I'd have to have evidence of some kind. So I found it. Then I called and gave him one last chance to come clean, which he didn't. While I had him on the phone, I sent him the picture I found, and after a lot of back and forth, he finally came clean. About *everything*."

I had her undivided attention now.

Emotions ate at me as I tried to explain. Anger burned in my chest while the pain of his betrayal stabbed the backs of my eyes.

"That girl wasn't the first one. Hell, I still don't know how many there were or when exactly it started. And the reason he has two identical shirts is because he couldn't remember what he did with the one I gave him. He thought he might've let someone wear it and never got it back, so he bought another one to keep me from asking where it was. I'm the one who told him he'd left it at my place, but before that, he thought some chick might've worn it home."

"Oh, Mercy…" Sympathy laced her eyes, which helped me pull myself together.

"Anyway, after I got off the phone with him, I went through Brogan's nightstand to get a tissue and found this." I handed her the notecard and then settled back against the headboard. I didn't need to read it, as I'd already memorized the lyrics. They crooned in my head with the sound of Brogan's voice.

Intensity builds,
The rolling thunder of ecstasy,
The pulsing cadence of fury,
The aching heartbeat of desire,
The roaring beat of lust,
Twisting, writhing in the lovers' dance
As I bared my all to Mercy

Stella finished reading the words—probably a few times with as long as it took her to put the paper down—and then lifted her gaze to my face. "I don't know what this means, Mercy. You gave it to me as if it's somehow supposed to explain why you ran off like a coward. From what I can tell, it's a love note. Not a Dear John letter."

"Listen to what he's saying. Ecstasy, desire, lust. He doesn't love me. It's clearly all about sex to him, and if that part of our relationship slows down or gets *boring*, who's to say I won't find him on a dance floor with another woman? Or worse…find them in bed together. We'll never last if we don't have real love for one another—a solid foundation to build a life on."

"Do you love him?"

I wiped a lone tear from my cheek, knowing it wouldn't be long before the flood of my heartache followed. "Yes. I've thought it for so long that I don't remember ever *not* loving him. It's like it was there the moment we met. Except, I haven't been able to admit it because *he* refuses to. It's like his avoidance of it has made me question if it's real, or if it's lust disguised as love."

"If you love him, why not just tell him? Maybe he feels the same as you, and he can't admit it for fear you're not there yet. Have you thought about that?" Stella had always been my go-to person in a crisis because she had a way of lightening any dark situation—albeit, she usually did so with humor rather than seriousness.

Damn her.

"Did you not read the card? What about those words gave you the impression he's in love with me but can't admit it out of fear of being rejected? He pretty much wrote a poetic porn scene." I wanted to swallow those words whole and pretend they had never been uttered. The thought of saying anything remotely negative about his lyrics made me feel like the biggest piece of shit on Earth, even if he never heard it.

"It's all about the interpretation, Best Friend. The one thing I know for sure is you can't expect to know how he feels if you aren't willing to give him the same."

"I can't say it first."

She sucked her teeth and rolled her eyes. "Are you twelve?"

"No. I'm in survival mode." I didn't know where that came from, but it was powerful enough to make me stop and think about it before offering more of an explanation. "Not only have I never felt this way about anyone before, I never imagined it was possible to. He scares me in ways that hurt to think about. But at the same time, he makes me so unbelievably happy—which terrifies me because that means he has the power to annihilate my heart. On one hand, the way I feel about him is the thing every girl searches for, and I've found. And on the other, it seems unhealthy in a very co-dependent way."

Stella put her hand on my knee and waited until I lifted my blurry vision to see her face. As she lovingly tried to clear the rivers of pain that drenched my cheeks, she said, "You left because you're scared he'll leave you first, and you know you wouldn't survive that. So, you pulled the plug before he could. I get it, Mercy. Trust me, I do. But if you love him even half as much as you say you do, then you owe it to yourself to talk to him."

She then grabbed my cell off the bedside table and handed it to me. Right before she left me alone in the room to do what I already knew I needed to, she offered a supportive hug and whispered encouragement. Then suddenly, I was alone.

And the loneliness was suffocating.

I tapped on his name and brought the phone to my ear while it rang. After several seconds, the line went silent. No more ringing. I wasn't sure if the call had been disconnected or if he'd picked up without saying anything. Rather than wait any longer, I croaked, "Hello?"

Then I heard the sigh. The broken, painful, crippling sigh of a man who'd lost everything. It once again released the flood of sorrow that threatened to leave me dry and empty. There was no way I could cry this much and still have enough tears to blind me.

"Why?" was all he could ask. His voice a scratchy, hollow pit of agony laced with pure and utter loss. Despite the rasp, it bellowed through the line and ripped me in half. Cut me to the bone. Where it embedded never-ending guilt into my marrow. "Is it because of what Indi told you at the bar?"

"No."

"Because I was going to tell you. I swear to you, Mercy. I never meant to keep it from you. There was so much going on, and I wanted to make sure that you chose to stay not because of what he'd done, but because you truly want to be with me. I never wanted you to question my motives for telling you the truth about Jordan."

My chest burned, as though his words had turned to acid as they touched my heart. "I understand that, Brogan. That's exactly why I left. I *need* to know that what we have is what we think it is."

"That doesn't make any sense. What does leaving me prove?"

"My heart had been freshly broken when we met. And while your heartache was a couple of years old, it was still fresh because you had never dealt with it. We ran off to get married on a whim. A spur-of-the-moment decision. Then Jordan pulled his stunt, begging me to go back to him. I need to know without a doubt that you didn't fight for me because the thought of losing another wife was too painful. I have to know that it was never a pride thing." My voice cracked, causing me to pause so I could collect my emotions long enough to get through this.

He took that second of silence and used it to his advantage. "I don't know how to prove that to you. Marrying you, wanting you to stay...none of that was done out of fear or selfishness. None of it was done for any reason other than you're *it* for me."

"If that's the case, then you don't have anything to worry about."

"Except for the fact you left!" His anger had spiked, which only made me cry harder.

"Listen, Brogan. Your show just started filming again. Focus on that. Get through that, and let me work through the chaos around me that has settled at my feet over the last several weeks. Right now, we've both had too much destruction surrounding us; let's sift through the debris and see where we are."

He was silent for a while, nothing but a low hum coming from his side of the call. Right before I spoke up to see if he was still on the line, he muttered, "Wading through the mess alone will only separate us more than we already are. We should be holding hands, helping each other every step of the way. Other-wise, we will never reach the end on the same side."

While I understood what he was saying, I had a hard time seeing past my own issues. "I guess we just have to trust that we will. And that when we make it out of the ruins, we will both be stronger for it. I don't want to be held up along the way. I want to make it to the other side, knowing I *can* do it on my own, so that when we have to weather another storm, I can lean on you and know I'm doing so because I trust you. Not because I'm too weak to stand on my own two feet. And I want you to know that I'm holding your hand along the way because I choose to...not because I'm dependent on you to save me."

His breathing hitched, amplifying his emotions.

And it nearly broke me.

"We've gone about everything in a jumbled order, Brogan. Even you can't deny that." I stared at the puddle of fallen tears on the pillow in my lap, watching it spread through the fabric. "We got married before we learned to trust the other. And we've been put through test after test ever since. I can't risk either of us waking up one morning and realizing that our bubble has popped. I need to know, before it's too late, that we aren't living in a realm of false hope."

"I guess that's where we differ then, huh? Because, you see, Mercy...I don't need to do this alone to realize anything. I'm one thousand percent certain that you're the other half of me, and it doesn't matter what storm comes our way, I want to face it *with* you. The universe can test us all it wants, because I have faith that we'll pass each and every time." His words might've been filled with certainty and positivity, but his tone reeked of defeat.

I hesitated, knowing nothing short of promising to get in my car and drive back would make this easier for him. Nothing would erase the pain and fear from his voice, other than my giving in. And I couldn't do that. "I'm happy that you're so confident. But this is what *I* need, Brogan."

"Seems you've already made up your mind."

No matter how badly I tried to rein it in, hold my emotions tight to my chest, and stuff down the frustration, it came out anyway. "I'm twenty-three. You're almost thirty with one marriage already under your belt. You've lived and learned. It's easier for you to trust your feelings and follow your gut. I'm not there yet. It's unfair of you to ask me to ignore the crippling fear that runs through me, simply because you don't feel the same. You've learned enough to believe in us. Allow me the same. That's all I'm asking."

"I'm not asking you to ignore anything," he argued calmly, possibly on the verge of giving up.

I took a moment and cleared my vision with the pillowcase. Then I took a deep breath, knowing I had to forge on and fight for myself if I ever planned to reach the place he was at. "I get that you don't like this. That this isn't the way you would choose to do things. But this is what *I* have to do, Brogan. I have to see this through. If not, then I will spend the rest of my life wondering."

"What is there to wonder about?"

While hearing him fight for me—for us—aided in my belief that we'd be okay at the end of this, there was a part of me that wished he'd concede and let us see this through. It was a comfort I reveled in, but at the same time, his insistence only made my decision harder to make.

"If fate really did put us together. Or if it was simply circumstance."

The silence between us stretched out, filled only with his concentrated breathing.

Finally, I decided to fill the void with the answers to the question I knew ran through his mind. "When you found me, I was utterly lost with nowhere to go—literally. I'd gone to town to stay with Jordan, whom I found on a dance floor with another woman. I had no car, no place to stay, and my luggage was at his house. You admitted that night that you look after Joe, a homeless man you have no connection to other than he lives on the streets of the town you live in. It's part of your nature to help those who need it."

"That's not why I offered you help that night."

"Maybe not. But it's certainly something I could spend the rest of my life wondering about, along with my true reason for accepting your offer. Did I do that because I didn't have any other option? Or was it because my heart knew something I hadn't realized yet? And less than a week later, we got married. Did I say yes because I was high on lust? Or was that fate, too?"

"Only you can answer these questions, Mercy." Frustration rolled in his deep baritone. Scratched in the grit between the syllables. While his desperation thundered in the silence that separated each thought, like a drummer in a hollow well. "But I don't know why you have to figure them out on your own. Why can't you find those answers with me?"

"It's the only way I'll know for sure. I figured that while you're busy filming the show, it made sense to do it now. This way, I can try to sort out a job—or at least narrow it down to which direction I want to look at—while you finish your obligations. Especially since those obligations have had such a difficult impact on our relationship." I tried to sound like I knew what I was talking about, but really, I'd dialed his number without a single idea as to what I'd say. And now, I just had to go with it. Open my mouth and see what came out.

"Any idea how long this will take?"

"No. It's best if we take this one day at a time."

Once again, the line went still. Then the harsh hitch of a sharp inhale rang in my ear, seconds before he said, "Okay. We'll do it your way. Just as long as you keep me informed with where your head's at along the way. I can't be left in the dark thinking you're coming back, only to find out at the end that you've decided this isn't the life you want."

It was my turn to remain quiet as I choked down an audible sob. The pain was almost too much to bear. Silent emotion poured out of me like a river barreling over the side of a cliff with no way to make it stop. I squeezed my eyes shut, lips pulled wide in a grimace I didn't allow many to witness, and gave my sorrow what it wanted—an outlet.

"You still there, Mercy?"

Finally, I dried my face, swallowed the knot in my throat, and muttered, "Yeah. I'm still here."

There was no way I'd managed to conceal the sound of my tears from my voice, but even if he had noticed it, he didn't say anything. Instead, he informed me that he had to get ready for work. It was obvious there was more he wanted to say, yet he chose to keep it to himself.

I had a solid reason to stay strong rather than run back to him right now. Not only for myself, but for him as well. I still wasn't sure why Jessica had returned, or what they'd spoken about. Hell, I had no idea if they'd seen each other since Friday night. And it wasn't that I didn't trust him. My biggest concern was that he wouldn't allow himself to be honest about his feelings for her after all this time as long as I was there. Without that, I'd never have all of him. Just like he'd never have all of me until I believed with my entire being that we were meant to be, rather than an impulsive decision.

With that in mind, I said goodbye and disconnected the call.

And allowed myself to feel every emotion that ran through me.

———

"Any idea how long you plan to shack up with me?"

I glared at Stella, trying to keep a straight face despite the dramatic show she put on in the kitchen. She thought it was hysterical to phrase things a certain way to make it sound like we were more than friends. In all honesty, it was funny. It gave my heart the break it needed from constantly thinking of Brogan.

"It's only been a few days. Are you already about to kick me out?"

She finished slathering peanut butter on a slice of bread and then licked the knife. "Technically. But only because my lease is up at the end of October. You're welcome to come with me if you want. However, as for you staying in *this* apartment, you have three months before you're out on your ass."

This was news to me. "Where are you going?"

"After I came back from visiting you, I decided it wouldn't be such a bad idea to move down there." She shrugged, as if what she said was nothing major. "I wanted to surprise you. Thanks for ruining that, by the way."

Her news stunned me silent for a moment, leaving me staring at her, blinking dramatically. "What are you going to do about a job? Where will you stay? You can't just pack up and move hundreds of miles away."

"You mean like you did...twice?" She shrugged, which was her version of a *mic-drop*. "I've spoken to the owner of that yoga studio you took me to when I was there. She said she'd love to have another instructor. I guess she's been wanting to open more classes but hasn't found anyone to cover the added shifts. And as for where I'd live, I've already found a townhouse close to the studio. I've got it all worked out. You have nothing to worry about, Best Friend."

"You're still planning to move there? Even though I came back to Ohio?"

She regarded me with pursed lips and a furrowed brow. "We both know you aren't staying here. Your future's with Wrong. I'm entertaining your cold feet at the moment, but don't, for one second, think you're gonna fool me."

"And what if he decides his future is somewhere else?"

"The only way that'll happen is if you already live somewhere else."

I wondered what it would be like to have as much faith as she did.

"Mercy…" She set the sandwich down and shifted on her feet to face me. "You've barely spoken to the guy. Honestly, how much longer are you going to drag this out? It's apparent from his posts on Wrong Inc's page that he's miserable. Throw the man a bone."

I glanced at my phone that sat on the counter in front of me. She was right. I'd resorted to stalking his page over the last seven days rather than talk to him, because even a simple text was too much to handle.

"What are you waiting for? How do you possibly expect to find out that he's in love with you if you don't give him a chance to tell you?" Again, Stella made a valid point. Maybe all this yoga and meditation had started to work in her favor.

"Nothing's stopping him from telling me how he feels. He knows that's what I need to hear, considering I've asked him a dozen times if he loves me. This would be the time to admit it if that's how he truly felt. Unfortunately, his silence is speaking a thousand words right now."

"Nothing's stopping him? Did you really just say that? How about the fact that you won't talk to him? Or possibly the fact that you up and left him without so much as a goodbye?" It was clear whose team she was on. And it wasn't mine. All she was missing was the T-shirt. "In case you weren't aware, guys are just as insecure about their feelings as we are—even the most alpha male of them all. Not to mention, after all he had to go through with his ex-wife, can you blame him for guarding his heart around a woman who can't seem to make up her mind if she even wants to be with him?"

Hearing that was roughly the equivalent of being hit by two freight trains barreling at me from opposite sides. It crushed me. And the worst part was...I somehow hadn't seen it coming. "How could I be so stupid?" I asked—not seeking a reply—as I dropped my head into my hands.

"I've wondered the same thing since the first time you questioned your relationship with Wrong. I mean, *come on*, Best Friend. It's Wrong Daniels. He's not the kind of guy you walk away from. I knew that *before* I ever met him and realized he's the epitome of Prince Charming meets Adam Levine."

I separated my fingers to glare at her without removing my hands from covering my face. "What would I do without you, Stella?"

"Walk away from the best thing that's ever happened to you," she said with a nonchalant shrug. "But for real...you can't let this drag out forever. And if he can't admit he loves you right now, give him time. While I understand you guys are married, you really haven't been together that long. And if you think about it, you spent half that time debating if you should stay or leave. You can't blame the guy if he hasn't gotten there yet."

"I fucked up, didn't I?"

"Royally." She laughed, which made me look at her. "But I doubt it's too late."

Stella took her sandwich and went to the couch, leaving me in the kitchen alone with my phone. I'd decided it would be best to send a text, but at the moment, I wasn't sure what I needed to say. Realistically, I only had to make him respond. It didn't need to be anything poetic or deep. All that could be saved for the phone call. Right now, I only needed to type out a message.

So what did I do? Went to Google to pull up his shop's page.

The very last post caught my eye and made me pay attention.

Two broken parts of the same,
Two fragmented halves,
Can love grow in the fractures of souls?
Can devotion consummate the shattered hearts?
Can tenderness bind the two to one?
Can I become we?
Can we become mercy?

My vision slurred. Then blurred. And for the first time in over a week, the tears that poured out of me weren't born in pain. They didn't come from feelings of loss or confusion. Instead, my chest swelled with pride. Butterflies took flight in my stomach. A smile stretched across my face, and utter happiness filled every crevice, every hole, every ounce of me at the acknowledgment of Brogan's words on his site for the whole world to see.

This was a part of him he'd refused anyone access to—except me. It was his secret. And now, not only was it out there like graffiti on the side of a building, but he'd done it for me. He'd written that piece for me. It was impossible to ignore the love he'd poured into that.

I had no idea how long I stood there, reading his distorted words through the blur of tears. I wanted to memorize them. Score them into my shattered heart. Breathe them into my fractured soul. But just as I had locked the first line into my memory, the phone was ripped from my hand.

"Don't." Stella had come out of nowhere. Her voice was

harsh, stern. No-nonsense. She held my cell against her chest and silenced me with her hard stare. "Talk to him before you start making assumptions. Hear him out. But above all else, give him the benefit of the doubt."

I had no idea what she was talking about. Confusion held my tongue while I stared at her, waiting for more information. Anything to let me know what she meant by that. And why she'd taken my phone.

Finally, she handed back the device, yet before letting it go, she added, "I mean it, Mercy. Wipe those tears away and go into it with an open mind. Think positively. Trust that there's an honest and reasonable explanation. Got it?"

When I nodded, she released the phone, but she didn't leave the kitchen. Instead, she took a step back, crossed her arms, and regarded me while I unlocked the screen. She'd seen something bad, something that would hurt me, and she had assumed I'd seen it, too. She'd taken my tears as pain, rather than happiness. To her, I was full of doubt, when really, his post had flooded me with hope. Which only left me with the question...*what did I miss?*

I pretended to send him a text, for no other reason than to get her off my back and buy myself some time to look into the cause of her concern. After tapping on the screen to mimic the formation of a message, I put the phone in my back pocket. "I'll let you know what he says."

"What did *you* say?"

I should've expected her to ask that. Yet I didn't. Meaning I had to come up with something that wouldn't make her question anything or catch on to what I was doing. "I asked him to call me when he had a minute to talk."

"That's it? No. Give me your phone. You suck at being you; I'm so much better at it. He might take that the wrong way and think you're going to end things with him. Then he won't call you."

I shoved her arm away. "You're being ridiculous. Even if he

does think that, it won't stop him from calling me. This is Brogan we're talking about here. He's not a coward."

Thank God that worked.

"You're right. Very well then…let me know when he calls. I wanna be there when you talk to him to make sure you don't mess this up for us—I mean, *you*." She flashed her typical shit-eating grin and went back to the living room.

Needing more privacy than her small kitchen offered, I told her I'd be in the room getting ready for the day. There was a chance that wouldn't keep her out, but at least I knew she'd knock before coming in. And to add another layer of security, I locked myself in the bathroom, putting *two* doors between us.

As I sat on the edge of the tub, I pulled up Google, knowing that would be the quickest and easiest way to get an idea of what she'd seen. Whatever it was, it seemed Stella had stumbled upon it, which told me I wouldn't have to do much digging to find it.

And I was correct.

My answer was on the first page of news that the search engine believed I'd want to see.

"Wrong Daniels' Ex Comes Back to Stake Claim After News of His New Marriage"

It wasn't news to me that Jessica had returned to town—I'd seen her at the bar the night before I took off. However, the picture of the two of them together was what surprised me. It wasn't from the bar, or even that night. It was from his shop. During the day.

Which meant he'd seen her at least twice.

Stella's voice ran through my head, reminding me that I can't trust everything on the internet. And while I knew that to be true, it didn't stop the doubts that lingered in the back of my mind. Eventually, those doubts left me questioning the reason for his lyrics on his page. The ones he'd written for me.

The ones that now felt more like guilt than a declaration of love.

I clenched my teeth and searched for other articles that might lend some insight into her presence and how often they'd seen each other. But the more I found, article after article, picture after picture of the two of them together, as well as only him, the more I began to wonder if this had been going on behind my back all along. There was no way this had all taken place over the last few days.

"Wrong Daniels Distraught Over Having to Choose Between Women"

"New Wife Gives Wrong Ultimatum"

"Jessica Daniels: I've Never Stopped Loving Wrong"

My stomach couldn't handle seeing any more. The images of Brogan and Jessica at lunch, holding hands while walking through a parking lot, and secret kisses shared behind the window of his shop, left me on my knees, hugging the toilet while I expelled everything I'd eaten since last night. And when there was nothing left, I pressed my cheek to the cold porcelain and just cried.

I was *fully* aware how stupid I was acting; how wishy-washy I had been. Yet I couldn't seem to switch off the emotion long enough to change it. I couldn't stop the agony from ripping me apart in order to accept the truth. The pain was physical, as if my body was literally being pulled in different directions. My heart one way. Brain another. Neither willing to concede or compromise.

While I knew there was a possibility that he'd realize Jessica was the one he wanted, I guess I'd held on to the hope that he would choose me. That he'd recognize what we had together and never want to give that up. After all, this was the whole reason I'd left to begin with—so that we could both come back together without an ounce of doubt that we were meant to be.

It was a risk.

I'd taken a gamble.

In the end, I was left with the losing hand.

24

BROGAN

One day without Mercy was like a lifetime without a beating heart.

Multiply that by three, and that was where I was.

I'd spent more time with a notebook and pencil in my hand since she'd left than I ever had before. While I had always written, it had never been a constant part of my life. Most of the time, I'd jot things down or scribble out a few thoughts when I needed to get something off my chest, but never *this* much.

When my marriage to Jess ended, I had no desire to pen a single word. When Mercy came into my life, there were moments I needed to express my feelings toward her, and that was the only way I knew how since we hadn't reached a point where either of us were ready to be that open with the other. But ever since she left, I hadn't been able to stop pouring my heart onto the pages of my tattered notebook. Filling the lines with the anguish, sorrow, loss, and love I felt for her.

My days were filled with ink and skin.

While my nights were reserved for lead and paper.

It was a good thing I had already declined another season on the show. After filming me sitting around like a lost boy for days, I doubted the producers were even interested in another season. This time wasn't like the last. Rather than turn into the playboy that increased the show's ratings, I grew quiet. Reserved. Locked within my own head while the world went on around me.

Honestly, I didn't know if they'd have enough to fill the proper number of episodes without the viewers watching me stare into space week after week. It was a good thing the others in the shop lived dramatic lives that would appease the viewers. I just didn't have it in me to give anyone what they wanted.

Anyone but Mercy.

And all she wanted was space to make sure we weren't a mistake.

My phone chirped from my pocket as I sat on the stool at the front desk. Normally, I would've ignored it, but now, every alert became more important than anything I might've been in the middle of, just in case Mercy had decided to reach out. And, as if the heavens had grown tired of my pleas, her name appeared on my screen.

I held up one finger to the client in front of me, who had come in to discuss a design he wanted me to do on his back, so I could open her text and see what she had to say. There was no telling how long this would take, but I didn't care. He wasn't here for a tattoo anyway, only to discuss the design so that I would be prepared for his appointment. He could wait.

Mercy: *Do you know what a painite is?*

Her question took me by surprise. There was no greeting, no *how are you*. Just a question about a word that made my heart stop. Not because I knew what it was, but because the first four letters spelled *pain*, and it worried me that she might've seen the latest drama on the internet and actually believed it. However, rather than assume my fears were correct—which would only make me sound guilty even though I wasn't—I decided to answer her question and leave it at that.

Me: *No. What is it?*

Her response was immediate.

Mercy: *A gemstone. It's apparently the rarest one.*

Following her explanation, a photo came through. It was of a stone, bloodred in color with bursts of crimson that shone through with the help of a light source I couldn't see from the image. While it did resemble a few other red-colored gemstones, I had to admit that I'd never seen it before.

However, that didn't explain her reason for asking.

Me: *Looks nice. Have you been shopping?*

I even added a smiley face at the end, just in case she didn't detect my teasing tone. But the small amount of humor that had bubbled to the surface during our brief chat on jewelry quickly faded when her next message came through.

Mercy: *No. I read your poem this morning. The one you posted on your page. And then I saw the pictures of you and your ex. It made me want to write something. I'm not as good with words as you are, but I understand now why you like to express yourself with poetry. It's easier to put your feelings into a metaphor.*

Without waiting for a response, she sent me a long message. After seeing the length of her text, I glanced up at the client in front of me, the one who continued to wait with patience. And with a forced smile, I excused myself, fully expecting him to be gone by the time I returned.

Behind the closed door of my studio, I sat on my stool and began to read her words. Her pain. Her fears and acceptance. And all the while, my heart fissured. Splintered. Broke into a thousand pieces that held on until the end. The pride I felt with the way she spun her lyrics into an image of longing and loss leaked between the cracks. Spilled over into my chest. Drowning me. Leaving me gasping for air—for hope that this wasn't a goodbye.

Reading her words felt a lot like reading my life in simile.

There were the moments of moving from one woman to the next. Then a part about being found by someone special, someone who cared for me. Until one day, she didn't. I had worried that person was meant to portray her, until I continued reading. Until I got to the part about the woman putting me aside, forgetting about me. While she still could've referred to herself, I doubted it. For there seemed to be too much pain *for* me in those words.

Then the woman—whom I assumed to be Jess—had tossed me aside.

It was what came next that left me choking on the shards of my heart.

Lost. Moving from one place to the next. Waiting. Waiting. Waiting to be found. To be taken home. To be loved and cherished again. To be worn by her again.

The heavens cried. Their tears carrying you away until the tides found you. The current picked you up, cradled you, and sent you on a journey.

I, too, was on a journey of my own when you washed up on my beach. At my feet. Practically in my lap. I saw you. I knew you —your value and worth.

With you in my hands, I smiled. I laughed. I danced and I sang. I felt like I had been found. Like I had been looking for you, Painite, all my life.

Yet we both knew that happiness would only last a moment

—a brief moment. For you weren't mine...never were. I wasn't a thief; I should not have taken something that wasn't mine to begin with. So with an aching heart, I set you back out to sea. Back on your way to the one you want more than me.

The surf lapped at my ankles like hands, desperately trying to drag me to you. Yet I didn't move. Didn't budge. I stood at the edge, feet buried in the sand for ten thousand lifetimes. Crying ten thousand tears. Begging. Pleading. Hoping and praying you'd come back.

But you never did.
The rare ones never do.

I composed myself long enough to stand up. And then I ran out the back of the shop, not caring in the slightest about returning to work.

———

I must've called Mercy a hundred times, yet she refused to pick up the phone.

However, I wouldn't give up.

When I couldn't get ahold of Mercy, I tracked down her best friend and tried that route. "So you have no idea where she went?" I didn't bother to hide just how frantic I was while speaking to Stella over the phone.

At the time, Stella wasn't home. But after I had explained it all to her, she left work and headed back to her apartment—the last place Mercy had been. When that proved fruitless, she tried Mercy's parents' house. Again, no sign of my wife.

I didn't hesitate. Instead, I quickly packed a bag and got on the road, heading to Ohio. My only hope was that Stella would find Mercy before I got there. Even if she didn't, nothing would stop me from tracking her down and assuring her that there was no one I wanted more than her.

"She could've gone to the store or any number of people's houses. I mean, I'm not her only friend in town. But I wouldn't even know where to start. I think it might be best if I just stay at my apartment and wait for her. Maybe have her parents call if she shows up—although, from what they said, they had no idea she had even come back to town. So that might be a dead end."

"I know she's upset, but if she would answer my calls, I could explain it to her."

"Listen, I love my best friend, but she's so damn stubborn when she wants to be. Mercy's the type of person who needs to look at all the facts before coming to a conclusion. The one thing that keeps her from reaching that point sooner is fear. What I *can* tell you is she always comes around. It may be on her own time, but she will eventually see the truth. We just have to wait for her to find her strength, because once she does that, she'll push past the worry of getting hurt and stop avoiding the situation."

While I understood what she was telling me, and it made sense, I refused to sit back and wait. Not when it came to Mercy. "Well, let's hope she reaches that point soon, because I'll be there in about ten hours. And I won't stop until I find her and make her listen to me."

"At least you have one thing on your side," she said, humor peeking out in her voice.

"And what would that be?"

"If there's anyone who can make her do what they want, it's you."

I couldn't fight off the need to smile. Right now, that was the only thing getting me through. It was my ray of hope. There was no way this was the end of us. I told her I wouldn't chase after her, but fuck that. I'd never stop going after the woman I loved.

"Just do me a favor, will you, Stella? If you find her, please don't let her out of your sight. And no matter what you do, do *not* tell her I'm on my way. I don't need to chance her taking off again." If I wasn't in such a panicked mood, I might've made a joke about how I felt like a bounty hunter. "You know her better than anyone, so if you think trying to talk to her might help, then I'd appreciate that, too."

"Mercy's one lucky lady, Wrong."

"Thanks, Stella."

I disconnected the call and then continued my long drive in silence. Nothing but the whine of the tires on the road and the wind filling the cab. Trees passing in a blur. The only thing playing in my mind was the thought of getting Mercy back.

And I *would* get her back.

25

MERCY

I couldn't hide forever…no matter how badly I wanted to.

At some point, I had to go back to Stella's place, even though the thought of it gave me anxiety. It wasn't Stella I dreaded; it was the lecture I knew she'd give. Once I finally turned my phone back on, I had more than a dozen messages from her—as well as from Brogan. His were the hardest to read. They may have been written words, but I could *feel* his pain. Hear his brokenness. And it killed me inside. Whereas Stella's texts pretty much told me how dumb I was.

Which, to be fair, I was.

But that's just it… Doubt had taken over, and he was a relentless asshole. Self-preservation had taken the front lines, building a wall around my shattered heart. Guarding me against the inevitable pain doubt had convinced me of.

And that wall was so tall and impenetrable that the sliver of truth playing in my mind couldn't gain traction. That voice was so soft, filled with honesty and warmth, heavy with promises that could never be broken. She spoke with such a soothing, poetic cadence that her confident wisdom was nothing more than a whisper. Unfortunately, that gentle, whistling breeze was no match against the solid fortress doubt had erected around me.

So, it didn't matter what Stella had to say, because my fear about everything going on seemed to be rather stubborn. There wasn't anything she could say that I hadn't already thought of. And so far, nothing had quieted the apprehension that blared in my head.

What I didn't expect, though, was to walk into a quiet, empty apartment.

"Stella?" I called out, wondering if she might've been hiding in a closet or tucked away in a cabinet. While I understood how preposterous that was, it was the only thing that would explain why her car was in the parking lot and all the lights inside were on, but I didn't see her anywhere.

After checking every room—it was a small space, which meant it hadn't taken me but ten seconds to affirm she wasn't here—I sat at the small kitchen table and called her phone. When she didn't answer, I sent a text. And then another. Followed by one more call that went unanswered.

I grew worried; it was almost eleven at night, and she was nowhere to be found. Granted, I had never lived with her to know if this was something she did often, but she was my best friend, so I would've known if she led a double life where she'd vanish into the night like Batman.

I figured I'd give her a little more time to either return my call or show up before I sent out a search party. And, while I waited, I thought it would be best to respond to Brogan. No matter how I felt, he didn't deserve to be ignored.

However, my texts went unread.

And my calls went unanswered.

At some point, I must've fallen asleep, because the next thing I knew, Brogan stood in front of me. It felt like a dream. There was no way he was in Ohio. In Stella's living room. At… I glanced at the clock on the wall. Almost midnight.

I jumped up and turned in circles like a ballerina. Still no sign of Stella. When I faced him again, the agony that lived in his soul seeped out through his pores. It broke my heart.

"What are you doing here, Brogan? Where's Stella?"

"She said she'd stay away for the night…unless you need her to come back."

I began to think this was, in fact, a dream, since nothing made sense. "So you've seen her?"

"Yeah. She went with me to see your parents."

This was *definitely* a dream.

He moved closer, took my hands in his, and guided me to take a seat on the couch while assuming the cushion next to me. "I realized I need to do things right this time. And that started with your parents. Now…it's time to make it right with you."

All I could do was shake my head, still not understanding what was going on.

"What's the story behind your name? Why Mercy?"

"You came all this way for that?" I stared unblinkingly at him, knowing I was missing something. "I've already told you, it's lame. It's stupid. You've built it up to be this big deal, and it's not."

Brogan squeezed my hands and scooted as close to me as he could without sitting on my lap. "I don't care about the story. I don't care how big or small it is, or how stupid you think the reason was. I keep asking because I want to know everything about you. Your name—how you got it, the meaning behind it—is part of who you are. The story itself isn't important to me. What I care about is the part that makes it *you*."

Well, if he had said that a month ago, he would've already had his answer.

I cleared my throat and glanced around the room, suddenly feeling silly. "My parents wanted to name me Marcy, but the name was spelled wrong on the birth certificate and no one caught it in time. And rather than change it, they decided they liked it and kept it."

The faintest smile crept across his lips. "Mercy suits you better anyway."

"Is that really why you came here?"

"Fuck no. I came to make you listen to me. To make you understand a few things. And then to take you home." He waited a moment, and when he didn't get any response from me, he carried on. "Jess was in town this past weekend for a wedding, and the night before filming began, she saw my Jeep at the bar and stopped in to see me."

I wanted to tell him I knew, that I had seen her there and watched them walk outside together, though I kept that to myself. I needed to hear what all he would say before admitting anything.

"She heard that I had gotten married. So while she was in town, she figured she would take the opportunity to congratulate me. That way, we could finally get closure on the disaster that was the end of our marriage. We didn't get to say much before Indi told me you were sick."

If only he knew the reason for my illness was because I'd seen him with his ex...

"Since we didn't get a chance to really talk, she stopped by the shop the next morning, on her way to the wedding. She was there for ten minutes, at most, but I guess it was long enough for someone to snap a photo."

"What about the other pictures? The ones of you two having lunch or holding hands in a parking lot? When were those taken?"

His weak smile might as well have been a knife in my chest.

"Babe, those are old. Those were all taken while we were married. I have no idea why anyone would choose to use them —other than to create drama surrounding the show. But the *only* one that's new is the one from the shop on Saturday." His eyes told the truth.

And I hated myself for not giving him that chance earlier.

"I thought I was doing you a favor by letting you see if she was the one you wanted." A tear slipped free, and Brogan cleared it away before it reached my chin. "I guess I needed to know, too. For my own sanity. I've done nothing but feel inferior to her ever since I watched the first season of the show. And you've referred to her as the one who got away. I needed to make sure you truly wanted to be with me...and not because she was gone."

He appeared baffled. Truly baffled. "How in the world could you possibly question my feelings for you? Or doubt that I would've wanted her instead?"

"You can't even say you love me," I whispered with a shrug. "And based on the piece of a poem I found in your nightstand, what we have is purely physical. At least, that's how your words made it sound."

He moved to the floor, where he sat on his knees with his hands on my hips, eyes blazing into mine. "I know what poem you're talking about, because I wrote it as part of a surprise—something I wanted to do for you the day you had your meeting at the school. And when I was packing my stuff to come get you, I noticed it was gone. But no, Mercy...that's not what I was trying to say. That wasn't what those words meant to me."

"Lust. Ecstasy. Writhing in the lovers' dance?"

He nodded, eyes set on mine like they had nowhere to go and nothing to see but the depths of my soul. "I believe the very last line was, *as I bared my all to Mercy*. I was trying to say that, even though we've explored every inch of each other's bodies, I've never felt more naked, more *bare*, than at the thought of telling you how much I love you."

The power of interpretation was a bitch.

He scooted closer and held himself to me with a firm grip on my thighs. "I do love you, Mercy. I'm sorry I haven't said it before now. I felt it. I knew it. But I guess I was too scared to admit it. Too scared you'd run. I've been living these past several weeks terrified that you'll leave. But I do love you. All of you. Always have and always will."

Even though I couldn't see him past the blur of tears that filled my eyes, I was able to notice something on his hand. On his left ring finger to be precise. I grabbed his wrist and pulled the fresh tattoo closer so I could see it better.

Along the top of his finger, where a wedding band would rest, was my name. Permanently marked into his skin with black ink. I found his stare and gawked for a moment before asking, "What's this? When did you do this?"

"Saturday morning."

I wasn't sure why, but knowing he'd done this prior to me taking off, before hearing my reasons for leaving…made me love him even more. Which I didn't think was possible. "But why?"

"Babe, how many different ways do I have to tell you that you're *it* for me before you finally accept it? You're not just my wife, you're the other half of my soul. The reason I'm here."

And because I couldn't just accept that—still unable to believe the truth that stared at me—I muttered, "You said you wouldn't chase me."

"That was until I realized I didn't want to wait. I need you with me, Mercy. Please, come home and be with me. For real this time." He reached to the side, next to the end table, and grabbed a backpack I hadn't noticed until now. From the inside, he pulled out a jewelry box and held up it up for me.

When he lifted the lid, a ballerina twirled, and piano music played. Which only made me cry harder. Through the tears, I noticed a gold band at the dancer's feet. He picked it up and held it out in front of me.

"I had planned to give this to you when you came back from your meeting with the school. But things didn't go the way I'd hoped, and after everything that happened that day, I forgot about it. Then I decided to wait. And now, I refuse to wait any longer before putting this on your finger. I said I needed to do things right this time, so when I spoke to your parents, I told them how much I love you. How I'll do everything in my power to make sure you're taken care of. And then I asked them…"

I gasped and covered my gaping mouth with my hand.

There was no doubt in my mind that this was a dream. One I never wanted to wake from.

"I asked them for permission to love you for the rest of my life. So, with that…" He took my hand in his and poised the band an inch away from my finger. "Mercy Wright, will you marry me? Will you have the real wedding you deserve and be my wife?" A smile broke free on his face. "Well, technically you already are."

"Yes." No word had ever felt more right on my lips. "Yes, Brogan…I'll come home. I'll be your wife. I'll love you forever —*but*, we need a plan. We need to discuss what's going to happen when we get back home. I still don't have a job, and your show has done nothing but interfere with my plans. Well, your show *and* Jordan."

"Don't worry about him. He won't bother us again."

That shocked me. "What is that supposed to mean?"

"Let's just say his job has moved him out of the area." The sly smile on his lips made my heart skip a beat. "And as for the show, I'll quit. I'll break the contract and end it right now. It's not important if it means I'll lose you. The money doesn't matter to me. *You* matter to me."

"You can't quit, baby."

"Sure I can." He was serious, which warmed my heart.

I playfully rolled my eyes and huffed. "Fine. Technically you can. But you shouldn't. We'll get through this last season, but to do so, we need to figure out a few things. Like how we'll deal with the media and gossip. I didn't handle it properly this last time. And for that, I'm sorry. But I honestly don't know how much more of it I can go through. How much more of my life I can allow it to destroy."

"Then we'll figure it out together. I'll follow your lead, Mercy. As long as I have you by my side, I'll follow you anywhere." Truth sang in his words, while sincerity blazed in his eyes. "And we can figure out what we'll do about your job. You wouldn't let me try to fix it before, but I'm sure I can do something to change their minds. Let me. Please. If it doesn't work, then we can look at other options. *Together.*"

I nodded, giving in. Because there was nothing else in the world I wanted to do.

Happiness dripped from his smile when he pushed the ring over my knuckle. "This was Nonna's wedding band. I've always had it, but I've never thought about giving it to anyone before. Until you. Like it was meant to be on your finger. I realize you don't have an engagement ring, but I plan to get you one when—"

"Kiss me," I interjected, not caring about a diamond. "Fucking kiss me already."

He pulled me into his lap, arms around me, jewelry box on the floor next to us.

"I love you, Brogan," I whispered against his lips. "Thank you for coming back."

"The rare ones are always worth coming back for."

My chest ached from being so tight, but there was no way I'd chicken out of this—even though Brogan had assured me that he wouldn't be upset if I changed my mind. I loved him. And he loved me. So there was no way I'd back out now.

The door to the shop had never felt as heavy as it did right now. Cameramen stood in various corners, mics on long sticks filling the space above their heads, while other video equipment hung from the ceiling to catch all angles. And all at once, every pair of eyes turned to me.

But I never looked away from Brogan.

The smile on my face burned my cheeks, and suddenly, no one else existed in the small space just inside the front door. All I could see was him. And all he could focus on was me. No matter how many times I had played this out in my mind, it never felt as good as this did.

"Morning, baby," I practically sang as I moved toward him.

Brogan leaned over the front desk and kissed my lips, longer than I'd expected. Oddly enough, not once did I believe it was for show, either. This was simply his way of loving me, with or without an audience.

"So this is the wife?" one of the men with a handheld camera over his shoulder asked.

Brogan turned toward him, his smile no longer brightening his face. "From now on, if my wife is in the shop, there will be no prompts. You can try to direct our conversation all you want, but we aren't actors. *This* isn't an act, and we won't play into it. So, if you want to film us, you'll have to take what we give you."

His dominance did crazy things to me.

When he faced me again, his smile back in place, he said, "Hey, babe. What brings you here?"

That made me laugh. Full-belly laugh. He'd just gotten done lecturing one of the crew members about how we weren't actors, yet here he was, acting as if he had no idea why I was there. When in reality, this had been planned since before coming home from Ohio.

I couldn't let him walk away from his contract with the show. It was the last season, so he only needed to get through the next five weeks of filming, and it'd all be over. We compromised by taking matters into our own hands. If they wanted to talk about us, we'd write the script. Share our story the way *we* wanted it to be told. Which led me in front of the cameras for the first time.

"I was in town getting my classroom set up, so I thought I'd come by on my way home to see you."

I'd reluctantly allowed him to try to make things right with the school, and to my surprise, he did. Granted, it had taken a very generous donation on his part to get my job back—which, had I known ahead of time, I wouldn't have let happen. In the end, I couldn't argue. Brogan wasn't the type of man to let things go—especially when it involved me.

"Well, I'm glad you did. I missed you."

I reached over the desk and held his face, pulling him closer to me. Against his lips, I whispered, "I love you, Brogan."

He hummed and said, "I fucking love you, Mercy."

EPILOGUE

MERCY

"Hurry up…you're making me miss the season premiere of the show." Stella huffed from behind me, though she hadn't hidden her teasing tone very well.

I turned to the side and glanced at her through the mirror. It took insurmountable strength to keep the smile off my face while I watched her dramatically slouch on the sofa in her dress like a drunken slob on prom night. Ever since Brogan and I had announced the date for our "wedding," she complained about having to miss the first episode of *Wrong Inc*'s final season. Which was a ridiculous thing to bitch about, considering she could record it and watch it when she got home.

To be fair…we'd picked this date on purpose.

I liked the idea of our friends and family being *with* us rather than *watching* us.

"I mean," she continued to whine, "it's not like it's a real wedding. You guys are already married—and have been for six months. This is nothing more than a party. You could've had a party anytime. Doing so on the night the first episode airs is just a bitch move."

Stella was lucky I hadn't taken any of this seriously.

"Keep it up, and I'll have a party every evening the show

274

comes on. And I'll *make* you attend." I eyed her through the mirror before returning to my mom so she could finish fixing my hair—there was nothing wrong with it, but she couldn't seem to stop fawning over me. It was a special day, and we had come so far since they had learned of my relationship with Brogan, so I gave it to her.

"It just needs a little more spray. Hold on."

"It's fine, Mom. I'm pretty sure the eighty-four thousand pins you added will keep it all in place until our tenth anniversary."

She rolled her eyes and smacked her lips. "Just a little more," she said while heading to the corner of the room for her giant bag of preparation items. Honestly, it was something a doomsday prepper would envy.

"I heard a little rumor." Stella's singsong voice caught my attention, forcing me to turn and actually look at her. "Is it true that Indi's getting her own show?"

I shrugged, not caring to discuss our friend behind her back. "You talk to her more than I do...shouldn't you know?"

Stella had moved to town a little over a month ago, and since then, she'd grown close with Indi—as well as everyone else at Brogan's shop. She'd made herself at home in our circle, as if she'd been there forever, and I couldn't have been happier.

She didn't seem pleased with my response, which was evident in her crossed arms and even more slouched posture. "Well, I know the producers approached her with the idea not too long ago, but she won't tell me if she's agreed to it or not. And since she works for Wrong, and you sleep with Wrong, I figured you'd have all the details."

Just then, Indi slipped into the room, closing the door behind her with her foot. I pointed to her while keeping my eyes on Stella and said, "Here she is. Ask her yourself."

Stella waved me off. "Already tried that. She won't give anything up."

"Has anyone ever told you that you're relentless?" Indi

asked with a swift roll of her chocolate-brown eyes. Then she handed Stella a covered plate. "There. Eat your brownies and be quiet."

Stella lifted the edge of the cling wrap and smiled. "I see right through you, Indi. This is a bribe. But it's a good thing I like your kind of bribery."

With an easy laugh, Indi made her way across the room to where I stood in front of the mirrored vanity. She held out an envelope, her cheeks glowing red with unspoken secrets. I wasn't sure which secret had caused the blush—the one about her getting her own show, or whatever she had to give me.

"Wrong wanted you to have this before the party got started." Well, that answered one question. However, it created another one.

Considering nothing about Brogan and me had been conventional since the day we met, we figured it would be pointless to start now. It was one of the reasons we'd opted out of the actual wedding and only planned a reception. There were lots of things about a ceremony that we would've wanted, but after sitting down and talking through it all, we decided that the tradition of it wasn't that important or worth the extra cost. So, we had agreed to take the money we would've spent and donate it to his charity to help feed the less fortunate—The Heart of Joe Foundation, named after the homeless man who had caused Brogan to speak to me that night outside Rulebreakers.

However, the one tradition Brogan refused to give up was not seeing me before the party. I might not have been walking down an aisle to him, but that didn't stop him from wanting to experience the feeling of seeing me for the first time right before we went hand-in-hand into the dining hall.

Which had left Indi to be the go-between all afternoon.

"What's this?" I asked, taking the envelope from her.

The hopeless-romantic part of her that she desperately fought to keep hidden came to the surface, brightening her face and dancing on her lips. There was a moment in time I'd assumed this was caused by jealousy, though I'd come to learn it wasn't. Envy, maybe. She'd admitted that a part of her yearned to find what I had with Brogan, yet she knew too well what it was like to lose it unexpectedly, which had kept her from searching for it. That killed me—knowing she purposely denied herself this kind of happiness. Indi was truly an amazing person, and she deserved so much better than being alone.

But that was something she'd have to come to on her own.

"I don't know what it says," she whispered through the emotion clogging her throat. "I haven't read it, no matter how badly I wanted to peek inside. But if I had to guess, I'd say it's probably his vows."

That surprised me, as we had decided against vows—not because they meant nothing to us, but simply because we weren't having an actual wedding. When the topic had come up, we'd decided to share and honor our vows in private, on a daily basis, and make that part of our life together. We had agreed that voicing our promises in front of others would simply be for show, that it would mean more if they were spoken inside of an embrace or over dinner or after a fight. We didn't need to make declarations in front of anyone else—only to each other.

Unsure of what to expect, I glanced down at the envelope in my trembling hand.

I lifted the flap and pulled out a yellowed piece of paper. The edges appeared to have been charred, making it look like an old letter. Carefully penned words decorated the front in black script, leaving behind a mental image of a feather in an inkwell. The lines of some letters had seeped into the fibers of the cardstock, adding to the overall presentation.

My eyes brimmed with tears before I finished reading the first line.

Stood now at the helm of a beautiful ship am I,
Another by my side as we plot our course, we sail,
From deepest ocean to deepest ocean,
On winds of joy and hope,
Her soul, my sanctuary
And I finally know why they called her mercy.

With the note still in my hand, I ran out of the room, leaving Indi, Stella, and my mother behind. They yelled for me to come back, asking what was wrong. I ignored their pleas. Disregarded their cries. I couldn't remain in that room for one more minute. One more second.

Barefoot and blinded by tears, I fled. The harsh beats of my heart and hollow thuds of my feet pounding the carpeted floor harmonized in my ears, the rapidly increasing tempo propelling me forward until I reached the end of the hallway.

The drums that had resounded around me slowed along with my pace, until the only rhythm that remained was the one my heart created. It was strong and steady. Confident yet impatient. Each eager beat pumped to the cadence of excitement and longing and anticipation.

I stilled and wiped my eyes, not caring about my makeup. I didn't give two shits if I had mascara all over my cheeks in place of blush, or if my eyeliner looked like it'd been drawn on by a blind and drunk squirrel after smoking pot. I only cared about what was on the other side of the closed door.

In the blink of an eye, I was in the room, the door now at my back. I didn't remember opening it or stepping inside or even shutting it behind me. I'd taken a deep breath to calm myself, and before I knew it, my breath blew past my lips as I stood there, staring into the frightened eyes of the man I loved.

"What happened, Mercy?" Panic filled his voice as he rushed to me, and then it ran through him as he held my face in his hands. "Fuck, babe…talk to me. Are you okay?"

I curled my fingers around his wrist to keep his warmth

against my cheek, and then lifted my other hand, which still held his note, to his chest. When I ran out of my dressing room, I had no clue what I wanted to say to him. But now that I was here, I realized it didn't matter. I didn't need a prepared speech to tell the man I loved how I felt. And without a second thought, I spoke the words that were in my heart.

"I love you, Brogan."

"I love you, too."

I shook my head, silencing his interruption. "I need to get this out, so please just listen until I've said everything I need to. Okay?" I waited for his hesitant nod before continuing. "From the moment we first met, I knew there was something different about you. Something special. And when I ignored everything else, it was easy to accept that. It was easy to see that you came into my life for a reason—and not a temporary one."

Brogan's brows pinched together, worry furrowing along his forehead.

Needing to reassure him, I squeezed his wrist and carried on. "I'm so sorry for allowing everything to become so loud in my head. For allowing it to create doubt. For running when I should've remained steady. Looking back, I realize I should've trusted you. I should've trusted *us*. Because my faith in what we have together has always been there. *What you mean to me* has always been there. My soul has known all along. So this is my vow. My promise to you. I'll never allow anything to come between us. Ever. I'll never run again, never give you a reason to chase me again. This is where I belong—where I *want* to be. Right next to you for the rest of this life and any other we have after this."

"Oh, babe…" He ran the pad of his thumb beneath my eye, clearing away the evidence of my tears. "That's what you ran in here for? Is that why you're crying? Do you think I question your love for me or expect you to run again?"

"No. I just needed to say that." I held the notecard between us and added, "We said no vows, but then you gave me this, and I realized how badly I wanted to share mine with you. No… It wasn't a *want* but a *need*. I *needed* to make that promise today. On our wedding day, before we allowed the rest of the world in."

"Mercy…you didn't need to rush over here to tell me all that. I already knew. But thank you. Hearing you say it means the world to me, even if I never doubted it. I love you so much. Everything we've been through has gotten us here, and no matter how painful it was at times, I wouldn't change a second of it. You're worth it all, Mercy Daniels."

He was right. We'd known each other for six days before getting married. It was just shy of eight weeks from the night we met until the night he'd shown up in Ohio to take me home for good. And in total, we'd only been together for six months. No one in their right mind would be as confident in a relationship in such a short amount of time. Yet we were. And we couldn't have possibly felt this way without all the obstacles we'd had to face.

Jordan had been the biggest problem by far. However, his persistence and interference and the doubt he'd caused had only strengthened what I felt for Brogan. It pushed and tested me, making me understand things that would've taken others ten times as long to comprehend. I hadn't been given the opportunity to ease into my feelings for Brogan. They smacked me in the face, stopped me dead in my tracks. And no matter how hard I'd fought against them, they won.

Each and every time.

Our connection was relentless from the start. It didn't matter how many times I'd questioned where Brogan had come from that night, how he'd ended up on that sidewalk or why I'd gone home with him, because the answer wasn't important. Regardless of what reason either of us could come up with, it would never make sense.

Because fate doesn't make sense.

I questioned it, analyzed it, picked it apart and tried to

understand the reasons for things, but I never found what I was looking for. Instead, I simply had to trust it. Believe in it. Follow my heart and *listen* to my soul. I realized now that I only had to pay attention to the signs; they were my only guide in this life. I couldn't wait for someone to tell me what to do—the breeze won't whisper advice in your ear. And I learned that I shouldn't assume a roadblock means the end of the road. It might be there to detour me. It also might be there to test me. The only way to know for sure is to tackle it head-on. But the biggest lesson I'd learned through this whole thing was:

Nothing in life comes easy.

If you want something, fight for it.

Make it happen.

And then never stop.

The universe may have a sick sense of humor, but if you play along, it'll leave you with a burning smile on your face and a soul full of happiness.

MERCY

Tied to the mast of a drifting ship was I,
My wheel lost, years before in a tempest of my own design.
Tossed was I from shallow bay to shallow bay by the silent
storm of solitude,
Sanctuary escaped me.
To the heavens, I cried for mercy.

When dawn broke on new life's day I saw her then,
Perfect yet damaged, whole yet...missing,
A puzzle yearning to be solved,
Her pieces scattered, lost?
The only clue, a vision on my soul.
And her name was Mercy.

In rolled a cotton fog of lavender that filled my senses and
loosened my bonds,
As the mist caressed paint scarred flesh,
it crackled with the chilled heat of passion rekindled.
The first time I tasted Mercy

"Save me and have me, fix me and I'm yours"

Mercy

With her words burning in my mind I tried,
I took from me, gave to her and left myself a broken shell.
I stripped all I could spare and more besides
As I emptied myself into Mercy

Intensity builds,
The rolling thunder of ecstasy,
The pulsing cadence of fury,
The aching heartbeat of desire,
The roaring beat of lust,
Twisting, writhing in the lovers' dance
As I bared my all to Mercy

Two broken parts of the same,
Two fragmented halves,
Can love grow in the fractures of souls?
Can devotion consummate the shattered hearts?
Can tenderness bind the two to one?
Can I become we?
Can we become mercy?

Stood now at the helm of a beautiful ship am I,
Another by my side as we plot our course, we sail,
From deepest ocean to deepest ocean,
On winds of joy and hope.
Her soul, my sanctuary
And I finally know why they called her mercy.

—*Kev Murtagh*

PAINITE

Shine a light on you, and you flash like fire. Red and warm. Bright. Dangerous, yet unmistakably safe.

Set you down, and you go unnoticed. Lost in the rocks with your rough, unrefined edges. Just another piece of earth along the way.

You are rare, Painite. Some say the rarest. But there are those who don't see it. They don't know it...your worth. Your value.

You were passed around like show and tell. Women taking their turns with you. Trying you on. Wearing you for a moment—just a brief moment—before it was someone else's turn.

Then she found you.

She saw something in you. Valued and cherished you. Polished you and wore you with pride. She made you feel as rare as you are, Painite. Until one day, you were just another gemstone.

Maybe you didn't fit her anymore. Maybe her style changed

and you no longer matched her outfits. Maybe you were reserved for the rare, special occasion.

Maybe.
    Maybe.
    Maybe.

Whatever the reason, you found yourself in a box with a ballerina on top. Though, she hadn't danced in a while. The music hadn't played in a while. The outside light hadn't peeked inside in a while. And all along, there you sat.

Waiting.
    Waiting.
    Waiting.

One day, the box moved. It fell. Tumbled to the ground where the splinters and long lost jewels scattered about. The ballerina would never twirl again. The music would never play again. But you'd be safe, Painite. You're rare. Precious. Valuable and worthy. Surely you'd be found and remembered. Worn again. Shown off like a brilliant diamond.

No.

You were swept up. Swept away. Carried out with the pieces of wood and broken mirror and shattered dancer. Lost in the shuffle; mistaken for something else.

Something less rare.
    Something less precious.
    Something less valuable and worthy.

Lost. Moving from one place to the next. Waiting. Waiting.

Waiting to be found. To be taken home. To be loved and cherished again. To be worn by *her* again.

The heavens cried. Their tears carrying you away until the tides found you. The current picked you up, cradled you, and sent you on a journey.

I, too, was on a journey of my own when you washed up on my beach. At my feet. Practically in my lap. I saw you. I knew you —your value and worth.

With you in my hands, I smiled. I laughed. I danced and I sang. I felt like I had been found. Like I had been looking for you, Painite, all my life.

Yet we both knew that happiness would only last a moment—a brief moment. For you weren't mine...never were. I wasn't a thief; I should not have taken something that wasn't mine to begin with. So with an aching heart, I set you back out to sea. Back on your way to the one you want more than me.

The surf lapped at my ankles like hands, desperately trying to drag me to you. Yet I didn't move. Didn't budge. I stood at the edge, feet buried in the sand for ten thousand lifetimes. Crying ten thousand tears. Begging. Pleading. Hoping and praying you'd come back.

But you never did.
The rare ones never do.

—*Kristen Clark*

LEDDY'S NOTES

I don't even know where to begin with this one. This book was easy and hard for so many different reasons. When I first started, the words flowed with little to no effort from me. They just poured out of me, as if they needed to be heard. But after a few chapters, my personal life took a hard hit, and writing became difficult. The story was still there, yearning to be told, yet I lacked the motivation to get it out.

Writing has always been my outlet. My therapy. From a very early age, if I was going through something, I'd work it out with fictional characters. Rather than write a story about people going through what I was, I'd use metaphors, create parallel issues for the characters to deal with. It was my way of taking a step back to sort through what was plaguing me. I've always been good at *giving* advice and spinning a situation so my friends can see the other side—devil's advocate, if you will. But I've *never* been good at doing those things for myself (or using my own amazing advice). So, writing has allowed me to give myself the kind of advice I'd give my loved ones.

Brogan and Mercy's story helped me in so many ways, but at the same time, it hit a little too close to home, which is probably the reason I didn't want to write very often. After all, I am the queen of procrastination. It's much easier to fix other people's lives than it is my own. But I digress. When I did sit down and write, I poured my heart and soul into their world. A lot of their emotion was personal, something that came from a place inside me I couldn't deal with on my own, so I lent it all to the characters. It was cathartic in a way. It was also very emotionally draining.

I didn't want to finish the book, and for the life of me, I couldn't figure out why. Part of me feared I'd get to the end without discovering any personal resolution. Another part of me clung to superstition and believed that the end of the story would signify some sort of finality to a relationship I don't want to lose. However, a large part of me didn't want to type "the end" because I just loved Brogan and Mercy so much. They are such a big piece of me, and the thought of closing their book pained me. I didn't want to let them go.

I'd like to say that finishing the book means I've worked through my own issues. But I can't. If anything, I think their journey made me take an even closer look into my life. It made me think of things I never wanted to, made me analyze myself and the people around me. It made me appreciate many relationships, while leaving me to question others. But I guess I can't complain. As long as it *got* me thinking, that's all that matters…right?

My only hope is that Mercy and Brogan has touched others the same way. That their story has allowed others to think and feel and analyze. That it's made you appreciate the journeys you've had to go through to get where you're at, or offer you hope that you'll get where you want to be.

If there's one thing I can say that I've taken away from their story, it would be to trust in fate. That very little in life is an actual coincidence. And to never allow fear to keep you from your destiny. Through this couple, I was able to learn that if you want something bad enough, if you *believe* in something enough, then it's worth fighting for. But you can't be the only one on the battlefield. And just because it doesn't immediately work out in your favor, doesn't mean it never will. Have faith that everything will end up the way it's supposed to, and nothing can go wrong.

Where there's a will, there's a way.

Find your will, and the way will present itself.

ACKNOWLEDGMENTS

Once again, I couldn't have gotten this far without my family. Every single one of you. The ones I share blood with, the ones I gained through marriage, and the ones I've adopted into my life by choice. Your support is immeasurable. Thank you all, for *everything*. I love you.

Steph—you are my woobie, my security blanket, the one person I can always count on when I'm homesick. We've been through lots of highs and lows, sunshine and rain, laughter and tears. And there will be loads more ahead of us. The one constant is that we go through it all *together*. You really are the ham to my cheese, the tuna to my fish, and the crack to my pipe. Love you, Woobs!

Kristie—since you can read my mind now, there doesn't seem to be any point in wasting your time reading what I have to say to you. You're welcome.

Crystal—I told you a long time ago that one of these days, you'd see proof that you inspire me. And I must say, there are *lots* of things in this one that were inspired by you. I hope you approve, because if you don't, then you get no more characters in my books! LOL! Love you, Best Friend. ITS for life!

Marlo—I absolutely adore you…more than you know. You're my lobster, and even though I do a shitty job at proving to you how much you mean to me, you've stuck by me. For that, you're a saint. You've definitely secured your place in heaven! Here's to another book I wouldn't have been able to do without you! (PS: I can't wait to come see your new house!!!)

Amanda—I shluv the shit outta you, Biffle. Let's hope this year gets you back at my side, where you belong. No lie…my life has been chaotic without you. It's time you leave that nine-to-five behind and come save me (from myself)!!

Brit—I've always believed that people come and go in your life; some stay for a minute, others for hours or years, and the occasional few who stay forever. Nevertheless, every relationship serves a purpose (whether it's for you or them). No matter how long God decides to let me keep you, I know your purpose in my life is everlasting, and the role you've played will never be forgotten. No matter what happens, I'll forever love the piss out of you and your socks!

Mila—here's to new beginnings and a beautiful friendship! I "hart" you!!

Emily (Social Butterfly PR)—I honestly don't know what I'd do without you! Thank you so much for sticking by me and putting up with my bullshit. I know it's not easy. You deserve a medal for all you've done for me. Seriously, a really big, shiny, gold medal.

Robin (Wicked by Design Covers)—you give my books a face. Best designer ever!! You rock!

Kristie—don't forget I can read your mind too. That wasn't nice. Take it back!

Kev Murtagh—I can't thank you enough for allowing me to use your words in my book. You truly are a lyrical genius, and I pray you never put your pen away. I hope you aren't disappointed in the way Brogan used your poem…I tried to add more guts and gore to make it less sappy, but the critics weren't having it. Seriously though, thank you.

Candace—believe it or not, but you were one of the biggest influences when it came to this book. Your advice to read poetry is what made this story what it is. Without you, Brogan would've been two-dimensional, and my writing would've been subpar. I will forever be grateful for coming across your book and finding you, and beyond thankful that you didn't tell me to fuck off when I reached out to you! LOL!! When you're amongst the big names, I'll get to say I know you!!

Angela—no matter what part you play in my life, or how long we go without talking due to our crazy lives, just know that you mean the world to me. I value your friendship and loyalty more than you know. You're the best!

Kristie—you about ready to move in with me yet??

Danielle—it's about time you realize you're worth more than to be some bitch's bitch! It's your turn to shine, girl! Go blind everyone with your talent! You have no idea how excited I am to see you succeed on your own. Love you to pieces!

Saya—just when I thought I'd never find an editor who could fill the shoes of my old one (seriously, she was my grammar bible), you came along, and I can't thank you enough for taking me on. I appreciate all you've taught me and all the time you've given to explain things to me. You really do make me a better writer.

Bloggers—I've said it before, but I'll say it again, you guys truly are the unsung heroes behind us all. I honestly believe none of us would be able to live our dreams without the support of each and every one of you. Thank you, thank you, THANK YOU!

Readers—whether this is the first book of mine you've picked up, if you've been with me from the beginning, or if you're somewhere in between, I can't thank you enough for giving me a chance. I value every opinion that's given, and it's because of you that I strive to better my work. It's because of you I continue to write. And it's because of you I get to do what I love.

Kristie—just think…if you lived here, I could be eating a cupcake right now.

ABOUT THE AUTHOR

Leddy Harper had to use her imagination often as a child. She grew up the only girl in a house full of boys. At the age of fourteen, she decided to use that imagination and wrote her first book, and never stopped. She often calls writing her therapy, using it as a way to deal with issues through the eyes of her characters.

She is now a mother of three girls, leaving her husband as the only man in a house full of females. The decision to publish her first book was made as a way of showing her children to go after whatever it is they want to. Love what you do and do it well. And to teach them what it means to overcome their fears.

ALSO BY LEDDY HARPER

Home No More

My Biggest Mistake

Falling to Pieces

Take Your Time

Beautiful Boy

Eminent Love

Resuscitate Me

Lust

Silenced

Dane

I Do(n't)

The Roommate 'dis'Agreement

Love Rerouted

Kiss My Ash

The (Half) Truth

Made in the
USA
Lexington, KY